W9-CKB-084

"I knew you'd come," she said with soft satisfaction.

"Were you waiting for me?" His voice cracked with a husky edge.

"No. But I knew you'd come."

"Why?"

"You couldn't resist the music."

That haunting melody. "It...called to me."

"*I* called to you."

It remained dark all around them, but Lucas could see her eyes sparkle in the darkness. How was it that he could see her as clearly as though every chandelier in the room was lit, and yet shadow shrouded everything else?

Ashlynne—no, *Ashe*—smiled again, a sultry, knowing expression, and she scooted around to face him. "Why did you come down here, Lucas?" she asked, and he blinked. She looked—and sounded—so...patient.

"I heard you playing."

"And that's all?"

"No." He reached for her, drew her upward. "Because of this."

He hauled her tight against him and caught her mouth with his....

* * *

The Unlikely Groom
Harlequin Historical #741—February 2005

Praise for Wendy Douglas's debut

Shades of Gray

"A heartwarming voice and a story
about the power of love."
—*New York Times* bestselling author Jennifer Greene

"Secrets, lies and revenge rule the day in this graphic
western drama. Danger mounts, passion flares, and lies
unfold as this stirring historical plays out
and characters evolve."
—*Affaire de Coeur*

WENDY DOUGLAS

THE UNLIKELY GROOM

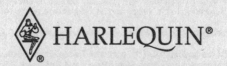

HARLEQUIN®

TORONTO • NEW YORK • LONDON
AMSTERDAM • PARIS • SYDNEY • HAMBURG
STOCKHOLM • ATHENS • TOKYO • MILAN • MADRID
PRAGUE • WARSAW • BUDAPEST • AUCKLAND

If you purchased this book without a cover you should be aware that this book is stolen property. It was reported as "unsold and destroyed" to the publisher, and neither the author nor the publisher has received any payment for this "stripped book."

ISBN 0-373-29341-0

THE UNLIKELY GROOM

Copyright © 2005 by Wendy L. Ferguson

All rights reserved. Except for use in any review, the reproduction or utilization of this work in whole or in part in any form by any electronic, mechanical or other means, now known or hereafter invented, including xerography, photocopying and recording, or in any information storage or retrieval system, is forbidden without the written permission of the publisher, Harlequin Enterprises Limited, 225 Duncan Mill Road, Don Mills, Ontario, Canada M3B 3K9.

All characters in this book have no existence outside the imagination of the author and have no relation whatsoever to anyone bearing the same name or names. They are not even distantly inspired by any individual known or unknown to the author, and all incidents are pure invention.

This edition published by arrangement with Harlequin Books S.A.

® and TM are trademarks of the publisher. Trademarks indicated with ® are registered in the United States Patent and Trademark Office, the Canadian Trade Marks Office and in other countries.

www.eHarlequin.com

Printed in U.S.A.

Available from Harlequin Historicals and
WENDY DOUGLAS

Shades of Gray #602
The Unlikely Groom #741

Please address questions and book requests to:
Harlequin Reader Service
U.S.: 3010 Walden Ave., P.O. Box 1325, Buffalo, NY 14269
Canadian: P.O. Box 609, Fort Erie, Ont. L2A 5X3

With much love for my mom, Lenore Romey, who never told me I should be outside playing instead of reading a book, and in memory of my father, Wendell Romey, the most patient man I've ever known.

And, as always, for Doug, who loves me despite all the trouble I cause, who makes everything work—somehow—and who has been known to offer that special endearment only a writer can appreciate: "Aren't you supposed to be writing?" I couldn't do it without you, darlin'.

I love you all.

Acknowledgments

Special thanks must go to Willie and Candy Seltenrich for their willing participation in this book. Legs all the way to heaven, Candy, and not one broken bone! Also to Heather Mase for filling in as the Paperwork Queen so I could finish this book and to Kathy Hafer for last-minute proofreading.

Chapter One

Skagway, Alaska, February 1898

Life was hell. It had been for longer than Lucas Templeton could remember, and there was no changing it. He'd gambled everything to learn that lesson—and he'd lost as completely as any man could. But that was old news and not particularly interesting any longer. Not to him, at least, and it was nobody else's business.

It was part of the past and that's exactly where he meant to see that it stayed.

Lucas lifted his shot glass and eyed the fine, clear whiskey with some appreciation. The glass was cool and smooth against his fingers and the alcohol shimmered with the taunt of a familiar amber color. The memory of its smooth, distinctive bite offered the lure of forgetfulness…if only he would give in to it.

He didn't doubt the whiskey's ability to make good on its promise; tonight he drank the expensive stuff, available to any man who could pay the price…and he could. He, in fact, owned the whole damned shebang—or at least this shebang.

He sipped the whiskey with an appreciation for which few men in Alaska seemed to have the patience and turned to survey his domain.

The Star of the North. Lucas smiled and nodded, satisfied by what he saw. It wasn't much, not by most standards anywhere else in the world. For him, it was everything.

One of the first saloons in Skagway, he had built it at precisely the right time. He'd had little competition at first and had unwittingly built the Star's reputation by dealing fairly with his customers and offering a reasonable comfort not often found on the frontier. Now, less than a year later, he continued to enjoy a particular success that few of the others had matched.

He'd often thought that those who'd come later hadn't wanted the triumph—or needed it—nearly as badly as he had. He'd even accepted that explanation for at least part of the difference.

But what about the rest of it?

He didn't know for certain, nor had he ever wasted much time trying to figure it out. That kind of thinking could only lead him back to the reasons that this saloon mattered so very much in the first place, and all that was better left in the past. He needed no reminder of the life he'd once led.

It was enough that *this life* compared in no way to the one he'd left behind.

No. He corrected himself with an irritable scowl and tossed back the rest of the whiskey. Not *left behind.* He hadn't left a damned thing behind. Everything he'd had had been stolen from him and he'd simply walked away from the devastation that had followed. There had been nothing left, no reason to stay.

And while it was true that he'd never planned a life such as this one for himself, it would do well enough. His success meant that he could do as he damn well pleased. He never could have done that in his other life. If it could be found in Skagway and he wanted it, he could have it.

Well, he might not go that far. An inherent trace of humility, the result of his Minnesota upbringing, stopped Lucas before he got too full of himself. He twisted his lips into a parody of a smile and dropped his glass to the well-used wooden table where he sat, then gestured to Willie, behind the bar, for a refill.

Undoubtedly, he reminded himself, he was in a much better position than most of the men who had poured into Alaska seeking gold over the past six months. And while he would have no trouble covering the expense of his choice of diversions, the reality of affording something and actually having it were two different things altogether.

He wasn't exactly sure how much he really wanted the things he could afford. It was damn sure that he didn't deserve them.

What do you think, you'll be tempting God again if you aspire for too much? scoffed an inner voice that sounded entirely too mocking for his taste. And if the question came closer to the truth than Lucas found comfortable, he chose to pretend otherwise. He had other things with which to concern himself, things more important than this ridiculous tendency toward indulging his overdeveloped sense of self-pity.

Right now, he should be concentrating on the Star and its needs.

Business had been off tonight. Not necessarily bad, just…off. The atmosphere had been fractious and Lucas had broken up more than one argument that had run closer than usual to turning into a real fight. It might have been the cold that had set tempers on edge; the temperature had plummeted of late, typical enough for an Alaskan winter but trying for those unprepared for it. The brisk north wind in Skagway only made it seem worse.

Or it might be something else entirely, like the latest outbreak of killings—one a day, some said. Lucas hadn't kept track, but he had no trouble believing the number. Ever since Soapy Smith and his band of troublemakers had taken over the town six months ago, lawlessness had soared and mayhem had become the rule of the streets.

"Here you go, sugar."

A husky voice interrupted his wandering thoughts and Lucas glanced around. Sugar Candy, as she was known among the men, swept up next to him. She carried with her the cloying scent of roses that he would recognize without ever having to see her. Tonight, she'd fixed her red-tinted hair into a cascade of curls that looked far too formal and proper to suit her formfitting green gown. The dress displayed with astonishing blatancy her full, ample curves and long, slender legs.

Legs all the way to heaven. He remembered hearing one man describe her that way. Lucas allowed himself a small smile. He could appreciate the sentiment.

"Thanks, Candy." He took the glass and did his best to ignore the way she preened under his attention. Such a response always made him uncomfortable.

He didn't drink right away but instead set the glass on the table, next to the empty one. Candy didn't move away.

"You want some company to go with that?"

He didn't, not really. And yet he didn't particularly want to sit here alone, either. He didn't need the chance for his mind to wander back to those places and thoughts better left alone.

"All right." He gestured to the chair opposite him. "Sit down."

And so, he thought, he would pass the night—and his

life—drinking expensive whiskey and wasting his time on a whore who meant nothing to him. It was exactly as he expected.

Exactly as he deserved.

And if he ever wished for something else?

Lucas blinked and shook his head. He didn't. He wouldn't. He knew better. He was lucky to have this much.

He picked up the shot glass and drank.

Ashlynne Mackenzie stepped into the saloon with no more fanfare than was necessary. Just the thought of where she was and what she was doing caused her to shiver. She managed to suppress it by sheer strength of will. She couldn't afford the weakness or even the appearance of it.

What was the name of this place? Ashlynne looked around but saw nothing in particular to distinguish this saloon from the others she'd been in tonight. It was loud and bright, cheerful in a frenetic sort of way, and a good deal warmer than the outdoors.

Even that couldn't make her like it here. She didn't.

A saloon?

A saloon. The truth repeated itself in a heavy, condemning voice.

Oh, God.

What was she doing here? But she knew. This was, after all, the fifth or sixth one she'd been in. Ashlynne couldn't remember for certain—and maybe, she thought, she didn't *want* to remember. It was bad enough that she found herself here at all. Worse, she didn't see Ian anywhere in this place, either.

Ashlynne swallowed a disappointed sigh and crossed her arms over her chest. The night was bitterly cold and a terrible draft blew in beneath the poorly hung door, but the chill had nothing to do with the way she stood. *That* was due to other, far more important reasons. Such as, with her arms clutched around herself and her hands tucked away, no one could see that she trembled.

Take your time, she reminded herself with as much cheerful encouragement as she could muster. She took a breath and looked around once more. The room stretched as deep as it did wide, with tables scattered throughout in no apparent order. A bar graced the far wall, a surprisingly sturdy wooden arrangement compared with some of the others she'd seen. The wall behind it boasted shelves that held an array of bottles and glasses. A gilt-framed mirror hung as the area's centerpiece. It was, by far, the most prosperous-looking place she'd seen in Skagway.

She didn't doubt that Ian's first choice would be a place very much like this.

Reminded of the urgency of her mission, Ashlynne turned to inspect the men who lounged at the various tables. They seemed contented enough, drinking the night away or staring dumbly at the capricious luck of the playing cards in their hands. But even looking again changed nothing.

Her heart sank. Ian wasn't here.

She would have to keep looking.

"You lookin' for someone, honey?"

"Come on over here, sweetheart, and give us a kiss for luck!"

The catcalls eliminated any errant sigh of disappointment. Her brief time in Skagway had already accustomed her to withholding her reactions. Ashlynne pressed her lips into a thin line rather than permit the scowl that would reveal more than she dared allow in a place such as this. Especially for a woman alone…

She turned to leave without ever having stepped more than a foot away from the entrance—and then she saw him.

It wasn't Ian. Instead a stranger threaded his way through the scattered tables and chairs. Heading straight for her.

She should have been swamped with disappointment that it wasn't Ian—or at least troubled by a new fear. Oddly enough, she was neither. She was, instead…captivated. By nothing more than the sight of this man. She'd never before been so taken by the mere sight of anyone.

He was big and muscular. Surprisingly so, she thought. He dressed in a fine broadcloth suit like those worn by the most elegant businessmen in San Francisco, and he was, she realized, even taller than Ian. That put him several inches over six feet and well above her own five foot five. And as he moved closer, his features became more distinct, appearing far less rugged than she would have expected for a man who seemed at home in the wilderness of Alaska.

Or in a saloon.

He looked to be in his prime, no more than thirty, and almost…aristocratic. His nose was straight, perhaps a little too big to be considered perfect, but it suited his high cheekbones and clean-shaven, square jaw. And while his dark blue eyes pierced her with the force of his stare, they did little enough to draw her attention away from his mouth. His lips were full in a classic bow shape, and the whole image gave him an improper, seductive air.

An air of wickedness. Something…irresistible. And something that enticed and repelled with equal fervor.

Or did that impression come from his overlong blond hair? It scraped well past his collar, almost to his shoulders, and tumbled into his eyes. The blunt cut looked tantalizingly tousled, as if he had done nothing more than run his fingers through it once he'd left his bed. Or perhaps someone else— one of the soiled doves who seemed to abound in Skagway?—had done it for him.

Ashlynne swallowed, astonished by the shamelessness of her thoughts. Her heart had found an extra, erratic beat that left her gasping. She tried to catch her breath but couldn't seem to manage it. Her heart stumbled, her breathing continued with no apparent rhythm...and the man kept coming.

What was wrong with her? He was just a man, after all.

He stopped an arm's length away and frowned. "Who are you?" he demanded without preamble.

"I..." His rudeness sent her thoughts tumbling with a new uncertainty and she couldn't quite formulate the haughty answer she might have liked. "I'm Ashlynne Mackenzie. Who are you?"

He blinked, as though he hadn't expected the question. But then, she hadn't exactly planned to make such a request of him and certainly not in such a saucy tone. She regretted it the instant it was too late. She wanted these people—these *strangers*—to help her; insolence would hardly encourage them to do so.

"I'm Lucas Templeton." The man surprised her when he answered, considering how very...detached he sounded. The fire in his eyes was gone, as well. Still, he didn't look away and the aloof distance in his stare left her feeling nearly as uneasy as had his earlier vehemence. She refused to let him see it, however.

"I own the Star of the North," he added after a moment.

"The Star—" She blinked and cast a cursory glance around her. It was an unthinking reaction; she hadn't forgotten for a moment where she was or why she was here. "That's the name of this place? The Star of the North?"

"You didn't know?"

She shook her head, thinking instead that she would be safe to settle her gaze somewhere near Lucas Templeton's shoulder. Unfortunately looking at him at all only made her more aware of his strength and size in an entirely new—and intimate—way.

She jerked her gaze up to his and held herself steady as she tried to regulate her breathing. "I'm sorry," she said, hoping her apology might give her a reprieve from the bone-deep intensity of his glare. "I've been in so many of these places tonight I lost track."

"So many?"

The question, low and incredulous, kept her eyes drawn to his, no matter that she knew better. In spite of the dim interior, she could see that his expression remained narrowed with distrust. In fact, he made no attempt to disguise it; he didn't blink or look away, revealing exactly what he wanted her to see.

"I…yes." She swallowed in an effort to free up an answer. Surely that would help with this breathlessness—wouldn't it? "I've been in a number of—"

"How many?" he interrupted.

"I beg your pardon?" Her spine stiffened despite her very precarious situation. Perilous predicament or not, she didn't tolerate anyone making such rude, autocratic demands of her.

"How many?" he repeated as he stepped forward.

He smelled of whiskey. Ashlynne caught the scent, a familiar one that made her want to back away. She resisted the impulse and the weakness it would reveal, reminding herself sternly that she had no excuse for it. She'd known exactly what to expect before she'd ever entered the first saloon. She'd grown up as a Mackenzie in San Francisco, after all. Her father had been very clear in his choice of vices and he'd trained his only son quite effectively to follow in his footsteps.

And if his daughter had proved to be an utter failure…well, fate had given her this unexpected chance to succeed.

"How many?" Templeton asked again. His voice came sharp with impatience this time.

Ashlynne stiffened and offered him a disapproving glare. "Five or six," she said woodenly.

"And why would you do that?" He paused and angled his head as though suddenly looking at her from a different perspective. "Are you looking for work?"

"No!" She meant to resist the provocation of this man's impolite questions, but the word came out too sharp all the same. "I am not looking for work. I'm looking for—someone."

Just because she answered, she didn't have to give him any more information than was strictly necessary. Even so, she couldn't afford to dismiss him too quickly; Lucas Templeton left little doubt that he was not a man to be denied.

Besides, she didn't yet know if he could help her.

She forced herself to ignore her inner uncertainties and looked at Templeton once more, straight-on this time. "His name is Ian Mackenzie. Have you seen him?"

Templeton shrugged with little apparent interest. "I don't know. I don't know every man who comes into the Star. I don't even know most of them. What does he look like?"

Anxiously, Ashlynne began her recitation. "He's tall, although not as tall as you are." Her gaze skittered away when she heard how personal her observation sounded and she hurried on. "His hair is dark and he's dressed…well—" she waved a hand toward the room in general "—I suppose like most of the men here."

Realizing what she'd done, she retucked her not-quite-steady hand under the opposite arm before anyone—most especially Lucas Templeton—could notice.

He didn't seem impressed with her words, nor did he show any interest in her movements. He lifted an eyebrow to disappear beneath the hair that had fallen over his forehead. "You just described half the men here."

"Yes, it would seem so." She couldn't argue with the truth. "We've been in Skagway a few days and—"

"A *cheechako?*" The word sounded like the same accusation as whenever else Ashlynne had heard it. No one wanted to be a greenhorn, it seemed; they all wanted the knowledge and experience of a seasoned Alaskan.

A sourdough.

"Yes," she agreed.

"What makes you think he'd be in here?"

Ashlynne swallowed a weary sigh. She had no intention of admitting to this man—or to anyone—that she had no idea where Ian might be.

He'd been so *good* on board the ship. Then they'd arrived and the frenzied excitement of Skagway had immediately taken hold of him, like the first taste of alcohol to a drunk. Ian had reverted to his old habits so quickly, Ashlynne still didn't quite know how it had happened.

She did know her brother, however—and better than she might have liked at times. The only things he might require for an evening's entertainment would be women, gambling and liquor. The Star of the North boasted all three.

Why *wouldn't* he come here?

"Is something wrong, sugar?"

A new voice intruded and Ashlynne realized that she'd missed the approach of another woman. A woman who belonged in a place like this.

The newcomer sidled up behind Templeton and slipped her arm around his waist to stand next to him, hip to hip. Her red hair appeared quite shocking at first, but a second look gave it more of a hint of the…exotic. She was tall— nowhere near Templeton's height but claiming several inches over Ashlynne—and she had the kind of figure that appealed to men. It was a perfect hourglass, accented most daringly by the snug fit of her emerald-green silk gown and its décolletage.

"Nothing's wrong, Candy." Templeton didn't turn to look at the woman as he spoke but continued to stare in Ashlynne's direction.

"What's *she* doing here?" Candy narrowed her eyes a fraction to shoot Ashlynne a look undoubtedly more distrustful than welcoming.

"Looking for someone." Finally, Templeton released Ashlynne from the grip of his glare and slanted a glance in Candy's direction instead. "His name's Ian Mackenzie. Have you seen him?"

The other woman shrugged in a seductive, graceful way that Ashlynne could never imitate—and why would she want to? She didn't want to be anything like these women who worked in saloons, and she didn't want to have anything to do with a man like Lucas Templeton.

"I don't know," Candy was saying. "I suppose I could have seen him." She looked at Ashlynne and winked, her painted lips curving upward with a knowing smile. "You know I don't always get their names, sugar. What's he look like?"

"Like most of the men in Skagway," Templeton snapped with clear impatience. "And he hasn't been in here tonight."

"Well, I'll be gla-ad—" Candy extended the word to two syllables "—to keep an eye out for him. If I find him…"

"Go on back to the table," said Templeton.

"But, sugar—"

"Go on." He indicated the room behind him with a jerk of his head but otherwise didn't move. "I'll be there in a minute."

Candy cast a frown of pure frustration in Ashlynne's direction, then flounced away with a sharp rustle of her skirts.

Could *she* ever achieve that same effect, both feminine and dramatic at the same time? The question stunned Ashlynne with its secret jealousy. She lowered her lashes in shame as the now familiar breathlessness began to fill her chest again. Oh, God, this night, this place…

"It doesn't look like I can help you." Templeton's voice, low and rough, didn't disguise his impatience. "Nobody named Ian Mackenzie has been in here tonight."

She swallowed a tired sigh and nodded with the same weariness. "Yes, of course. It's as I expected. Thank you."

And then, before any other foolishness—or Lucas Templeton's handsome face—got the better of her, she turned away. Gathering her determination—and whatever composure was left to her—Ashlynne stepped out into the cold night air and started for the next saloon.

Things continued to go from bad to worse!

Left to his own devices, Lucas discovered with some disgust that he'd lost any real taste for whiskey or women. He frowned. He'd been content enough to relax and sip his whiskey, with or without Candy's company. So why had that changed? He refused to believe it had been because of Ashlynne Mackenzie's very temporary interruption.

But that thought did bring up another question. What the hell did she think she was doing, going from saloon to saloon looking for her wastrel husband? Lucas could hardly berate her for her choice of mates; he didn't know enough about her situation to do so. But her reckless actions would be risky enough in most *civilized* parts of the world. To do so *here,* in Skagway? She must have been out of her mind—or as naive as she looked.

Recalling his first sight of Ashlynne, Lucas might have smiled if he hadn't sensed such…trouble about her. She'd stood by the door, so clearly out of place and with her arms crossed protectively over her chest. Her dark blue cloak had wrapped around her like a suit of armor. She was of average height, though the rest of her shape had been far less apparent. She'd peered around the room with obvious unease, as though she'd just stumbled into a nest of vipers.

That thought, finally, gave Lucas a crooked twist of a smile. Some might well say that she had—and she hardly looked the part for such a task.

She couldn't have been older than twenty, or just past the age. Her hair was the color of mink and she'd scraped it back from her face in a severe hairstyle that should have done nothing to make her look attractive. It had, in fact, accented each of her features at their most elemental: high forehead, arched cheekbones, painfully straight nose and full, finely shaped lips. Her eyes had provided the most surprise; they'd flickered with a golden light that was nothing if not the color of whiskey.

Lucas settled back in his chair at the same table where he always sat and thought about Ashlynne Mackenzie's eyes. He hadn't seen anything quite like them, expressive and yet guarded at the same time. But then, that described nearly everything about her. She was nothing like the working girls who made their ways north. Aside from that, she was worlds different from Emily.

His stomach knotted and he signaled for another drink. Maybe he hadn't been in the mood moments ago, but now, suddenly, he needed the alcohol. The last thing he could tolerate were comparisons between Emily and a woman he didn't even know. There could be no comparison. Emily had been…special. Unique. A woman not quite of this earth. And Ashlynne Mackenzie was…not. She was simply one more woman who had most likely made a questionable match and now had to live with the consequences.

It was none of his concern.

"You thirsty, sugar?"

Candy sidled up from behind him, scattering his thoughts as she delivered whiskey in a fresh glass. She bent low, hesitating long enough to draw considerable attention to the thrust of her breasts. Balancing herself with one hand on his shoulder, she offered him a seductive smile and leaned close, running her fingers down his chest and toying with the buttons of his vest beneath the suit jacket. Instinct urged him to pull away, but something else—some latent sense of self-preservation—stopped him. He needed to put behind him these unnerving memories of Emily, these unwelcome thoughts of Ashlynne Mackenzie. There could be no better way to do it than with another—and most certainly available—woman.

He lifted one corner of his mouth in a smile. "Where have you been, Candy? Looking for a better man?"

She gave him a wide smile of her own, made up of equal parts knowing seduction and wicked invitation. "There isn't a better man in all of Skagway, sugar. I was just giving you some time to remember there's no better woman than me."

Lucas couldn't help himself. He laughed at Candy's audacity and took a moment to remind himself of just how much a man he was. Not only that, but Candy was most definitely a woman. It didn't matter that he wasn't a man worth wanting—at least not in the traditional sense. Anything between Candy and him had nothing to do with that.

It was only sex and nothing permanent.

He reached up to tangle his fingers with hers. "Just what did you have in mind?" he asked in a voice pitched low enough to sound deliberately suggestive.

Candy smiled, a familiar expression that spoke of both seduction and attraction—and generated little response within

Lucas. Uneasy, he searched for another smile, a real one this time, and parted his lips when she leaned farther down.

Her mouth settled over his with unerring precision and Lucas waited for his body to awaken. Of the few girls with whom he'd spent any time, Candy had always been one of his favorites. Tonight, though, when she sent her tongue forward to twine around his, he knew only a mild aversion for her kiss. Neither the taste of her nor the cloying scent of rosewater enticed him to want anything more. Certainly he had no urge to take her to his bed—or anything else. Rather, some deep, elemental part of him wanted to pull away, to rub his hand across his mouth and wipe away the taste of her.

Don't be crazy, he told himself impatiently, and opened his mouth to deepen the kiss. He'd let his emotions, his thoughts, become too stirred up tonight—and not in a good way. He needed to find a release for the tension that coursed through him.

Not just any release, but a sexual one. He made the point for himself deliberately.

Lucas reached up to shove his fingers into Candy's carefully styled hair and anchored her mouth against his. She made a deep, guttural noise that he took to mean approval—or agreement, at the very least—and her tongue picked up the dance, swirling through the cavern of his mouth. It plunged deeper, darted away, then plunged again before she finally wrenched her mouth free.

"You want to go someplace, sugar?" Her whisper sounded like more of a pant and she arched her breasts toward him with brazen disregard for others in the room. "We can go in the back. Or we can go to my place. It's—"

A sharp sound cut off her invitation. It came strange and unexpected and not immediately identifiable. The others in the Star fell silent, as well, all listening. Lucas paused to catch his breath, more labored than he might have expected after Candy's kiss, and the sound echoed in his mind. Scuffling noises from outside gave him another clue, and then it hit him.

Gunfire.

The sound had been a pistol shot, and in Skagway, that could mean only one thing.

Trouble.

Chapter Two

The Star of the North went abruptly silent and the air grew thick with tension. Lucas didn't have to wonder why. Anyone who'd spent more than a day in Skagway would know that, chances were, Soapy Smith or one of his men was responsible for the gunfire.

But what, exactly, had they done now?

A woman's scream tore through the eerie silence, which changed everything as far as Lucas was concerned. Soapy Smith or not, women had mostly been protected from Skagway's troubles in the past. At least the kind of trouble that involved gunfire.

Lucas shoved Candy away and surged to his feet. Most of the others around him had begun to move, as well, and now they all headed for the door. The crowd bottled up at the entrance, but Lucas didn't let that slow him down. Using his size and his shoulders to his advantage, he demanded, "Let me through," in a voice of authority that guaranteed others would comply. He'd acquired that certain tone when he'd first opened the Star, and it worked as well now as whenever he'd used it in the past.

"Wait for me, sugar!" Candy cried from behind him.

Lucas ignored her and shoved his way through the door and out into the cold. He hadn't stopped to grab his heavy coat and now held himself stiff against the first shiver produced by the bitter winter wind. He put the frigid temperatures from his mind.

Groups of men had begun to gather in the nighttime streets and Lucas elbowed his way through the milling throng, again using his size to his advantage. No one seemed of a mind to argue and a path cleared for him until he reached the front of the crowd.

A few men had brought lanterns and now held them high, illuminating various patches of the shrouded, darkened street. Lucas peered into the shadows, searching for any sign of the ruckus. A man, judging from the size and mode of dress, lay unmoving and crumpled in the street. The body was twisted at an odd, unnatural angle that warned the man was dead. A smaller figure knelt next to him.

The woman who had screamed?

An unwelcome, ancient urge—could it have been decency?—sent a frisson of unease chasing up his spine. Instinct prodded him to go to the woman and her dead companion. To do what he could?

He shook his head, nothing more than a sharp, single movement, but he would have liked to have kept even that much to himself. What was wrong with him that he would consider helping anyone? He knew better. He could do nothing. If there were things that needed doing, then he was not the one to attempt them.

Another Lucas Templeton might have felt differently, might have made another choice, but that Lucas no longer existed and hadn't for years. *This* Lucas knew better. This Lucas had been created by a lifetime of mistakes, bad judgments and failures, and he'd learned every one of the lessons he'd been meant to. He knew when to up the ante and when to fold— and now was hardly the time to raise the stakes.

But where was Deputy Taylor to help that poor devil in the street? Or, for that matter, Reverend Dickey? Lucas peered into the shadows that surrounded the crowd but spied neither man. He knew how the law operated in Skagway, particularly if Soapy or one of his cohorts was involved in the fracas, and Lucas figured Taylor would show up in his own good time.

But what about the preacher? Where the hell was religion when a man needed it?

"What happened?" he asked no one in particular.

"One of Soapy's men got him."

The answer came as little surprise; it would hardly be the first time. Rumors of Soapy's activities had been varied and persistent. Men complained frequently of being swindled by crooked card games, false business fronts, robberies—and even murder.

"What started it?" he asked.

"They was playin' cards." Lucas didn't look to see who answered. "I weren't there when the ruckus started, but the way I heard it, the dead feller lost all his money to one of the boys and then he called Soapy's gang a bunch of cheaters. S'pose it went downhill from there."

Downhill? Under other circumstances, Lucas might have smiled to himself, thinking about it. Alaskans and those who had survived the hardships of life in the north had a certain way of understating any given situation. But then, he supposed, men who lived with difficulties such as those faced every day in this part of the world saw life from an entirely different perspective.

Enough to accept without question the wish of one man to shoot down another?

A gust of wind whipped itself up and raced down the street. Lucas tensed to hold back a fresh shiver, but his own discomfort suddenly lost its significance when he realized the wind carried with it a soft cry that he might otherwise have missed.

"Oh, Ian."

He jerked his head up to stare at the figures in the road. They hadn't moved.

Ian, the voice had said.

Ian?

Aw, shit. Lucas narrowed his eyes and drew his brow down into a fierce grimace. He stared into the street, at the dead man and his companion, and knew he couldn't be mistaken.

He *wasn't* mistaken.

The cry, uttered so breathlessly on a choked sob and carried on the wind, had been a woman's. She'd said *Ian*.

Son of a bitch. A growing list of other cusswords rolled around inside Lucas's head and he took great satisfaction in listing every one of them. He deserved them. He *needed* them.

Ashlynne Mackenzie crouched next to the dead man in the road.

She had found her husband.

But why did she have to squat there, so alone and helpless? Irritation scored him suddenly, frustrating him that no one went to her aid. They—all of them—couldn't just stand here and watch, leaving her to suffer alone that way.

Why don't you help her?

Dammit. He frowned again, this time just because he wanted to. Why the hell had he ever come out to investigate this damned ruckus in the first place?

Shit.

The cusswords began a new parade through his mind but provided him with little satisfaction this time. He didn't want to help Ashlynne Mackenzie; he didn't even want to *think* about her. He had turned his back and walked away from helping people years ago.

You look out for yourself now, he reminded himself firmly. If that meant nothing more than offering a bit of entertainment, a place to go and a few hours of forgetfulness for an ever-changing group of lonely miners, then that was enough for him. All Lucas wanted was to make a decent living away from the demands of *civilization.*

He didn't go out of his way for anybody—and he wouldn't do it for Ashlynne.

No, the best thing he could do would be to turn and walk away from this debacle. And he would. Just as soon as someone else stepped forward to help her.

Lucas waited, but no one moved. He didn't realize that he had, either, until he heard a familiar voice from behind him.

"Sugar, where're you going?"

He ignored Candy's question and kept walking.

The man came to her almost as if in a dream. Ashlynne hadn't realized he was here at first; she seemed able to do nothing but kneel on the rutted, frozen ground and stare at Ian's prone body. And cry. The tears, though, had begun to dry the moment she'd sensed another presence next to her.

Never cry in front of strangers.

Ashlynne could hear Grandmother Mackenzie's admonishment as though the old woman remained of this earth and stood here, right next to her. She didn't; the old woman had passed on years ago. Ashlynne was alone now, so how could she possibly take Grandmother's advice? Everything was wrong—terribly, terribly wrong—and it would never be right again.

Ashlynne's dilemma didn't seem to matter to the man who

crouched next to her. He refused to be denied, instead urging her to her feet and away from…here and Ian. She heard the words and even understood his meaning, and yet she couldn't move.

She could do nothing.

He wanted her to leave, to go away with him. But she couldn't! Not yet. That would mean leaving Ian lying in the road, alone and cold and…dead.

Ashlynne gasped and choked back a new sob that suddenly threatened. *Dead?* It couldn't be so! *There must be some mistake,* she told herself frantically. She must have come out of that last saloon and stepped into the wrong place, like Alice through the looking glass.

"Ashlynne." The man knew her name. How was that possible? But he touched her and her curiosity dissolved like a fleeting wisp of smoke. He took her arm and encouraged her to stand. "You can't stay here like this. Come with me."

"I can't!" She jerked her arm from his grasp. "I can't just leave Ian alone here. Not like this."

Inexorably he took her arm again. "He won't be alone. I promise you. Look, here's Reverend Dickey now. He'll take care of Ian. Won't you, preacher?"

"Of course."

A new voice entered the conversation, the tone gentle but no less firm. A hand patted her shoulder lightly with a touch that reassured, completely unlike the tempered steel of the other man's grip. "You go with Mr. Templeton now and leave everything else to me."

She heard the plea, but she couldn't bring herself to move. She didn't look at either man, could only stare into the shadows that surrounded Ian's body and hid the finer details of his face, his form. Could it be…what if he wasn't really dead! He might be only asleep or wounded—badly, of course, but still alive. If they could find a doctor, he could heal any injury Ian had suffered and prove that this was all just some terrible mistake.

With new hope in place, Ashlynne reached anxiously for her brother. Her hand trembled as though palsied.

"Come on, Ashlynne," urged the man, Templeton. His tone was as unyielding as she'd ever heard and it carried none of the underlying kindness of Reverend Dickey. It was Templeton who pulled her to her feet.

"We can't do anything for Ian now," he added, "but the preacher here can see that everything's taken care of."

Everything would be taken care of? The idea carried with it an odd giddiness and hope flickered to life as she snagged onto the reassurance of it. "You're sure?" She hardly recognized the sound of her voice, thick with unshed tears and quivering with uncertainty. "Ian and…everything?"

"I'm sure."

Everything would be taken care of.

The possibility drew her like a freezing man to the blaze of a fire. But could she truly leave Ian's body in the hands of strangers? It didn't seem right somehow. She would have never considered such a thing in San Francisco.

But in San Francisco, she wouldn't have been surrounded by strangers. In San Francisco, this never would have happened.

Everything would be taken care of. The weak part of her, the weary soul scraped raw, urged her to say yes. She longed to have someone's help, even if for just a little while. A little while in which she didn't have to think, plan, decide. A little while for her to find the strength to regain her bearings. If she could do that, she would be all right again. She was certain of it.

She had to be.

But could she trust these men? Certainly if anyone could help Ian now, it would be a minister. And she remembered Templeton. He was the man from the Star of the North. That had been the only saloon where someone had spoken to her in a way other than to make a vulgar comment or crude invitation about how she might spend the rest of the night.

Lucas Templeton might not have been precisely a gentleman, but he hadn't propositioned her, either.

Ashlynne found herself moving, as though prodded to it by her thoughts. She stepped back but then stopped at the last moment to stare down at Ian's body. It was only a shell, she reminded herself halfheartedly as she recalled the lessons of other ministers when she had faced other deaths. It was empty now and no longer housed all that had made her brother the unique person he'd been.

"Goodbye, Ian," she whispered, and the wind carried away the soft sound. "I'm sorry." An arm encircled her shoulders loosely, and then Lucas Templeton led her away from Reverend Dickey and Ian and the remains of their shattered dreams.

She accompanied Templeton blindly, simply putting one foot in front of the other in a semblance of walking that seemed to satisfy him. And she found the movement worked to her advantage, as well. It gave her a new sense of purpose, an activity that she didn't have to think about. As long as she continued to move, her mind and body remained occupied.

"Be careful." Lucas spoke close to her ear and his arm tightened around her shoulders as he led her up onto the wooden planks of the boardwalk.

She followed without comment or hesitation. For the moment she could think of nothing more than holding herself together. Guarding herself until she could find a stoic facade to present to the outside world.

She was a Mackenzie, after all, and there were certain

rules to be followed whenever trouble threatened: hide your tears, show only your strength, never retreat and, oddly enough, live life to the fullest. She'd never been particularly good at any of those things, but surely she could manage it this time. Somehow.

This time she needed at least the appearance of maintaining her composure as she never had before.

"Here."

Lucas took hold of her elbow and steered her through an open doorway. A blazing chandelier bestowed a sudden shock of light all around her and Ashlynne blinked. The Star of the North. She recognized the place immediately. It had been no more than an hour since she'd been here and it looked exactly the same. Ridiculously normal. The only difference she could see was that most of the earlier patrons were gone. They had all gone outside to see—

No. Don't remember it now. Put it from your mind. First, you must find your strength. The rest will be waiting when you're ready for it.

The advice echoed in her mind and, for a moment, she could almost believe that it was Grandfather Mackenzie who stood next to her this time. He would have given her that guidance exactly so, had he been here.

He wasn't, of course. Granddad had been gone for more than five years now, Grandmother even longer. They'd welcomed her parents to that celestial plane more than six months ago and now Ian would join them. They had all gone, left Ashlynne alone and—

Stop it! For God's sake, just stop thinking!

She listened to her better judgment because she could do nothing else. If she didn't, she'd fly apart into a thousand pieces that could never again be fitted together. Desperately she followed Lucas as he wound his way through the scattered maze of tables and chairs, until he stopped at one that looked just like all the others.

He pulled out a chair. "Sit down."

It was simpler to follow his instruction than to argue, and she had no words in any case. She had decided not to think— and it was just as well. Her legs felt suddenly weak, her knees on the verge of collapse. She'd kept herself moving through the street by sheer force of will, but now, when presented with another choice, her physical strength deserted her without warning. She sat down hard on the plain wooden chair.

"Do you want to take off your cloak?"

Ashlynne looked down at herself. The heavy woolen cloak—one of her few purchases for this trip to Alaska—covered her from neck to ankle, and suddenly she'd never been so grateful for a garment. It felt…good, heavy. Its weight somehow gave her a sense of security that otherwise seemed missing. She shook her head and crossed her arms over her chest, as though warning Lucas not to force the issue.

He didn't. In fact, he walked away and left her sitting alone.

Seizing any distraction, Ashlynne watched Lucas as he approached the bar. He moved with a casual grace that came unexpected from a man of his size. She'd thought the same thing when she'd first seen him and the impact hardly lessened upon second notice.

How was it, she wondered, that he had been the one to come to her aid? No one else had. Peripherally she'd been aware of others who'd stood around her in the street, staring and whispering among themselves, but none of them had approached her. Then Lucas had been there, kneeling next to her, and he'd helped her away from there. He'd seen to it that the reverend would take care of Ian, and he'd provided a safe place for her in the warmth and comfort of the Star of the North.

A saloon, she reminded herself.

The truth—that she found herself in this place *again*—hovered just beyond her ability to do something about it. It was wrong; she knew it with a vague uneasiness. She should have been aware of other emotions to concern her, as well, but...there was nothing. Rather, an ephemeral discomfort merely taunted her with the elusive impression of her complete and utter failure.

She had let Ian down and now she was a disappointment to herself, as well.

And still, she couldn't do anything to change what had happened.

"Here."

Ashlynne blinked, grateful for the diversion. Lucas stood next to the table, pointing to a steaming mug waiting on the table directly in front of her. She stared at it as though not quite comprehending exactly what it meant.

"Drink it. It'll help."

She nodded, not certain that he was right but touched by the gesture all the same. She recalled other times, when friends and relatives had made the same kind of offer or she'd done something similar for them. Remembering it now, she doubted that it had been of any real help. Still, it had been kinder than nothing at all.

Slowly, Ashlynne reached for the cup and slipped her not-quite-steady finger through the handle. Coffee. She could smell it, see a sliver of steam waft upward. She curled her fingers around the warm mug and brought it close enough to peer inside.

It was black, as these past days had taught her to drink both her coffee and tea. Sugar and cream had long ago become luxuries, a part of any fond memories of better days gone by. Ian had teased her that she would come to like the taste of the strong, bitter coffee favored by these Alaskans, and she had denied it with a certain laugh. Distance and necessity might require it, but she would never like it.

Oh, Ian.

Ashlynne gasped at the memory, her breath deserting her as a shaft of pain arrowed through her. It seemed for a moment as though she couldn't stand it and she gulped the coffee without thinking.

Heat scored her throat, and for reasons more than simply the temperature of the coffee. A different kind of fire scraped over her mouth, her tongue and down to the depths of her belly. It burned, stealing the last of her breath. Her eyes watered and her head swam with a crazy lightness.

"Wha…" The words wouldn't come and she was left wheezing for air. She clutched her throat with one hand and swallowed, then tried again. "What is that?"

"Coffee."

She blinked and shook her head. "No. That's not like…any coffee…I've ever tasted." The words came slowly as she struggled for breath.

Lucas tugged at the chair opposite hers. Wood scraped against wood as he dragged it across the plank floor and sat down. He leaned back and pointed to his own mug, waiting on the table in front of him.

"It's Irish coffee, of a sort, I suppose."

"Irish coffee?" Speech became easier as the breath rasped in and out of her lungs. She was Irish and she'd never heard of such a thing!

He shrugged. "Coffee with a dash of whiskey. Supposed to be Irish whiskey, but we use what we have in Alaska."

"Whiskey!" She all but dropped the cup in her haste to return it to the table. "Whiskey?"

Lucas nodded. "We sell a lot of it here. In Skagway and especially the Star."

"But…whiskey?" she repeated. The reminder of where she was and all that had just happened slammed into her with all the impact of a bullet. "I'm…well, ladies do not drink whiskey."

"The ones who come in the Star do. That or champagne, and champagne doesn't mix with coffee. I thought you needed the coffee more."

He looked at her, but his expression told Ashlynne nothing. His blue eyes reflected the fathomlessness of a shimmering, shadowy pool. They drew her, tantalized her but promised nothing at all.

"I…" She stumbled, uncertain exactly what she wanted to say. "How could you have served me whiskey? Whiskey!" she added one last time.

Lucas straightened but only enough to reach for his cup. If she'd been a betting woman, which she was not and never would be, she'd wager that his coffee was laced with whiskey, as well. He took a long drink and then very deliberately placed the mug on the table.

"What's wrong with whiskey?" he asked with a smooth laziness that she didn't believe for a minute.

Ashlynne straightened, even gripped the wooden arms of her chair under the urge to explain the evils of liquor and places like the Star of the North. As if to punctuate the speech she would make, she jerked her head aside to indicate the bar itself…and then her equilibrium wavered for a moment. She took a breath and paused. Frowning, she waited for things to settle back to where they should.

"Yes?" said Lucas, sounding smug, as though he doubted that she could answer the question.

"If you don't know, Mr. Templeton," she said, adding a certain emphasis to his name, though her voice came out with none of the strength she meant it to, "I certainly can't explain it to you. I can tell you, however, that *I don't drink spirits.*"

Lucas nodded, one corner of his mouth lifting in a semblance of a smile. "I can't say that comes as any great surprise." He paused, slanting her a look she couldn't quite interpret. "But it seems like now might be a good time to start."

"Mr. Templeton!" Fortunately a good sense of her outrage underscored her tone this time.

"What?"

"That is a wicked thing for you to say."

He stared at her for a moment, his face without expression. "It's not what I say that should worry you, Ashlynne. With your low opinion of me and the Star, it's your being here at all that should concern you."

Chapter Three

The words weren't rough enough. Lucas had wanted to say something…else. Something that would shock Ashlynne and send her running from the Star. He'd known from the beginning that he didn't need or want her here, and her prim insistence that she didn't drink spirits had only confirmed his conviction.

She was a teetotaler—and trouble.

How did he think his weak, sorry excuse for an accusation would convince a woman like Ashlynne Mackenzie to retreat? She had accompanied her husband to the frontier of Alaska, for God's sake. And, teetotaler or not, she'd found the will to go from saloon to saloon, looking for the drunken wastrel to whom she was married.

A woman who did those things was not a coward. A woman like that was beyond anything in his experience, but he could be certain that she wouldn't run from a few provocative words—and the sorry dare he'd come up with couldn't even be considered provocative.

She was also a woman whose husband had just been shot. Murdered. And for that reason alone, Lucas's more cowardly self couldn't find, let alone use, any harder, more ruthless words. No matter that it was a mistake and he knew it, he simply couldn't force himself to be deliberately cruel to her. Not tonight.

It was too bad, too. A firmer declaration would have made life simpler for them both.

"Drink your coffee," he said instead.

"I told you. I don't drink spirits."

"There isn't enough liquor in there to make you a drunkard, Ashlynne. Drink the damned stuff. You need it. Hell, *I* need it. It was damn cold outside." He took a healthy swig from his own cup.

"I beg your pardon!"

She drew herself up like an outraged little hen, an image that might have made Lucas smile under other circumstances. He didn't consider it now, not even when she gave him a frown that he guessed was meant to put him in his place. He stared back impassively.

"Hades will freeze over before I am crippled by a need for *alcohol* in order to survive," she said, her voice as frosty as the coldest Alaskan night. "I will endure whatever I have to, for however long I have to, and without the aid of a crutch like *whiskey*."

"Aha." He nodded as though understanding suddenly—and he did. "The ills of the world are laid at the feet of that demon liquor. Is that right?"

"Yes."

"And is that because Ian had a little trouble holding his drink?"

The question sounded like more of a taunt than Lucas had meant, but he didn't offer an apology. He might not have it in him to be deliberately cruel to Ashlynne, but that didn't mean he could be kind and gentle, either.

He couldn't. Nor did he care about finding such softheartedness within himself. *That* could only lead to more trouble, and he'd had enough of that already.

He had to admire Ashlynne's composure, however. She blinked at him like a confused little owl and said, "I don't want to talk about this." Her voice sounded prim, proper, much as he expected, but then she exposed a sudden desperation when she reached for her coffee and drank.

Did she realize what she'd done? Apparently not, he decided when she gasped and wheezed something that sounded like *ack*. Her eyes widened, grew watery and remained as clearly amber as the whiskey that laced her coffee.

She'd almost fooled him into believing she had more strength than she could possibly possess.

Lucas chose to ignore both her physical reaction and the reasons for it; she wouldn't appreciate anything he said. Instead he watched as she sat there, trussed up in her heavy cloak and, once she rid herself of her cup, with her arms crossed protectively over her chest.

What did she think she was guarding herself against? he wondered as a faint smile tilted up the corners of his mouth. There was nothing and no one in the Star—or all of Skagway—who could cause her any more harm than her husband already had.

The smile died and Lucas angled his head in her direction. "Why don't you take that cloak off before you get overheated? You'll get sick."

She glanced down at herself. "I…" She shrugged, as though unable to make the decision whether or not to do as he suggested.

And that was odd, Lucas thought as he watched her. She'd been quick and decisive in her disapproval of him and the Star—and alcohol in general—but she couldn't decide whether or not to remove her cloak? Had that second taste of alcohol undermined the strength of her reasoning? Or had the reality of her predicament finally struck her?

"Unless you have somewhere else to go?" he prompted when she didn't move.

"I…no." She dropped her gaze to the front fastenings that held her cloak secure, moving slowly to work each one free. Finally, when the last one had been unfastened, she shrugged the heavy garment from her shoulders and it fell away, draping down over the back of the chair. "There. Is that better?"

Lucas raised an eyebrow. "You tell me. You're the one who could have become sick."

"I'm…fine."

She was more than fine. He could see that in an entirely new way. She wore a plum-colored gown with a high collar and long sleeves. The only adornment was a bit of black piping and black buttons that decorated the front in an eminently proper style. But the respectable cut and fashion of Ashlynne's clothing could not disguise the lush shape of her body.

Her cloak had done an admirable job of concealing her form, making Lucas more appreciative of what he now could see. Her breasts curved in generous proportion, and her waist dipped inward with an enticing flare. She had the kind of shape that any man would admire.

What the hell had Ian Mackenzie been thinking of to bring his wife to Skagway? Particularly a wife who looked like Ashlynne?

"What are you going to do now?" The question slipped out before Lucas could think better of it. He didn't really want to know the answer, didn't want to learn anything about her past or future. Certainly he didn't want to understand the woman herself.

But then second, perhaps wiser, thoughts assailed him. Maybe such a question was for the best, after all. He wanted her gone from his life for good—and the sooner the better. A reminder of the reality of her situation might be the best way to accomplish that.

"Tonight?" she asked softly. "Or in the future?"

"Is there a difference?"

"Well, no. I don't suppose there is."

"And?"

She glanced away. When she looked back at him, it was for only a moment. "I don't know." She shook her head. "I have nowhere to go."

"Tonight?" He repeated her question. "Or ever?"

"Ever."

Damn. He narrowed his eyes and told himself not to respond to the look of forlorn confusion that paled her face. Ashlynne Mackenzie must have somewhere else to go. She had to. She couldn't stay here, at the Star.

At least he could be certain that she'd have no desire to remain in a saloon.

I should have walked away and let Reverend Dickey take care of her.

"What about family, friends?" he asked.

"I don't have a family. Not anymore. Ian was the last one." Her voice grew thick with the words and she paused, blinking quickly, repeatedly, as she fought back tears. "I never had many friends. Certainly no one close enough I could turn to now.

"I'm…alone," she added after a moment.

Alone.

Lucas was alone, too. Well, he had the Star. A place to call his own. It had started out as nothing more than a way to earn a living, but now it had become his home, and friends like

Sugar Candy and his bartender, Willie, had become his family.

Ashlynne said she had no one. Lucas could believe it was true, at least in Skagway. But at home, wherever that was? There must be someone.

Lucas leveled her a deliberate look but used the guise of reaching for his cup to mask his intent. He needn't have bothered; she had dropped her gaze once more, seeming fascinated by her hands, her lap—or something else entirely that he couldn't see.

She had paled, even, from earlier, and her mouth seemed slack. Lucas drank from his mug and looked closer. Her expression appeared all too shocked, confused. Had her admission surprised even her then?

"Go back where you came from, Ashlynne." Lucas spoke suddenly, using words he could say flatly and without hesitation. "Family or not, you have friends there. You don't want to stay in Alaska."

She shook her head as she looked up at him. "You don't understand." She sounded almost desperate, as though she needed to convince herself, as well. "There is no one there for me. There is no one at all. And even if there were…"

She paused for so long he gave up expecting that she would continue. When he would have spoken, prodded her, she finished, "Even if there were, I couldn't get there. I don't have a return ticket…and I don't have the fare for one."

"You don't have—" Lucas cut himself off, suddenly recalling pieces of what he'd learned on the street.

"Are you telling me," he began again, "that Ian lost everything? All your money?"

"Yes." The word was barely audible. "And that isn't even the worst of it."

Lucas's heart sank. Good God, there was more?

"What else?"

"It's my fault."

Ashlynne made the admission before she could give in to the cowardice that made her want to pretend otherwise. But she couldn't claim an innocence she didn't deserve. In truth, she was to blame for everything that had happened.

"What's your fault?"

"All of it."

"All of it," Lucas repeated, but nothing in his tone made the words sound like a question. "Do you have more to tell me?"

"I…" She paused as she tried to think carefully about what to say and how to say it. Lucas made it more difficult than it should have been, staring at her with those sharp blue eyes that seemed to look right through her to the very depths of her soul.

Apprehension stalked her, as it had for days now. It made her angry and irritable and reckless, which explained why she'd gone looking for Ian in the first place. Now it annoyed her into reaching for her coffee and she swallowed a mouthful before she could think better of it.

She realized her mistake the moment it was too late. She might have allowed petulance to get the better of her, but her pride permitted her to do nothing less than swallow the coffee…and the whiskey. The liquor tasted stronger than she remembered—or was it only that the coffee had cooled considerably since she'd tasted it before? She uttered a soft, decidedly unfeminine grunt as she shuddered.

"Think of it this way. Irish coffee is medicinal," suggested Lucas with unmistakable humor glinting in his eyes.

"Don't be ridiculous." She gasped more than she spoke. "There is nothing medicinal about whiskey."

"You might be surprised at how many tonics you can buy from any druggist that are mostly alcohol."

She didn't believe him, but she didn't have the interest or energy to argue with him. Not now. Maybe tomorrow or another day, when she could think again with some semblance of intelligence. At the moment she seemed only able to *feel*—and her emotions didn't seem all that dependable. They had careened up and down and around all night, urging her in one direction and then another without pause or logic, and she didn't trust a one of them.

"Now," said Lucas after he'd taken a drink from his own cup and settled back in his chair. "Do you want to tell me why this is all your fault?"

"No." She bit off the word, taking satisfaction in the sharp, disagreeable sound. "I can't say that I want to tell you anything at all."

He leveled an impatient frown of disapproval in her direction. "You've got someone else who wants to listen? Someone who's interested?

"And who'll help you?" he added after a significant pause.

Ashlynne tried to swallow a sigh, but she couldn't quite manage it. "There's no one," she stated, because it gave her at least the illusion of certainty. "I told you that. But can't this wait?" She brushed an unsteady hand over her forehead. "Do we have to talk about this now?"

"When would be better for you? When you're all settled into this new life that you've got waiting, now that you're all alone?" She couldn't mistake his sarcastic tone.

Ashlynne swallowed and dredged up the will to answer from somewhere, though she doubted seriously that she had the strength for it. "You're right, of course." She refused the tears that prickled behind her eyelids and forced back the fear and grief that waited just beyond the ironclad grip she held over her composure.

Lucas stared at her silently.

"All right." She took a deep breath. "It's my fault because it was my idea to come here."

Lucas angled his head to one side and seemed to watch her with more than a trace of curiosity. There seemed to be something else in his expression, as well, though she couldn't tell just what.

"What do you mean by *here?*" he asked. "It was your idea to come to the Star? Or to Skagway?"

"Alaska. The Klondike. I'm the one who wanted to prospect for gold."

He didn't believe her. She could tell by his narrowed eyes and the skeptical twist of his lips. He shook his head, shoving the hair out of his eyes when it tumbled over his forehead. "Women never choose adventure or places like Alaska."

"What…" Ashlynne shook her head in startled astonishment. The movement gave her a bit of a light-headed feeling, but she did her best to ignore it. "What a narrow-minded thing for you to say." She answered Lucas's ridiculous claim instead. "What about your girl Candy over there? How did she get here?"

Ashlynne pointed to where Candy circulated among the men on the other side of the room. The other woman touched one man with a familiar hand on his shoulder, bent low to whisper in another's ear. She chatted and laughed with them all, her manner casual and friendly and even intimate.

A startling regret washed over Ashlynne as she watched Candy's relaxed camaraderie with the men. An equal sense of shock followed almost immediately. How could she, Ashlynne, experience such a sense of disappointment? It was completely inappropriate! But…she had never felt that kind of easiness with another. No one. Granddad and Grandmother had always held themselves stiffly aloof from most emotion, and Ashlynne had been so very different from her immediate family—her parents and Ian—that they'd never been close.

She hadn't even felt that kind of familiarity with Elliott and he had been—

She cut off her thoughts with a ruthlessness she hadn't needed in a long time, perhaps not since Elliott himself had taught her the necessity for it. But she needed the ability with a real desperation tonight. She simply couldn't afford for her thoughts to divert in that particular direction. Not along with everything else that had happened.

And particularly not when facing a man of Lucas Templeton's considerable will.

She ignored the distant warning in her head and drank more coffee. It didn't burn with quite the same fire as earlier, although she wouldn't say that the taste had much improved. Still, it gave her something to do with her hands and worked as an effective distraction from the conversation she didn't want to have in the first place.

"Are you telling me that you're a woman like Candy?" asked Lucas, sounding both curious and dubious—and distinctly amused.

"I—" She flushed. "No." She shook her head emphatically and tried to ignore that same dizzy feeling that had overcome her earlier. "I have no intention of working in a *saloon*. But that doesn't change the fact that coming to Alaska was my idea."

"The lure of the gold?" Lucas's smile didn't reach anywhere near his eyes. "You and Ian planned to be rich, like the Carmacks and the Berrys?"

"You see?" Ashlynne pointed at Lucas, making her argument with fingers that had long ago ceased to tremble, but then she turned to fanning her face with her hand. The room had begun to seem overly warm.

"George Carmack and Clarence Berry had their wives with them when they struck gold," she added. "You can't tell me that Kate Carmack and Ethel Berry were dance hall girls—or anything else. I know better."

"I see you've learned about your predecessors to the Klondike."

"Yes." Ashlynne nodded, but briefly. "It seemed important to learn all we could. To be prepared." But her heart fell upon hearing the words. Despite whatever they might have thought, she and Ian had been sadly *unprepared* before arriving in Skagway.

"It's different here," she confessed in a soft voice, because the truth had always been the one thing on which she could depend. "Nothing like I expected."

"You aren't the first to say that."

"I didn't want to come this way." She shrugged. "I wanted to go to St. Michael and take a ship from there down the Yukon River to Dawson City."

"The all-water route." Lucas nodded with apparent approval. "It's a less arduous trip that way, that much is certain. Better for a woman."

"It's also more expensive. Ian said we couldn't afford it. Besides, the Yukon River is frozen this time of year and Ian wanted to travel now. He said we were better off coming early, through Skagway, and purchasing our outfit here, rather than paying to ship it from San Francisco. We could be ready as soon as the snow melted."

"And did he tell you how difficult it would be to cross either of the passes to get from here as far as Bennett? The Chilkoot is brutal enough, and the White Pass is no better. And that's only the beginning of the trail."

Ashlynne started to shake her head, then remembered her earlier dizziness and thought better of it. What if she was catching a cold? Or, worse, some strange Alaskan malady with which she had no experience.

She answered simply instead. "I don't know how much Ian knew before we left, but I began to suspect the truth of what we faced on the *Aurora Borealis*. The other passengers told me what they knew, and it did sound…daunting."

In truth, Ashlynne had been appalled to hear of the hardships that stampeders faced when climbing either the Chilkoot or White passes. But, as she'd quickly learned, those who wanted to go to the Klondike had no choice. There was no other route from Skagway to Dawson City, and the Canadian Mounties required those entering the Yukon to possess nearly a thousand pounds of goods and supplies. The only way a man—or woman—could comply was by carrying his outfit up and over the pass, trip after trip after trip.

"I thought we could do it." She tried to sound more confident than she actually felt. "Ian did, too. He told me so—but then, he didn't fear anything."

A boisterous shout from a noisy card game drew her attention and Ashlynne glanced to the back of the room. If Ian had been alive, he would have been there with the others, betting his last dime—or anything else with which he'd had to gamble. She didn't doubt it.

She frowned and turned back to Lucas. "The atmosphere of Skagway—the excitement and gambling and drinking—all took hold of him. It was like a…sickness. It didn't take even a day before he fell in with a bad influence and…well, you know the rest of it."

"And you consider yourself responsible for that?"

"It was my idea to come," she repeated tightly.

"You aren't responsible for anyone's actions but your own."

She smiled but with neither amusement nor understanding. "That sounds very nice, but it's not true. Not in this case. I knew we were taking a chance in coming here, but I thought we took a bigger chance by staying in San Francisco. Ian had too many acquaintances who were a bad influence, and we'd already lost nearly everything we had. *This* seemed like the right thing to do. I'm not so sure anymore, but at the time, it felt as though we were fulfilling the family prophecy."

"The…what?"

"Grandfather Mackenzie had found his first success in the California gold rush. He was shrewd and frugal and earned a great fortune—which my parents promptly spent. Wasted. When they were killed in a carriage accident months ago, they left nothing of Granddad's fortune. But I thought that Ian and I could have a new chance in the Klondike. A fresh start. Just when the time came that we had nothing left, George Carmack struck gold at Dawson City. It seemed like destiny—a sign from God."

Would He find it sacrilegious that she said such a thing? Ashlynne didn't know. Her family hadn't been religious and so she hadn't grown up in the church. But surely God would forgive her for her lapses in judgment, both tonight and in the recent past. Wouldn't He? She'd done her best.

Aware of how pitiful her best truly was, Ashlynne snatched up her coffee cup and drained it. If only she could find her bearings again…

"What did your parents have to do with your husband's family fortune?" Lucas's question came unexpectedly.

"My husband?" Ashlynne frowned. "Who are you talking about?"

"Ian." Lucas returned her frown. "Or…" He paused and the silence began to seem somehow exaggerated. "Were the two of you just…lovers?"

"Lovers! Who?"

"You and Ian."

"What about Ian?" Ashlynne shot Lucas another glare of confusion. Either he made no sense at all or she had become completely overwrought and hadn't realized it until this moment.

"You said that Grandfather Mackenzie found his success in the California gold rush." Lucas spoke slowly enough, but his tone smacked of more frustration than patience.

"Yes."

"And that was Ian's grandfather."

"Yes." She nodded briefly, careful of that highly unsettling dizziness. "Ian's and my grandfather."

"You and Ian shared the same grandfather?"

"Yes. Of course we did. Why wouldn't we? Most brothers and sisters share the same family."

Lucas blinked and for a moment his expression seemed to close down. Then his eyes widened and, remarkably, he laughed. "Son of a bitch," he said softly as he shook his head. "Ian wasn't your husband. He was your brother!"

Chapter Four

Lucas had been a fool.

A small part of Lucas exulted at the discovery; the rest of him recognized the difference for all the danger it posed. Ashlynne Mackenzie hadn't the protection, dubious though it might have been, of being a grieving widow; she'd never been a wife. She was, instead, a single woman. A woman stranded in Skagway without family or money.

A woman completely alone, not only in Alaska but in the world.

And wasn't he a man who had once fancied himself as *saving the world?*

No! His sense of self-preservation reared up to demand that he listen. *You don't save the world or people or anything else. Not anymore. You might have done that sort of thing once, but that was a long time ago. And you weren't very good at it, now were you? So don't think about making any noble gestures now.*

"Wherever did you get the idea that Ian and I were…married?" Ashlynne asked, sounding more confused than amused. But then Lucas's own amusement had disappeared the moment he'd understood the complications of this new truth.

He avoided looking at her as he reached for his coffee. Draining the last of it, he signaled Willie for another. For only himself, of course. Miss Ashlynne Mackenzie didn't drink spirits, after all.

He shrugged as though Ashlynne's question had been insignificant. "You must have said something."

"I'm sure I didn't say anything of the sort."

"Well, I didn't just pluck the idea out of thin air."

"I think you did." She straightened and frowned in a most argumentative way, aiming a dark, disgruntled look at him. "I think you made an assumption based on nothing more than your own antiquated ideas."

"Antiquated ideas?" Lucas's sense of humor returned and he laughed. "A man who owns a place like the Star of the North doesn't have *antiquated ideas*."

"*You* do," she insisted, her brow drawn in obvious disapproval. "You're the one who said, 'Women never choose adventure or places like Alaska.' That's an antiquated idea if I ever heard one. You think that only married women would want to travel, and then it would be because their husbands made them."

"Ashlynne, I do not—"

"You do so. If you didn't, you wouldn't have assumed Ian and I were husband and wife."

Lucas stared, wondering at this sudden quarrelsome side to Ashlynne's nature, when she'd been polite, even distant before. Had her grief finally overcome her other emotions? Or could she be this angry because he'd misunderstood her relationship with Ian?

Worse, could the whiskey have begun to affect her mood?

"Here you go, sugar."

Candy's words and the scent of roses preceded her arrival by mere seconds. She swept up from behind him, carrying two steaming mugs that she placed on the table with a feminine flourish. She set one in front of Ashlynne and the other within Lucas's reach.

"I didn't want two," he said, his voice sharper than it should have been. But…dammit! He wanted to end these moments with Ashlynne; he didn't want her in the Star and he didn't want to help her. He wanted her out of his life and gone from his memory, and plying her with whiskey *or* coffee would hardly accomplish that.

"*I* might have wanted something else," put in Ashlynne, her voice decidedly grumpy. "But you wouldn't know that—would you?—since you hadn't the courtesy to ask."

Who was she to chastise him? "You said you didn't drink spirits."

Ashlynne opened her mouth as though to argue the matter further, but Candy spoke first.

"You two can argue your differences on your own. One-Eyed Pete's waiting for me." She started to leave but then stopped and glanced back over her shoulder. She shot a pointed smile in Lucas's direction. "Don't forget, sugar. Just call me if you want…anything."

Candy flounced away with a laugh, swinging her hips and tossing her head like a filly in heat. Lucas wanted to appreciate the sight, but he couldn't seem to find his usual sense of admiration for her tonight.

"That woman is shameless."

He glanced at Ashlynne and found her staring after Candy. Her brow was wrinkled with disapproval. He swallowed a weary sigh. "She's a dance hall girl, Ashlynne."

She transferred her gaze to him. "And a…"

"A what?"

"A…" She hesitated again. "A…prostitute."

Lucas couldn't help himself; he laughed again. "Well, yes, I suppose she's that, too."

Ashlynne snatched up her fresh cup and took a healthy drink. "I don't know how you men can make light of such things. Prostitution is immoral—wicked! Why, this place—this whole town!—is immoral and wicked."

"Then why don't you go back where you came from and leave us to wallow in our immorality and wickedness?"

She took another, sizable drink, stared for a moment at the cup, then replaced it on the table with a new frown. "I told you. I don't have a ticket or the money to purchase one."

"I'll give you the money." The offer was out before Lucas could think better of it. But as the words echoed between them, he realized just how much sense it made. Ashlynne couldn't afford to leave—and he couldn't afford to allow her to stay. The piddling price of the fare back to Seattle or San Francisco would be a fair enough exchange for his peace of mind.

She, on the other hand, reared back as though he'd just suggested that she shed her clothes and dance naked on the tabletop. "Absolutely not!"

Lucas frowned, annoyed as much by himself as Ashlynne's reaction. His offer had been honorable, and she had no business behaving as though it wasn't. Worse, her current position drew every bit of his attention to her lush, completely feminine curves. His body noticed immediately, straining awake and reminding him, in fact, that he hadn't put her attractiveness from his mind at all.

"What do you plan to do instead?" he snapped without a hint of sympathy.

"Well…I don't know. But I have no intention of taking money from strange men."

"I'm not a stranger. You know my name, after all."

"That isn't enough," she insisted. Firmly.

"You should be relieved I made the offer. I didn't ask for any...favors in return."

"Mr. Templeton!" Her complexion paled and her eyes widened with apparent shock. When she spoke again, however, it was with a cool certainty that came as a surprise. "There is no chance that you would have gotten such *favors* from me," she said stiffly, all but draining her cup.

Ashlynne sat back decisively, but then peered into the depths of her empty mug. She sighed and glanced up at him. "Why don't you people have cream or sugar?" she asked with plaintive frustration.

Lucas blinked. Ashlynne's mood seemed to be changing with nothing more than the ticking of the clock and it had gotten worse as the night had passed. He understood that her emotions might be unstable after the traumatic turn of events, but it seemed that the whiskey had only heightened her reactions.

"Cream and sugar are too expensive," he answered carefully. "A person can probably find some sugar in Skagway if you've got the coin, but never cream."

Ashlynne sighed again. "I think I hate this place."

"So why not let me send you back Outside?"

"Outside where?"

"San Francisco or wherever you came from. Outside of Alaska."

"Why didn't you say that, then?"

"I did. Anyplace away from Alaska is Outside."

"What do you call the beauty and grandeur of nature beyond these walls?" she demanded smartly as she waved to the room in general. Her spark, however, and her gaze seemed to be fading. "You can't escape the wilderness in this place. I've seen that for myself."

"That's simply the great outdoors."

"*Cheechakos,* Outside—you Alaskans have your own vocabulary."

Lucas nodded, not that Ashlynne paid enough attention to notice. What she said was true, however. Most things about Alaska and Alaskans were different from elsewhere in the world. The disparities repelled as many people as they attracted.

Now, of course, the gold drew them, as well. Just as it had drawn Ashlynne and her brother. But the land, the elements and the hardy breed of both pioneers and Indians who had already settled this frontier were unforgiving. The wrong step could cost a man his life.

It had cost Ian Mackenzie his.

And what about his sister? What *would* she do now?

The world was a terrible place and the heavy thudding inside Ashlynne's head was God's way of proving it to her. She didn't know enough about God to be certain, but she suspected what He wanted of her. It was what He'd always wanted of her—and what she'd always failed to accomplish. He meant for her to give up her headstrong ways, to learn to think before she acted, to trust others and to forgive them for their shortcomings.

She had never even come close to managing it. Now she couldn't even consider it.

She couldn't seem to think at all.

Instinct demanded that she hold her arms, her legs—everything—stiff and steady. Better yet, that she give up movement entirely. She tried, but the blood continued to pound through her veins and her head drummed with a heavy, relentless beat that left her hardly able to think. In fact, the drumming and pounding produced a steady rhythm that paced her heart and seemed to aim specifically for the most sensitive spots in her forehead and behind her eyes.

Ashlynne caught and held her breath, but that only seemed to make things worse. She gave in with a weary sigh and allowed her breath to trickle out, bit by bit. At the same time she relaxed her muscles and tested her extremities: fingers and toes, hands and feet, arms and legs. They all worked, though she couldn't imagine quite how. Her body's natural reaction must have been responsible, for she couldn't seem to manage much else.

She shifted with a trifle more bravery and discovered a new ache, this one low in her back. Ashlynne pried open one eye and gradually realized at what an unnatural, crooked angle that she lay. Just as bad, her tongue felt thick and fuzzy and her mouth carried a dry, awful taste, as though she'd eaten dirt and ash—or worse.

Gingerly, hoping for some relief, she tested her lips with her tongue. They felt dry and cracked, too, but she'd come to expect that from Alaskan winter weather.

Alaska.

With just the word, everything came tumbling back into her mind in one great rush. She sat up with a gasp, at the same time clasping one hand to her throat as though that would stifle any other noise. It might have done the job, but the relentless pounding in her head only increased.

Moving carefully, she pressed her fingertips to her temples and gingerly massaged her forehead. She dared no other movement as she peered about her…and then she discovered herself in a small room, dark and gloomy. An odd assortment of crates, barrels and boxes surrounded her, all stacked in haphazard disarray. A mop and bucket, broom and dustpan and other assorted cleaning supplies filled one corner.

Daring a braver look, she turned by slow degrees to investigate the rest of the room. A line of pegs, used as clothes hangers, marched across the wall and a small chest of drawers squatted next to them. A cracked piece of mirror hung crookedly on the wall above it.

Her heart stumbled as did her breathing and Ashlynne lost any chance to ignore the reality of her situation. She had never before seen this room and she had no earthly idea where she was. She was in someone's bed—but whose? She tried to scramble to her feet but found herself virtually wrapped in a cocoon made up of her heavy woolen cloak. It tangled around her legs and kept her imprisoned on a bed that was actually more of a cot, she realized as she struggled to free herself.

"Be careful."

The voice, low and husky, was also male. She recognized it immediately and absolutely.

Lucas Templeton.

Ashlynne gave a sharp little grunt of surprise. The noise sounded most unlady-like, but she didn't care. She forced herself to settle back on the bed as she wriggled around to free her legs as best she could, and at the same time, she scanned the room to find him.

In the far corner, disguised by shadows and her ignorance that he was there, she finally spotted him. He slouched in a chair with enough lazy grace that suggested he was a man who would be comfortable wherever he went.

She'd gotten the same impression of him last night.

He stared back at her, his gaze somehow unexpected. He looked unsurprised to see her or her reaction, as though he had been lounging there and watching her for some time now. Most certainly as she slept. Had he reached some obscure conclusions? And about what?

Aside from that, had he slept? And if so, where? Dull

shadows clung to the far corners of the room and gave his eyes a sleepy, heavy-lidded appearance that suggested so. Perhaps she'd awoken him.

Other than that, he looked much the same as he had last night: tousled and wicked and all too male. She didn't want to notice—hated that she did. She had so much else at stake, so much else with which to concern herself, and yet she couldn't deny that she was aware of Lucas in a way that went clear through to her soul.

What should she say to him? Especially now, after everything that had happened.

"Where am I?"

It was all that occurred to her. Worse, her voice croaked with an embarrassing thinness. Ashlynne swallowed and forced herself to maintain a steady gaze in Lucas's direction.

"In my bed." He shot her a heavy glare that seemed pointed at the same time and told her nothing.

She frowned. It made her feel better and she hoped it would put Lucas in his place. Her unseemly awareness of him or not, the man remained a scoundrel. He very deliberately wanted to make things sound as bad as he could, and that wasn't fair.

He was the one who'd given her the whiskey, after all.

Oh, dear Lord. Ashlynne dropped her gaze to her lap and her hands went icy cold. *Whiskey,* she remembered, and a new wrinkle in her memory smoothed itself out. She'd had several cups of coffee laced with whiskey and swallowed them down without so much as a second thought. In a saloon. On the night of her brother's murder.

How could she? She'd never done anything that dreadful! Worse, that disrespectful. What kind of woman had she become?

But she wouldn't—couldn't—take the time to answer the

questions now. Self-reproach could—and would—come later, once she was alone. She wanted no witness for the emotional storm that waited just beneath her ability to control it.

For the moment she forced herself to look at Lucas once more. She leveled a steady gaze in his direction and spoke in a clear voice. "So this is *your bed*." She paused. "Or your cot, as it were."

"Complaining about the accommodations?"

"Not at all. I'm more interested in knowing exactly where your bed is."

Lucas shrugged. "Where else? In the back room at the Star."

The back room of a saloon. Ashlynne's heart dropped. Humiliation urged her to hide her face in her hands, but she resisted with stiffened shoulders and clenched fists. She wouldn't give Lucas Templeton the satisfaction of seeing her like that—and she couldn't afford to give her weaker side the victory.

She forced herself to maintain direct eye contact with Lucas and to ignore the sour churning that had roiled up in her stomach. "How did I get here?"

"I brought you," he said as he pushed himself straight and unfolded his body from the chair. He moved in one grand, sweeping motion that seemed completely unsuitable for a man his size.

He should have been more awkward, clumsier, she thought with a spurt of irritation. It would be only fair. Handsome men shouldn't have every other ability at their beck and call, as well.

And she shouldn't be noticing the man or how he moved.

"I didn't know what else to do with you," he added after a moment. "You couldn't seem to tell me where you were staying." He gave his lips a brief twist that she suspected was supposed to have been a smile. Even so, he didn't appear at all amused.

He started across the room, taking a lazy detour that skirted a crooked stack of crates. The path brought him perilously close to the bed and Ashlynne's instincts screamed at her to scoot back. Stubbornly she held herself still.

He passed by to stop at a window that Ashlynne hadn't noticed before. A bit of light seeped from beneath a dark piece of brocade fabric that had been tacked over it in an odd-looking curtain.

Lucas tugged the makeshift drapery away from the window and hooked it around a nail to stay back. Light flooded the room, a pale, thin brightness that she recognized already as a winter day this far north. In summer, she'd been told, the midnight sun could be blinding. At the moment *this* was enough to force Ashlynne's eyelids to snap closed and she jerked her hand up to shield her face.

Each movement pained her and she struggled against myriad physical ailments, refusing to acknowledge them. She dared not, not now that she'd remembered her drunken revelry was to blame. She was not like her father or brother. Demon alcohol would never get the better of her.

"What time is it?" she asked as she blinked to clear her vision.

She heard a soft rustle and then Lucas said, "Going on noon."

"Noon!"

Her eyelids popped open and she stared between Lucas and the window. He didn't seem to notice; he'd glanced down to replace his watch in the small pocket of his vest. When he looked up again, his smile appeared all too smug and he leaned his shoulder against the wall.

How could he appear casual and relaxed and dangerous all at once?

"What's the matter, darlin'?" he asked. "Are you feeling a bit worse for the wear?"

Dear Lord. *Noon.* She had never slept so late.

She looked away, unable to hold his gaze, and stared down at the woolen cape in her lap. Somehow she'd managed to wad it into a wrinkled ball that seemed to represent the shambles of her entire life. Shame sent the blood racing up her neck to her face and her cheeks burned with fire.

"I—I have to go!"

Ashlynne tore at her cloak, shoved it from her legs and onto the floor. She stood, stumbling in her haste, and only then did she slow down. *Careful,* she reminded herself sharply. Now wasn't the time to show Lucas how flustered she really was.

She took a deep breath and did her best to ignore the renewed pounding in her head. Gingerly she controlled her movements as she brushed the wrinkles from her skirt and adjusted her waistband. Her blouse would simply have to remain somewhat untucked, her bodice wrinkled, but she smoothed loose wisps of hair away from her face.

Finally, when she could avoid it no longer, she leveled a steady glare at Lucas. He stared back, just as she'd known he would.

"Thank you for…" She paused, struggling with how best to phrase her appreciation and yet conceal the confusion and fear that wrangled for dominance within her. "Helping me last night," she finished, knowing the words were inadequate but without anything better. "I don't know how I would have managed otherwise."

"Where do you think you're going?"

"To find the sheriff and Reverend Dickey." She didn't mind when her tone came out a bit sulky. Lucas needn't make such autocratic demands; it was none of his business where she went and what she did.

But…he *had* been good enough to help her last night and she would always appreciate that. "Can you tell me where the sheriff's office is located?" she asked in a more conciliatory tone.

"We don't have a sheriff."

"Well, there must be some law enforcement here."

"Deputy Marshal Taylor. But you don't want to go to him."

"Of course I do!" Ashlynne pulled herself up to stand as tall and imposing as she could. Even at that, she was hardly a match for Lucas's size and she knew it. She conjured up a deep scowl to help with the illusion of strength. "I didn't see him last night and I have a number of questions—not the least of which is if he has any idea who murdered my brother!"

"You won't get answers from Taylor."

"Surely he must have begun to investigate the—" she paused, swallowing the sudden lump at the back of her throat "—shooting by now. He must know *something,* and he won't know where to find me."

"You don't want to see Taylor," said Lucas again, his tone growing more insistent. He straightened from his casual pose and offered an answering scowl. "He won't tell you anything. If you know what's good for you, Ashlynne, you'll just forget it."

"Forget it?" Ashlynne's voice rose in octave and strength. "How can you suggest such a thing? I would never do something like that! Ian was my only brother, the last family I had left. I have no intention of forgetting what happened to him. I mean to make certain that justice is served, and I'm sure that Deputy Taylor feels the same way."

"Don't be naive."

"Naive? I only expect the law to do its job."

"Listen, Ashlynne." Lucas started in her direction, then he stopped and shook his head. "*Deputy* Taylor doesn't give one good goddamn about the law. Or you. He's Soapy's man, and if you don't want to end up like your brother, you'll leave it alone."

"Soapy's man? What are you talking about?"

"Rumor has it that your brother got himself involved in a card game with one of Soapy Smith's henchmen. It might have been crooked—hell, it probably *was* crooked. Doesn't matter. Ian accused the man of cheating and you know what happened after that. Whichever of Soapy's men it was, he's long gone. And even if the shooter comes back to town, it won't matter. Soapy's word is law around here, and nobody's going to take up for a *cheechako* they can't remember."

Undisguised fury fired her blood. "*I* remember him."

"Fine." He answered in a tone angry enough to match hers. "Remember him. Build a shrine to him. Do anything else you want. But for God's sake, leave the law out of it. You'll only draw Taylor's—and Soapy's—attention to yourself. And that's the last thing you want to do."

Chapter Five

She hadn't listened to him.

Lucas stalked down the boardwalk that fronted Broadway, ignoring the whispers and sidelong glances. He had neither the patience nor the time for polite chitchat and he wanted everyone to know it. He'd been careful to build his reputation as a man who kept his distance from others, but today that didn't seem to matter to anyone besides himself.

He'd broken his own rule last night, and that, it seemed, had changed everything. At least as far as his fellow Alaskans were concerned. He'd taken Ashlynne back to the Star after the shooting—rescued her, people were saying. Now they wanted to know why…and what else might have happened after that.

He wasn't telling anyone a damn thing.

Frowning, he added a steely glare of disapproval to keep the curiosity seekers and gossipmongers from approaching him. There wasn't anything to tell, except that Ashlynne Mackenzie didn't drink spirits…and she didn't listen to advice any better than she held her liquor.

The damn woman had ignored everything he'd said. She

hadn't even pretended to listen. She'd simply settled her cloak around her shoulders, turned her back on him and walked out of the Star without a backward glance.

He hadn't wondered where she was going. He'd known. She was on her way to see Taylor, no matter what Lucas had said...and he'd meant to let her go. She needed to learn the truth about Soapy Smith's hold over Skagway. If she had to do it the hard way, then that was a choice she made on her own. Lucas had given her the chance to do things the easy way, and she hadn't believed him.

He refused to follow her in this folly.

He'd had second thoughts almost immediately—and he'd squashed them down just as quickly. He'd gone about his morning routine, changed his shirt and splashed cold water over his face. Surely *that* would clear the cobwebs from his cluttered mind.

It had done precisely that...though not in the way he'd meant it to. Thirty minutes later he'd headed out after her— and the second thoughts had returned twofold. This time for far different reasons.

He hadn't listened to any of them.

Second thoughts weakened a man, crippled him...even killed him. They'd done their best to kill the old Lucas Templeton. In his place, like a Phoenix rising from the ashes, another man had come to life. A man who followed his instincts.

Even when he knew he was making probably the biggest mistake of his life?

The biggest mistake of *this* life, he clarified for himself. He'd made far bigger mistakes in his former life, but they didn't count for anything anymore. He couldn't let them.

The life he'd made in Alaska was the only life that counted for anything.

Blinking, Lucas walked away from his maudlin thoughts

by stepping down to the icy, half frozen and half muddy, rutted street. He crossed at the intersection and then stepped up onto another section of boardwalk. The walks weren't particularly well built, but they kept a man's feet free from the muck and mud and manure created by the steady stream of horses and wagons that churned up the roads, even in the middle of winter.

No matter how far he went, he couldn't escape himself. And no matter how hard he worked to force it away, there was one question that refused to leave him in peace: why had he listened to the part of him that insisted on going after Ashlynne after she'd walked out?

But he knew. It was that damned sense of decency that he'd thought he'd left behind him eons ago. It had reared its ugly head last night and gotten him into this mess to begin with. Couldn't a good night's sleep—or at least a few hours of dozing in a chair—have cleared up that bit of nonsense once and for all?

Apparently not. Lucas couldn't seem to forget that Ian's murder changed everything for Ashlynne. She might not understand—or want to acknowledge—the significance of her altered circumstances, but that didn't change the truth of it any. Her brother's death put everything at stake for her and in an entirely different way.

If she had grasped that one unchangeable fact, she wouldn't have marched off to find Deputy Taylor.

Lucas shook his head. Ashlynne had no idea what kind of trouble she would be inviting if she asked the deputy to find Ian's killer. Justice, vengeance—her reasons didn't matter. Taylor wouldn't hear of it, Soapy wouldn't stand for it…and Lucas couldn't seem to force himself to let her fend for herself against the others.

The marshal's office wasn't far now, but Lucas found he

had to look to find it. New structures seemed to spring up in town every day. Some were constructed of lumber, while others were nothing more than canvas tents. Still others were a combination of both. Skagway boasted hotels, restaurants, outfitters, a hardware store and a druggist. There was even a hospital and Reverend Dickey's Union Church, built last fall.

The sound of voices, one raised in anger, echoed from up ahead of him and a moment later Ashlynne backed out onto the boardwalk. "The proper authorities *will* hear of my treatment here today, sir. You can be certain of it." She slammed the door shut behind her.

So he'd been right, Lucas thought as he approached her from behind. Surprisingly, perhaps, he didn't notice any particular satisfaction within himself at the knowledge.

"You found Deputy Taylor," he murmured carefully.

Ashlynne went still. Tiny hairs rose on the back of her neck, revealed by the loose upsweep of her hair. Even beneath the protection of her cloak, he could see the way in which she stiffened her shoulders and straightened her spine. Second after second ticked by, until slowly, finally, she turned to face him.

She nodded, though her controlled expression revealed nothing. "Yes, I found him."

"And?"

She blinked, a slow, calculated movement that recalled nothing of the earlier confused owlishness of a woman who wasn't quite centered. "And you were right, of course." She made the admission with some defiance. "Is that what you wanted to hear?"

He ignored the question. "What did he say?"

"What did you expect he'd say?"

"Tell me," he insisted.

"He refused to investigate Ian's death. No one witnessed

the shooting itself, according to the deputy, which means that I have nothing but gossip and innuendo to support my claim."

She shook her head and uttered a brittle laugh that held more pain than amusement. Lucas did his best to ignore both.

"That isn't all," she added before he found an appropriate reply. "The deputy is…unhappy that Soapy Smith is so often blamed when things happen in Skagway. He warned me against speaking publicly about Ian's death. Soapy is an *upstanding, law-abiding citizen*—" her emphasis on the words seemed to indicate that she quoted Taylor directly "—and he's been unfairly targeted by jealous, careless stampeders."

The lawman's claims sounded no more convincing to Lucas than they had to Ashlynne—but that could have been Lucas's own fault. He could have easily prejudiced her against Soapy before she'd ever set foot in Taylor's office. Still, Lucas hadn't anticipated the deputy's threat—and he had no illusions about the way in which Taylor had meant his words. And yet, having heard them now, he couldn't say that he found himself particularly surprised, either.

But what did that mean for Ashlynne?

"I tried to warn you," he said, feeling no particular satisfaction in reminding her of the fact.

"So you did." She raised her eyes to meet his. The amber color had darkened to a bruised ebony that couldn't disguise either her pain or her confusion. "But I just don't understand, Lucas. Why wouldn't a man of the law want justice? Didn't he take an oath to uphold the law?"

The sound of his name on her lips—his *given* name and not that formal, disapproving *Mr. Templeton*—took hold of something within Lucas that made his blood run cold. His nerves awakened as though he'd just received an electrical shock, and his body tightened with an overwhelming physical awareness for Ashlynne.

And for the man he had become.

Forget it—and the way you feel. He uttered the chastisement harshly, only just managing to keep it to himself. *And forget the oath that you took at one time in your life.*

"An oath doesn't mean a damn thing if you don't believe in it," he said ruthlessly.

"You think Deputy Taylor doesn't believe in the law?"

Lucas shrugged. "I don't know. I don't give a damn. What I *do* know is that he believes in Soapy Smith and himself more than anything else."

"But how can he ignore the truth?"

"You can be sure that Soapy didn't pull the trigger himself, Ashlynne." Neither of them could afford to forget *that* truth. "He's very careful about things like that."

"That doesn't mean he isn't the man who's responsible," she insisted stubbornly. "You know it as well as I do. You told me so."

"I—" Lucas cut off his reply when a man stepped out onto the boardwalk from a nearby saloon, one of Lucas's competitors. He didn't know the man by name, but he recognized the face.

One of Soapy's men…and Lucas and Ashlynne remained standing outside the deputy marshal's office. Worse, if anyone cared to overhear, they were talking about the very things that Taylor had commanded her to keep private.

"Come on." Lucas grabbed her arm and tugged it through his, keeping hold of her forearm as he pulled her down the boardwalk. He steered them back the way he'd come—and away from Soapy's man.

"Where are you staying?" he asked.

"Wait!" Ashlynne tried to resist, but Lucas would have no part of it and hurried her along.

"Tell me where you're staying. When you're not sleeping

in my bed, of course." He added the last deliberately, meaning it to upset her enough that she'd quit fighting him and follow his lead with a bit more cooperation.

His words had the opposite effect. She stopped more suddenly than he could have imagined and dug in her heels, refusing to move another inch.

Dammit! *You should have expected it,* he told himself with no small irritation. Ashlynne had done nothing the way in which he'd anticipated that she would.

"Why?" She jerked her arm from his.

"Ashlynne, come along." He shot her a glare as hard as stone and said in a voice that was no softer, "You don't want to openly defy Deputy Taylor. Not now, when he just warned you away."

"How do you know what I want to do?" She planted her hands on her hips and glared back at him.

He would have had an excellent view of her figure if she hadn't been wearing that ridiculously bulky cloak, now cinched at the waist by her hands. As it was, he found it far too easy to recall exactly the curve of her hips, her waist, her breasts. Until he looked into her eyes.

She was doing her best to appear angry and purposeful—and she probably even felt that way. At least in part. But a flicker of uneasiness—even fear—lurked in the depths of her gaze. That, and a certain weariness, as well. And if she looked a bit worse for the wear today, well, he could hardly blame her.

She hadn't scraped her hair back with the same painful neatness as she'd worn it the night before; rather, she'd secured it in something of a loose bun. The softer look appealed to Lucas on a very basic, masculine level and his blood warmed despite the chill of the afternoon.

Stop noticing her as a woman! he snapped to himself.

Aloud, it took little effort to roughen the tone of his voice enough to get her attention. "You don't strike me as a stupid woman, Ashlynne. We both know what you should want to do—and that is *not* to act on a rash impulse. You tried that once already today. You might want to think carefully about just what you want to do next."

She stared at him with some apparent curiosity, as though she actually considered his words. A part of him breathed a sigh of relief at the unexpected cooperation, but the truth was he doubted that he'd done all that much to encourage it. It seemed unlikely that any woman in her position would forget a confrontation with a man like Taylor all that easily. After that, Ashlynne could hardly deny that Lucas only spoke the truth now.

She blinked and turned in the direction they'd been heading. "You're right," she said. "I'm staying at the Clifford House." They walked in silence until she asked, "Why didn't you take me there last night?"

Lucas shrugged, wishing not for the first time that it had been possible. "I told you, I didn't know what else to do with you. I didn't know where you were staying and you couldn't seem to tell me."

Her breath caught with a sharp hiss and she slanted him a glare of clear frustration. "I told you I don't drink spirits."

"Last night wasn't a typical situation. The little bit of whiskey you had won't ruin you."

"It wasn't a good thing for me, either."

Lucas disagreed, but the finality of her tone told him there was no point in arguing with her. Frankly he didn't care enough to quarrel with her over it. He owned and operated a saloon; she disapproved—highly—of such places.

What did it matter if they disagreed? Now that she'd seen the truth of what to expect from Taylor and his brand of law enforcement, she would be on her way back Outside on the next available ship. Lucas would remain here, where he belonged, and they would both be the better for it.

Ashlynne's head hadn't stopped pounding since she'd first awoken. She should have asked Lucas for a headache powder or returned to the Clifford House for her own, but she hadn't been certain that conventional medicine would work for an alcohol-induced illness. Her only memories of Ian's or her father's cures included drinking again the first thing the very next morning—and she would never do that.

A fresh wave of humiliation washed over her and she wanted to both cry and chastise herself at the same time. How could she have done such a thing as to drink alcohol—at all—but, even worse, immediately after her brother had been murdered?

Her thoughts produced strong emotions that only encouraged the dull thudding in her forehead and behind her eyes. Or was it because of her confrontation with Deputy Taylor? Or, worse yet, finding herself with Lucas again, after he'd witnessed her latest downfall?

No, she decided as she stared at Mr. Clifford, the proprietor of the Clifford House. It was *his* fault.

Clifford was a big, burly man with a barrel chest and an unshaven face. He stood behind a rough wooden counter, all he needed for a front desk in his hotel. He didn't waste money on fancy decoration or a luxurious lobby, he'd claimed when Ian had checked them into the Clifford House three days ago. Neither, it seemed, did he mince words or spare anyone's feelings by being polite.

"What do you mean, I can't stay here?" she asked carefully.

Lucas had remained silent thus far, but that, perhaps, was

only because she'd stepped in front of him to face Mr. Clifford by herself. That Lucas had accompanied her and remained an intimidating presence just behind her complicated matters enough.

Why did she have to *feel* him there, behind her? She didn't want to be so aware of him, but she couldn't seem to escape her sensitivity for him, either.

"I heard what happened to your brother." Mr. Clifford didn't disguise his disapproval. "I ain't lettin' no woman stay here who don't have a man to look after her. I ain't runnin' a bawdy house."

"Mr. Clifford!"

Ashlynne drew herself up with her own haughty disapproval and glared at the man. Any thought of appeasing him disappeared like so much smoke. She retreated behind the formal facade her very proper grandmother had used to great success in her day. "I am offended by your insinuation, sir. You are perfectly well aware that I am a *lady*."

A momentary satisfaction warmed her when Clifford had the grace to flush with apparent shame, but his disgrace didn't last nearly long enough to suit her. All too quickly he narrowed his eyes, and she couldn't mistake his knowing expression when he nodded toward Lucas.

"If you don't mind my askin', Miss Mackenzie—" did Clifford stress her name just a bit? "—what's *he* doin' here with you?"

Ashlynne had no intention of revealing the details of last night's debacle or today's disappointments. It was no one's business.

"You said you'd heard what happened to Ian," she reminded him instead. "Mr. Templeton was kind enough to come to my aid last night."

Clifford nodded. "Yep. I heard that, too. And I notice you

didn't come back here—till now. And you're…with him. So you musta stayed with him last night."

"I appreciate your concern," she began, but Mr. Clifford didn't let her finish.

"Hell, for all I could guess, you coulda run off with some fancy man or one of Soapy's boys. Now it looks like maybe I was right about that."

"Clifford."

The man's name sounded cold and sharp, like the crack of a whip, and not a polite form of address at all. Ignoring Ashlynne, Lucas stepped around her, his full attention trained on the other man. She would have liked to have said something, stopped him from becoming further involved, but at the moment she couldn't imagine how to do it. She couldn't even guess what he was thinking.

"What do you want, Templeton?"

"Where were you last night?" Lucas's strangely casual tone gave Ashlynne a new uneasiness.

"What do you mean?" Mr. Clifford's frown indicated his own confusion.

"It's a simple enough question. Last night when Ian Mackenzie was shot, where were you?"

"You accusin' me of somethin', Templeton?"

Ashlynne's heart sank and her head pounded with the steady rhythm that matched her heartbeat. Dear Lord, she only wanted to lay down somewhere, to close her eyes, to massage her temples and forget. Just for a little while. Instead she faced fight after fight, antagonism after antagonism.

If she hadn't been so angry, she might have given in to the tears she'd been holding back since last night.

"I'm not accusing you of anything," denied Lucas before she could say anything. "I'm really more interested in where you were *after* Ian Mackenzie was shot."

"I don't know what you mean." Clifford had begun to sound more sullen than curious.

"Did you go outside—to the street—to see what happened?"

"Yeah. Just about everybody else did, too, from the look of the crowd."

"It seemed that way, didn't it?" Lucas agreed. "And how many of those people who went out to look offered Miss Mackenzie some assistance?"

"I—"

"Were you one who did?" Lucas spoke over Mr. Clifford's explanation.

The other man flushed. "Well, I—"

"I was there, too, Clifford. I saw the crowd. I saw everything, and *no one* went to Miss Mackenzie's aid."

Understanding finally dawned, and while Ashlynne appreciated Lucas's point with weary surprise, apprehension snaked down her spine all the same. Mr. Clifford may not have offered his assistance last night, but having Lucas point it out didn't seem to be in the best interest of her chances for continuing to stay at the Clifford House. Particularly when she didn't have the money she'd need to pay the exorbitant rates.

"Lucas…" she began with some uncertainty.

Mr. Clifford, meanwhile, spoke at the same time. "I—"

"Now that you understand how Miss Mackenzie found herself at the Star last night," Lucas interrupted them both, "I'm sure you'll agree that she had little choice." One corner of his mouth lifted in a smile that offered little sincerity—but did Mr. Clifford realize it?

Apparently so, Ashlynne decided when the man insisted, "That don't explain why she didn't come back here for the night."

"I'm terribly sorry, Mr. Clifford." This time she deliberately stepped around Lucas, again putting herself between the two men. She'd been foolish to allow Lucas to accompany her at all, let alone speak on her behalf. She hadn't been thinking clearly—but then, when was the last time her thinking had been as sharp as she needed it to be? With this dull, deep-seated grief waiting impatiently just behind the throbbing in her head, she couldn't be sure of anything.

But Mr. Clifford couldn't know that—and there was no chance that she wanted Lucas Templeton to realize it, either.

"I'm afraid I wasn't in any condition to return here alone last night. There was much to do, and I hate to admit it, but I was…a bit distraught." She tried to smile, though in a brave, wan sort of way—which wasn't so far from the truth. "I'm sure you understand."

"I understand just fine." Clifford scowled all the same. "I understand your brother got hisself killed and now you're on your own. Well, I ain't havin' none of that here. I don't take no charity cases."

"Of course not. I wouldn't expect it of you." She took a breath meant to force back the desperation that hadn't completely left her since Ian had failed to return to the Clifford House last night. "I was hoping, however, that you'd allow me to stay again tonight. I have…plans that I must make."

"I don't have any room for tonight."

"My bed and Ian's were both paid in advance for last night," she pointed out in a voice she hoped sounded more reasonable than desperate. "We didn't use either of them."

Mr. Clifford drew his brow down in a new scowl. "I don't care about that. I coulda rented them two and three times over iffen I'da known you wouldn't be usin' 'em. You paid for 'em for last night and they was yours for last night. Tonight's a different story."

"Clifford," Lucas began in that same no-nonsense voice he'd used to get Ashlynne into trouble already, but the other man shook his head, refusing to hear another word.

"Nobody gave me nothin' I didn't work for," said Clifford with a snort of disapproval, "and I ain't givin' nobody nothin' they can't pay for."

"I'm not asking for charity," Ashlynne insisted, though even she had to admit it was a thin distinction. "I only need a room for the night," she added with as much dignity as she could muster.

Mr. Clifford blinked and for a moment she believed his expression seemed to soften. Then he said, "I am sorry for what happened to your brother, Miss Mackenzie, but it ain't my fault. I can't help you now without cash up front. A woman with no man is either a whore or broke, and I ain't takin' a chance on either one."

"Mr. Clifford, I..." Ashlynne meant to defend herself, but the words ran out almost before they began. She could claim her virtuousness from here to kingdom come, but what good would it do her? That was another of the old lessons she'd learned so long ago.

There was one basic truth that remained absolute: she hadn't the money to pay for even one night.

"What if I take responsibility for the bill?" Lucas asked.

"No!" Ashlynne's refusal came immediately. She simply couldn't let Lucas do more than he already had. Her one night in his saloon had caused her enough trouble.

The offer seemed wasted when Mr. Clifford muttered darkly, "It don't matter. All my rooms is rented for the night."

"Can I persuade you any differently?" Lucas punctuated the question by pulling a roll of bills—cash money like Ashlynne had never seen—from his pocket.

"Lucas, please! You cannot pay for my room. I forbid it."

"It don't matter how much money you got, Templeton, or how much Miss Mackenzie wants to stay here. I ain't got no rooms."

Mr. Clifford paused long enough to dart a considered gaze between Ashlynne and Lucas and then back again. "I'll tell you what, Miss Mackenzie. I'll have my boy deliver your things to Templeton's place. Yours and your brother's. You two can sort things out there."

"I—*what?*" Shards of icy disbelief splintered down Ashlynne's spine and she stared blankly at Mr. Clifford. Lucas, she noted, said nothing.

"Now, I wasted enough time. I got things to do."

And that seemed to end the conversation for Mr. Clifford. "My boy will be at the Star within the hour," he said, then disappeared through the door to his personal quarters.

That was it? Ashlynne swallowed. Mr. Clifford wouldn't help her?

He'd left her alone with Lucas. Again.

The awful, weak feeling she was beginning to hate more than any other churned itself up inside of her. She swallowed and clenched her hands into fists so tight that her nails bit into her palms. She didn't release them.

"Now what am I supposed to do?" she muttered before she could think better of it.

Chapter Six

$\diamondsuit\!\!\sim\!\!\diamondsuit\!\!\sim\!\!\diamondsuit$

Lucas didn't answer the question, a mercy for which Ashlynne was immediately and deeply grateful. The words echoed around her and her stomach dropped to her toes with embarrassment. Worse, the pounding in her head grew stronger.

Uncertain of what else to do and unwilling to say the wrong thing again, she turned toward the door. Lucas was there ahead of her, the apparent gentleman as he ushered her from the Clifford House without a word. Ashlynne said nothing, not even a murmur of thanks as she strode next to him down the boardwalk, together and yet apart. Neither choice really satisfied her.

The idea of being alone drew her with its promise of solitude and yet it terrified her for the very same reason. Once she truly was alone, there would be so much she could no longer avoid considering…remembering. But the opposite meant being with Lucas and that pleased her no better.

Gentlemanly behavior or not, she had little confidence in Lucas Templeton's trustworthiness. She had seen his exemplary moments and yet she couldn't help wondering about his sincerity. Her experience had shown her that most people in Skagway had an ulterior motive for the things they said and did.

Lucas would, too.

The silence between them continued as they walked and as the moments passed, it began to wear on Ashlynne. Nothing eased the awkwardness, not even the noise of Skagway's streets, ever churning with prostitutes, stampeders, wagons and horses. Ashlynne pretended a keen interest in the activities, but Lucas made no such effort. He merely stalked along next to her, his expression harsh and stoic as the dancing north wind fluttered the hair at his collar and over his forehead.

No, the idea of breaking the stalemate didn't appeal to her in the least. On the other hand, ignoring the silence between them, the distractions *and* Lucas himself grew increasingly difficult with each step. Worse, she thought with a spurt of frustration, her most private thoughts offered no better alternative. *There* waited only the agony and uncertainty of questions about her future to which she had no answers.

Panic crowded at the back of her throat, robbing her of breath until it was almost gone. Ashlynne gasped for air and lengthened her stride, trying to outpace Lucas. She tried to swallow as she wrestled with her anxiety, hoping to ease any other sound that would betray her.

Hurrying ahead, she stepped down at the crosswalk and plodded into the churned-up mud of the road, then crossed to the other side of the street and hastened up onto the boardwalk. Lucas's boots thudded behind her as he followed more closely than she'd anticipated.

Why couldn't she get a moment alone…a chance to think? Instead it seemed that things only continued to get worse and worse.

"Come on." Lucas spoke suddenly and held the door as he motioned her inside the Star of the North. Only then did she realize how far they'd walked.

"Sit down." He gestured to the room in general. "I'll get you some coffee."

"*Just* coffee?" Ashlynne asked, adding the emphasis without thinking. "Without whiskey?"

"*Just* coffee," he snapped, his voice noticeably sharp as he stalked away.

Exhausted suddenly, both emotionally and physically, Ashlynne made her way to the same table that had stood witness to her downfall last night. She sank onto the hard wooden chair and shrugged her cloak from her shoulders, glancing around her with no real purpose. Even so, she noticed the number of men who drank and gambled, even in the middle of the afternoon.

Shameful, she thought stiffly. *Weak-willed and self-indulgent.*

Exactly like most men she'd known in her life—her father and brother among them. And Elliott, as well.

Scoundrels, all three.

Unexpected tears prickled behind her eyelids and Ashlynne dropped her gaze to the tabletop, horrified to find herself so close to the edge of breaking down. She sucked in a desperate breath and blinked until the urge to cry gradually faded.

Lord, she was tired. Exhausted and no longer able to control the direction of her thoughts. She would have leaned forward, rested her elbows on the table and her cheek against her palm, but she knew better. It would reveal too much. But…just how long did she expect she could maintain this calm, emotionless facade?

It was time she faced the truth, though the thought of it

made her feel sick and disloyal. She hadn't the luxury of giving in to her feelings, however; she could only think in ways that were both sensible and practical. It was the only chance she had at safety.

The truth was she had little choice in the way things happened. She must give up her pride to rely on Lucas and his generosity for as long as he was willing to offer it. For now. Until she could find some way to establish herself in Alaska.

And how will you be able to do that? scoffed a disbelieving voice. She was alone, as alone as a body could be, and completely unsuited for the rough wickedness of a boomtown like Skagway—or so she realized now, when it was too late.

"It doesn't matter," Ashlynne muttered under her breath, her tone as determined as she could make it. "I'll find a way through this."

She must.

Ashlynne glanced around, as though she would find an answer—or perhaps some source of strength. She didn't, but she spied Lucas waiting next to the bar. He was a man not to be missed, taller and broader, more muscular—more *everything*—than any other man here. He dressed like a gentleman in a sea of wool and denim. More than that, his mouth hinted at illicit secrets about which she had no business wondering, while his slumberous eyes and tousled hair confirmed his explicit sensuality.

A sensuality she should have never noticed.

But how could she *not?* Something about him called to her on a very deep and basic level. He needn't do anything to demand her attention; he had it…and more. At times, he stole her breath and filled her with a wicked excitement that left her weak and shaking. Other times he scared her senseless.

And he was all that she had.

A heated flush raced through her, from the top of her head

to the soles of her feet, and her breath stumbled in her chest. Ashlynne dropped her gaze to her lap, where her hands clenched in useless fists, and prayed the awful reactions would stop. She couldn't allow this overwhelming reaction, not when it made her feel hot and cold at the same time and set her to trembling so badly she could hardly breathe.

Her mouth suddenly arid, Ashlynne touched her tongue to her lips. She knew all too well where such wanton thoughts could lead, and merely the idea of such…intimacy with Lucas robbed her of the ability to breathe. It frightened her as nothing else could and wouldn't leave her in peace.

The memory of waking in Lucas's bed, seeing him sprawled in the chair across the room with sleepy eyes and tousled hair, haunted some vital, feminine place deep inside her. She hadn't known herself capable of such a reaction, and now that she did, she couldn't get the image out of her head.

Her pulse went tripping to double speed and a new feverishness heated her skin until it ached. Ashlynne swallowed, shifting uneasily under a new unfamiliarity with her body and its reactions but unable to escape them. They crowded over her, producing sensations that left her nervous and excited and intrigued despite herself.

With a single-mindedness that had seen her through other difficult times in her life, Ashlynne wrenched a deep breath from somewhere and forced her thoughts to scatter. If she must face them, it would be later. For now her primary concern must remain her most pressing problems: a place to stay and a way to earn a living.

"Here's your coffee."

She jumped, glancing up at the sound of Lucas's voice. He approached carrying two steaming mugs, and a wave of déjà vu pulled her straight in her chair. Frowning, she took the blue-enameled cup from him. How had the important deci-

sions of her life been reduced to sitting here in this saloon—
at this very table—and drinking coffee with a man who was
little more than a stranger?

She peered into the pungent depths of the cup and sniffed.

"It's just coffee," said Lucas, an edge to his voice.

Ashlynne nodded. Unwelcome, a spurt of guilt warmed her
cheeks. Perhaps she had been too quick to disbelieve him; he
had been more generous than he had any obligation to be.

But…to trust a man? She couldn't remember the last time
she'd done so.

Last night. Her sense of self-protection provided a quick
reminder. *You trusted Ian to go out alone last night, and look
what happened.*

Rather than acknowledge the things she couldn't yet face,
she sipped from the cup and concentrated on the bitter taste
of the coffee. Without the sharp fire of whiskey, the flavor
seemed immensely improved. And perhaps one day she
would accept cream and sugar as a thing of the past.

Lucas took a seat across from her and drank from his own
cup. She hadn't the courage to ask him if he, too, drank just
coffee. It seemed unlikely that he did.

"So," he said as he placed his cup on the table. "Here we
sit, waiting for Clifford to have your things delivered. And
then?"

"I'm sorry?" It was an unworthy question and Ashlynne
knew it, just as she knew what Lucas asked; she simply had
no answer for him.

"What are you going to do next?"

She stalled, taking a small sip of coffee, but the weight of
his gaze made her uneasy. Finally, when she suspected that
she'd delayed long enough, she shook her head and forced her
gaze to Lucas's. "I'm…not sure," she admitted slowly. "But
I'm certain I'll think of something."

"Ashlynne." Lucas leaned forward and his hair tumbled over his shoulders and into his eyes. He shoved it back with undisguised impatience, his expression oddly fierce and angry and earnest all at once. "We both know what your answer should be. That you're going back to San Francisco immediately."

"Go back?" She plunked her cup on the table hard enough that coffee spilled out over the rim; she hardly noticed. She blinked furiously instead and glared at Lucas. *"Leave Skagway?"*

"There's nothing for you here. Not without Ian."

"Well, I can't leave, either."

"Why not?"

She could have answered in a dozen ways, but she chose the reason that mattered most to her heart. "I don't know who killed Ian."

"Dammit!" Lucas muttered another cussword or two under his breath, soft enough that Ashlynne couldn't hear. She didn't ask him to repeat them.

"What's wrong?"

"What's wrong!" He glared at her as he shoved his cup onto the table. "You sound as though you have no inkling what I mean."

"I don't."

"The hell you don't. Didn't your conversation with Taylor tell you anything?"

"Yes. It told me that I'd have to get my answers elsewhere. But that doesn't change anything. Other than knowing—all right, *suspecting*—" she inserted when Lucas narrowed his eyes "—that Soapy Smith is responsible for Ian's death, I'm sure of little else. I owe it to my brother to find out who did this and to see that justice is served."

Lucas sat as stiff as if he'd become frozen in place.

"Haven't I convinced you that there is no justice here? Didn't your run-in with Taylor make that clear enough?"

Stubbornly, she shook her head. "Justice may be missing at the moment, but that doesn't mean I can just accept the unfairness of it. Ian deserved better."

Lucas dropped his eyelids, but for only a moment. "He was a gambler, Ashlynne. He lost all your money and got himself into one hell of a lot of trouble. He left you stranded."

"He was my brother. All that was left of my family." She answered softly, undeterred by his terse words or the cold anger that sharpened his eyes to an icy blue. How Lucas felt didn't—couldn't—matter.

"He's dead."

Ashlynne flinched when he said it; she couldn't help herself. "Yes, I know. But he didn't deserve to die that way and I can't turn my back on what happened.

"Besides." She took a breath and tried to smile, but gave up the effort when it felt as weak as it did sad. "That isn't the only reason. I wasn't lying when I told you I couldn't leave. I don't have a return ticket or the money to purchase one."

Lucas's jaw tightened. "And I told you I'd give you the fare."

"I don't take that kind of charity from strangers."

Lucas paused and the silence between them filled with a growing intensity. "How much of a stranger can I be, darlin'?" He looked and sounded different than before. His eyelids drooped in a lazy blink and his rough voice sounded...suggestive. "You slept in my bed last night."

"Oh, stop it!" She shot him a scowl that was as frustrated as it was furious. "What happened last night was completely innocent and you know it."

He shrugged as though it made little difference. "Maybe so." And then the seductive, flirting stranger disappeared as quickly as he had come. "But my question remains unanswered. What do you propose to do now?"

"I…" She caught a breath and took a moment to think. "I should see Reverend Dickey and make arrangements for…Ian." Sudden tears threatened once more, but Ashlynne was better prepared this time and she blinked them away before Lucas could notice.

"And then?" Lucas watched her, considered her…dared her.

Buck up, she told herself, somehow finding the strength to straighten her shoulders and stiffen her spine. "Then I must find work."

"Doing what?"

His demand seemed relentless, the words flinty. Even so, she had no better answer for him than she'd had for herself. She only knew what she couldn't do. Ashlynne had seen enough to know she couldn't lead the kind of life that Candy led.

And yet, how many choices did she have? Her fellow passengers from the *Aurora Borealis* had all gone their separate ways. Deputy Taylor had turned her away, as had Mr. Clifford. And while Reverend Dickey might have offered to care for Ian, he hadn't been around since then to offer any comfort to the living.

Lucas had been the only one.

An idea struck her then, quite unexpectedly and admittedly borne of desperation. It made no sense…but what else did she have?

Trembling inside and determined not to show it, Ashlynne struggled for a steady smile and peered at Lucas with a confidence she didn't feel. "I can work for you. As…as—your housekeeper."

Lucas heard the words clearly enough, but he couldn't quite bring himself to believe them.

Ashlynne couldn't be serious—could she?

Another look at her earnest expression told him that, indeed, she was as serious about this as she had been about anything else. She appeared remarkably sure of herself, calm and even expectant.

And why not? Lucas demanded of himself with some disgust. He had done damn near everything he could think of to please her, and from almost the very first. What more could a woman in her position want from a friend or stranger? He'd even become her own private champion as soon as he'd discovered Ian's murder.

And now?

"I don't need a housekeeper," he said, careful to keep his tone steady and uncompromising.

"Of course you do!"

Did her smile waver or did it simply broaden? She smoothed a fluttering hand over her forehead and said with all apparent earnestness, "I may not have been at my best earlier, but I did notice your storage room was…well, quite a mess, actually."

She smiled again, this time with less certainty, as though she regretted her frankness. But she recovered quickly enough and gestured around her. "Look over there. The tables are stained—sticky! The floor is dirty, and who knows what these miners have tracked in? I'm sure your man behind the bar could use some help and—"

"Ashlynne—"

"Those are just a few of the things I could do. You have laundry, other cleaning and cooking chores. That sort of thing."

"The Star doesn't have a kitchen."

"But…" She visibly swallowed. "Where do you cook?"

"I don't. I eat in restaurants or have it delivered here." He paused, then added with a deliberately wicked smile, "Candy brings me…special delicacies sometimes."

"Well…" Ashlynne blinked but then offered him a weak if game smile. "You could add a kitchen if you wanted. And *then* I could cook for you. I—I'm sure it would save you money. I haven't had much chance to work out the details, but there is so much that I can do. I can figure it all out as soon as I'm settled."

Lucas frowned to show he wasn't convinced. "This is a saloon, Ashlynne—a place that serves whiskey and caters to drinkers, gamblers and…" He paused, looking for a delicate way to phrase the truth, then wondered why he even tried. She needed to remember the harsh realities of what being in the Star meant. "Prostitutes. Whores," he added with more callousness than was necessary. "You don't approve of any of that, so why would you want to work here?"

Her eyes widened, the shimmering whiskey-gold betraying a moment of uncertainty, but then she dropped her gaze and shook her head. "I—"

A ruckus at the front door interrupted whatever she might have said. Fighting his impatience, Lucas glanced across the room and recognized Henry Clifford's helper. The boy—approaching manhood within the next year or two—stumbled in through the doorway with a large trunk hefted over one shoulder. He peered around the room with the avid interest only an adolescent boy could muster.

"Put the luggage there by the door," Lucas called. He pointed to where it would be out of the way and ignored the youngster's interest.

"Yes…sir."

Lucas turned back to Ashlynne but she didn't notice. She was watching Clifford's helper, everything about her stiff with disapproval. Feeling that way, how could she claim to want to work here, for him?

"That's all of them."

Lucas glanced to where the boy had stacked three trunks, one on top of the other.

The young man stood gawking all around, taking in the sights the Star had to offer—and then Candy sashayed into the place with a delighted squeal. "Just who are you, you handsome young man?" she demanded with a laugh, reaching out to link her arm with his.

The boy blushed a bright, brilliant red and ran from the saloon as though his hind end was on fire. Lucas gave up an amused chuckle, despite himself. Ashlynne's frown, he noted, only deepened.

"What's all this?" Candy turned away from her lost conquest and pointed to the stack of trunks.

"Don't concern yourself." Lucas's amusement vanished and he looked at Ashlynne. "How much did you bring with you?"

She smiled, though it looked small and unconvincing. "Ian and I each had our own trunk and we shared one. For things we thought we'd need in the Klondike."

"And how did you think you were going to get all this to Dawson?"

"I…" she began but her smile faltered. She shook her head and gave a small sigh. "It never occurred to us. We were on the *Aurora Borealis* before we learned about the trail out of Skagway. By then, it was too late."

"I see." And Lucas did. Like so many others, the Mackenzies had understood nothing about the life for which they were headed when they'd started out for Alaska. And now…well, now it didn't seem to matter so much. Ian was dead, Ashlynne was alone—and she wanted to be Lucas's housekeeper.

His housekeeper? Goddammit!

"It'll never work," he muttered to himself, but she heard him.

"It *will,* Lucas. I can do the work! I know I can! I can do so much to help, so much to make—"

Her voice fell off in the oddest of ways, as though her air had suddenly been cut off. As though she'd just realized something vital or had an unexpected change of heart? She dropped her gaze from his.

"Yes?" he prompted, trying not to sound eager. Perhaps she had finally wised up and realized that staying in Skagway was not only futile but hardly in her best interest. "You can do so much? So much what?"

She didn't answer and didn't look at him.

"What's wrong?" he demanded.

She shook her head and pulled in a breath deep enough that he detected the gentle rise and fall of her breasts. *Don't notice!* he told himself. But the fitted bodice of her plum-colored gown made looking far more delightful than anything he'd seen in years.

"I'm sorry." She didn't look at him still. "This isn't the time for foolishness. I can't lie. You'd find out the truth soon enough." Slowly, clearly reluctant, she dragged her gaze up to meet his. "I can work for you, Lucas, and I *will* work hard. But I have no real experience at such things. All I know is from when I did domestic chores at our home in San Francisco. When my parents were…without funds."

Broke, Lucas thought, and wondered if her father had been a gambler like Ian. Most likely, if he could believe the bits of information he'd pieced together so far. And a drinker, too.

But he only asked, "Why are you telling me this, Ashlynne? There can be such a thing as too much honesty—particularly if you want me to hire you. You haven't much to recommend you so far."

Her expression softened, just enough to give him an idea of the despair she had done so much to conceal. "You've

been good to me. Better than anyone else." The admission
didn't seem to make her completely happy. "You're the only
one."

Dammit! Why had she said that? And why did she have to
look at him with that expression, all deep and anxious and forlorn? The combination hit him like a fist in the gut.

"I need this job, Lucas. I can't be a prostitute like Candy.
I won't! But I'm not stupid. I know my choices are limited.
Who in Skagway has the money or the need to hire domes-
tic help? Especially with limited skills? Someone like your
Soapy Smith? Or Deputy Taylor? No, no one else is going to
hire me. You're the only one."

Goddammit, she said it again.

She'd said other things, as well, and he couldn't forget any
of them. Ashlynne had spoken the truth; Lucas didn't doubt
it. Her choices *were* limited, and if he refused to hire her, then
what? She might speak out against prostitution now, but what
would happen after a few nights on Skagway's streets? Would
she be so defiant then?

Is that what you want? he demanded of himself. He knew
that if he refused her, it *would* happen. The past few years had
given him a very clear understanding of life in a town like
Skagway. So…could he do it?

"You've been very kind," Ashlynne said, an unmistakable
thread of urgency weaving through the care in her voice. "I
want you to know that I appreciate everything you've done.
If you can take this last chance on me, I'll work hard for you.
Harder than you can imagine."

Lucas stared at her, at her smooth, pale skin; her fine, delicate features; her whiskey eyes and mostly tamed hair. At her
womanly figure, all curves and tantalizing softness.

Indeed, some man—most men—would want her for themselves. Many in Skagway would be contented enough to have

her for an evening, or only an hour if they could afford no more. Ashlynne Mackenzie was too unique, too beautiful for any man to ignore. And once it became known that she was a woman without protection, there would be no saving her.

Don't you have enough sins on your soul? demanded his conscience harshly. It sounded a bit like Emily at her most appalled. *Do you intend to add this girl's virtue to your list?*

Lucas shook his head without quite meaning to. No matter what else he might do in this life, he didn't expect to save himself. His sins were too many; he had gone too far over the edge for that. But was he so without heart that he could carelessly cast Ashlynne into a life of prostitution? For no reason other than his own selfishness?

What would Emily think of the man he had become?

"All right." The words were out before he could stop them and then it was too late. "I'll hire you."

Chapter Seven

∽◉∾

He'd agreed! Elation soared through Ashlynne much like Skagway's gusty north wind. Working for Lucas was far from a perfect solution; it required a compromise of her beliefs that was almost more than she could bear—at its worst, her very self, it seemed. It would put her in close proximity with him, which perhaps seemed less than wise considering her physical awareness of him. But what choice did she have?

Ian's death had changed everything; she was only just beginning to understand the truth of it. It took her plans for the future and utterly destroyed them. It left her wondering if she even *had* a future, and as the hours had passed and she'd accustomed herself to continuing without him, it made her certain of something else. Survival—and nothing else—was all that mattered.

Survival meant that if she didn't make this compromise, she would lose everything—and she hadn't that much left to her beyond her willingness to work hard and a bit of self-respect.

"You'll pay wages?" she asked before she lost her nerve. "And provide room and board?"

Lucas glared at her, his eyes narrowing with mistrust. "Room and board?"

"I need somewhere to stay." It took all she had for Ashlynne to sound practical and businesslike despite the nerves that fought to unsteady her.

"Why is that my responsibility?"

Why, indeed. Already he had done more than his share to help her, but she couldn't allow that to influence her. Ashlynne cleared her throat. "You heard Mr. Clifford. He doesn't have any rooms. And even if he did, he wouldn't allow me to stay. Maybe you know of another hotel or boarding house where they'd feel differently?"

Deliberately, Ashlynne turned the last into a question. Lucas could make his own suggestion if he had one. He did nothing but tighten his lips and shoot her a stiff frown.

"Room and board," he repeated and shook his head, ignoring the hair that tumbled over his eyes. Ashlynne wasn't so distracted. She noted the sharp, vibrant blue, the way his lips tightened, the blond tangle of hair.

And she hated that she noticed.

"And where, exactly, do you plan to stay?" He flung his hand wide. "Under one of the tables? Or maybe back by the poker game?"

"Don't be silly." She relied on her own frown to demonstrate her seriousness. "The Star of the North is big enough for space other than the storage room where I slept last night."

"This is a saloon," he snapped impatiently. "I make my living from whiskey and gambling. I don't leave room for anything else."

Goaded by his angry tone, Ashlynne inspected the room through different eyes. Since he'd mentioned it, she could see that every available space was filled with tables and chairs, and the gaming area looked roughly twice the size of the storage

room that occupied the opposite corner. But there, in the
back...

"Where does that staircase lead?" she asked.

"To the second floor." Lucas stated the obvious, sounding
bored—or was it sarcastic again? She couldn't be sure and
Lucas's guarded expression gave her no other clues.

"Yes, I know." She worked to sound patient. "But what's
up there?"

"What's usually on the second floor of a saloon?"

He wanted to frighten her by sounding angry; the underlying
disdain and rough edge to his voice told her so. He couldn't
quite carry it off, however. His eyes darkened with a slumber-
ousness that seemed somehow wildly alive at the same time and
gave him a strange intensity that seemed almost...electrified.

But why?

She glanced back to the staircase. What could possibly be
located on the upper floor that would elicit such a reaction
within him, and how could she possibly expect to understand
Lucas's odd behavior? Her personal experience with saloons
involved nothing more than the events of—what?—the past
eighteen hours.

Eighteen hours?

A sudden lump in her throat made Ashlynne swallow. Less
than a day? How could it be that no more time than that had
passed? Her entire life had been turned upside down. She'd
seen things thrown topsy-turvy before, but never like this.

Ashlynne opened her mouth to tell Lucas exactly how
things seemed to her at the moment...and then a faint memory from years gone by flitted into her consciousness.

There had been another day when all her illusions were utterly shattered. It had been as many as ten years ago and Ian
had come to her in an odd, exultant mood that she hadn't recognized at the time.

He'd been increasingly impressed with himself back then, as their father had begun to take an unprecedented interest in his only son. Three years younger, Ashlynne had noticed the changing relationship and, as much as it shamed her to admit it, she had been sick with jealousy. Any attention their parents had ever paid to her usually came in the form of acute disappointment.

On this particular day, Ian had been even more jubilant than usual. "Father took me out with him last night."

"Yes, I know." Ashlynne had answered carefully, trying to sound unimpressed.

"He took me to a—" Ian had stopped, then laughed and finished. "A drinking establishment. A place where there were women."

"Women?" Not yet in her teens, Ashlynne had been young in so many ways then—surprisingly naive, she thought now, considering the lifestyle her parents had led. "Ladies who drink liquor?" Even now, so many years later, she remembered how properly appalled she had sounded—and how silly.

Ian had found her innocence wildly funny. "Of course there are ladies who drink liquor! *Mother* drinks liquor, for God's sake!"

"Well…yes." Ashlynne had pretended a worldliness she didn't feel—and which she doubted that Ian had believed, in any case. But still she had tried. "What does that have to do with the women you saw last night?"

"Can't you figure anything out for yourself?" He had laughed again, sounding completely amused by her stupidity. "These weren't just women, you idiot! They were prostitutes. Father took me to a brothel. They serve liquor on the first floor—and women on the second. And I had them both."

Even now, heat shot through Ashlynne. Fire blazed up her

neck and across her cheeks and seemed to sear her lungs, making it almost impossible to breathe. Her mouth had gone dry again and the pounding in her head returned twofold. Only a fervent need to keep her humiliation to herself kept her from gasping in pain.

"Ashlynne?"

She forced her gaze up to meet his. Lucas looked as wanton and wicked as any man she'd ever seen, his hair tumbling over his forehead, his eyes glittering, and his lips full and parted, as though waiting to kiss the next woman he found.

And more.

And, as shocking as it seemed, a very real part of her wanted to be that woman.

She swallowed. "Are you telling me this is a brothel? That you employ prostitutes upstairs?"

He smiled just a bit, a strange expression that looked both taunting and wholly immoral. Her heart pounded so hard in her chest, she thought surely he must be able to hear it.

"Would you get on the next ship back to San Francisco if I did?" he asked.

Was that his game? To humiliate—or frighten—her into leaving?

"No." She allowed no uncertainty in her tone. She couldn't.

His expression fell away to one of fury. "Goddammit, Ashlynne."

"I will not leave," she insisted with more bravery than she felt. "I have responsibilities—commitments. Including one to you. We agreed."

"*You* decided. I was coerced."

"You agreed."

He snatched up his cup and drained the last of it. "All right. Let's say I agreed."

"Do you employ prostitutes upstairs?"

"No." His voice carried all the stinging snap of a whip. "I sell liquor and gambling, not women. Candy's here to convince the men to spend their money. If she wants to take some miner back to her bed when she's done here, that's her business."

He paused long enough to warn her he spoke with some reluctance. "The upstairs is empty."

Ashlynne's relief at his words lost some of its influence when she realized exactly what *empty* meant. She could have the entire second floor at her disposal.

Why had he taunted her that way?

"I could live there, then," she suggested in a casual tone that wouldn't reveal how badly she wanted him to agree.

"No." He dashed her hopes with the word.

"Why not, if it's empty?"

Lucas raised his cup without answering and signaled for another drink. Ashlynne stiffened. He was going to drink more alcohol?

She said nothing. Yet. The question of where she would stay still had not been decided.

"Why not?" she repeated instead.

"It's unfinished."

"Is that all?" She caught her lip between her teeth rather than smile in renewed excitement. Lucas, however, continued to frown, his expression thoroughly out of sorts. "That doesn't bother me in the least."

"It bothers me," he returned. "Unfinished means there's nothing but a few walls up there. No doors. No locks."

She shrugged. "I didn't have a lock at the Clifford House, either. Just some canvas partitioning off rows of cots."

"Here you go, Lucas."

The bartender arrived with a glass. Not another blue-enameled cup but a shot glass. Filled with the vile whiskey she hated so much.

"Thanks, Willie."

For the first time, Ashlynne looked closely at the man who dispensed liquor from behind Lucas's bar. Willie wasn't as tall as Lucas but he was solidly built, a man who could take care of himself. His light-colored hair was more blond than brown and the expression on his round face looked like the model for good cheer.

She watched through lowered lashes as Lucas shared a wicked smile with Willie, then he took a slow, clearly contented sip of whiskey. He settled back in his chair as though he meant to sit and enjoy himself for a good long while.

And despite it all, she had to try again. "I don't care about doors or locks. I only want a place to stay."

"A woman staying upstairs alone? An unmarried female?" Lucas couldn't have sounded more incredulous, the sparkle in his eyes looking suddenly dangerous. "When I've got a saloon full of men—*lonely men*—downstairs? It would be a cold day in hell before I allowed that to happen."

Ashlynne supposed he meant what followed to be a laugh, but it sounded more like a snort. "It's going to be bad enough when word gets out that you're here at all," he added.

She shook her head. "I won't tell anyone."

Lucas gave a bark of real laughter this time. "You won't need to, honey. People in Skagway are already talking about you. There aren't enough women in all of Alaska to allow you to pass through unnoticed. Once they find out you aren't a grieving widow…well, things will change. You can bet on it."

"What do you mean by that?"

"Everything. You've already generated enough interest." He sipped his whiskey and considered her. "It might be good for business, I suppose…" He paused and drank again. "But it'll damn sure be a pain in the ass."

"I beg your pardon!"

"What?"

"You—your language."

Lucas laughed again. "You don't like the way I talk?"

"No, I don't."

"Then you can always go back to San Francisco."

Ashlynne glared at him. Checkmate. He had her and he knew it.

"I am not leaving."

"Then you better get used to hearing cusswords—and a whole lot more than that, honey. If you're going to live here, you'll see and hear worse—and not necessarily from me."

"Then I can stay?"

He stared at her, losing every bit of his amusement in no more than the beat of a heart. He blinked and then, finally, he shrugged. "You'll have to take the storage room. I'll move upstairs."

Euphoria flooded through Ashlynne, and relief made her feel almost light-headed. She swallowed to hold back both the laughter and the tears that tried to press forward. She had earned his agreement again!

She had a place to stay.

"I—" Ashlynne cut herself off. The woman she had been yesterday would have apologized for inconveniencing him. The woman who had lived through the past eighteen hours knew better. He might view an apology as a weakness and she couldn't afford so much as the impression of such a thing.

"It seems, then, that we have a deal." She held out her hand and reached across the table to seal their bargain with a handshake.

Lucas hesitated. Or did she only imagine it? she wondered as he slowly offered his own hand in return. His fingers closed around hers and their palms nestled against each other as though made to fit together. His hand swallowed hers and his skin all but scorched hers with its intrinsic heat. She couldn't pull away...but how long could she withstand the force of this man and his touch? Especially when it made her think of so many other things.

"We have a deal," he said softly, perhaps ruefully, and he withdrew his hand. Slowly. "Now I suppose I should take you to your room. Willie will bring your trunks later. You can start work tomorrow."

Lucas rose in a swift, fluid motion and Ashlynne did the same. He carried his glass with him. "Come on."

She followed him from the table, her thoughts racing. An errant question returned from their earlier conversation, and she asked, "Lucas?"

"What?" He didn't turn to look at her as they neared the storage room—*her* room, she reminded herself with a sliver of glee.

"How will people know I'm not a widow?"

He opened the door and pushed it wide before he turned back to her. "What did you tell Taylor?" He caught her eyes with a deliberate question in his. "That your husband or your brother died? And what about Clifford? You checked in at his place as brother and sister. And the preacher? Are you going to lie to him and tell him you're burying your husband?"

Of course. Ashlynne shook her head. She should have thought of such details herself.

"You might as well learn one thing right now, Irish." Lucas spoke without a thread of kindness in his tone. He swallowed all the whiskey in his glass and shot her a steady look. "A place like Skagway doesn't leave room for secrets. We're too far away from wherever anybody calls home. News from Outside travels up here slow, and that leaves just about everything open for gossip."

He stepped back, away from her, and gestured for her to enter. "If you've got any secrets, you damn well better keep them to yourself."

Lucas sat at his customary table, drinking his customary whiskey and watching Ashlynne as she worked in the far corner of the room. She'd found herself a scarred-up old piece of wood and stacked up empty crates to create a counter of sorts. That had become her work area. At the moment she'd added a bucket and porcelain bowl to serve as a dishpan, and she was washing dirty glasses.

Lucas grunted and sipped his whiskey. Her tidy little work area looked completely out of place—too homey for the Star—but he let it go for the moment. He had a more pressing problem to consider first.

He had to get her to quit grieving.

He frowned as she fished the glasses, one by one, from the soapy water and rinsed them in the nearby bucket. She wore a plain black skirt and white blouse, the uniform she seemed to have adopted as her working attire. Her mink-colored hair was wound up in a soft bun at the back of her head and her apron covered her from bodice to ankle.

It didn't hide a damn thing, as far as he was concerned.

Lucas could still see every one of her curves, all but feel the softness of her skin as his fingers touched her…almost taste her.

Goddammit!

He swallowed half the whiskey, hardly noticing the burn as it slid down his throat. Instead he scowled at the tidy, feminine picture she made.

It had been nearly a week since Ashlynne had persuaded him to hire her, a week during which he'd spent every waking hour questioning both his judgment and his sanity. What the hell had he been thinking? Had he lost his common sense to an early bout of cabin fever?

No. He almost wished he had. He'd done the only thing he could under the circumstances, and he knew it. Lucas might not have been the one responsible for getting her into the mess of her life right now, but that didn't mean he could turn his back on her. Not when he knew it would only make things worse.

He didn't have much decency left to him and the truth of it was, most of the time it didn't worry him overmuch. Emily's memory, however, demanded that he do the right thing from time to time and this seemed to be one of them.

His wife had always had a soft spot for the less fortunate.

Even so, the reality of what he'd done ate at him every damn day. To make matters worse, no matter what Ashlynne had said to convince him to hire her, she'd lied.

She wasn't adjusting to her new lifestyle at all.

It had been six days since he'd hired her and five since the brief service for her brother. She'd been appalled to discover that burial couldn't take place until the spring when the ground thawed. Lucas hadn't seen her smile, not even once, since then. She didn't speak to others unless spoken to. She rarely made eye contact and she very deliberately kept herself aloof from all activity around her. And she seemed to do it in a way that would assure everyone else understood what she was about.

You should be happy. She's keeping herself away from the men. Lucas had told himself the same thing countless times each day. Somehow, he couldn't accept it. She seemed to be simply fading away.

Absently he sipped from his glass and watched as she dried the now clean glasses. She moved with an economy of movement, her hands both gentle and nimble as she smoothed cotton toweling over each of the glasses. It took nothing at all before Lucas's imagination transformed the image and he had her hands on him, streaking across his chest and down to where he wanted her to touch him most. Her fingers would curl around him and—

Son of a bitch.

He grunted and tossed back the last bit of whiskey, shifting as his body suddenly rose to life. What the hell was wrong with him, sitting in the middle of the Star and making himself hard by fantasizing about a woman who was as priggish as she was edgy? If he wanted a woman that bad, Candy had issued an open invitation.

Candy. Lucas looked around until he found the sometime-prostitute. She held court at a table of men, most of whom he didn't know. It didn't matter. As immodest as it might sound, Lucas knew that if he'd wanted her right now, she would have left them all to be with him.

But he didn't.

Lucas turned back to Ashlynne. The difference between the women startled him as much as it had whenever he compared them. Ashlynne Mackenzie had no business being in the Star. She wasn't a woman made for manual labor and broken hearts; she should be pampered and indulged. She should be back in San Francisco, married to some nice, polite young man who would keep her comfortable in a fancy home and give her lots of babies.

She shouldn't be in Alaska at all—and she sure shouldn't be around him.

Lucas lifted his glass once more and discovered it was empty. He surged to his feet with a frown and stalked across the room to plunk his glass on the bar. "Give me a refill," he said to Willie, "and another whiskey."

Lucas snatched up both glasses with a muttered thanks and skirted the wooden length of the bar, approaching Ashlynne from behind. "Here."

"What?" She turned, coming within an arm's length of him, and then she stopped, but not before he caught the soft scent of lavender. Lucas couldn't remember having noticed that about her before, but somehow it didn't surprise him, either. It was light and fresh and feminine, refreshing after the heavy rosewater that Candy preferred.

"What do you want?" Ashlynne asked when he didn't say anything.

"Here." He thrust the glass toward her. "Drink this."

"I will not." She scooted back and held her dish towel up in front of her like a weapon. "That's whiskey, and I've already told you I don't drink spirits."

"It didn't hurt you the other night. This little bit—" he raised the glass "—won't make you a drunkard."

She wrinkled her brow in obvious displeasure. "It won't do me any good, either. Why would you even *suggest* such a thing?"

"You need it."

"I *what?*" she demanded. Outrage made her voice loud enough to attract attention from across the room. Lucas didn't turn to see if anyone had noticed.

"I do not need alcohol!" Her tone remained brittle. "What kind of a man are you to suggest such a thing to me—and why now?"

"I'm a man who's tired of watching you mope around here like you've done for the last week. It's time you got over whatever's stuck in your craw. If you need to get drunk to do it…" Lucas shrugged. "You won't be the first."

She stiffened as though she'd just bitten into a sour apple. The reaction thrust her breasts into sharp relief, and though he knew better, Lucas could almost imagine he saw the outline of her nipples beneath the cover of her apron and blouse.

"I happen to be in mourning," she said in a voice so icy it

would have made him shiver, if he hadn't already spent years accustoming himself to the cold of life in Alaska. But at least it diverted his attention from her breasts.

Now it was time for Ashlynne to accustom herself to this life she'd worked so hard to attain.

"You can't afford to be in mourning, Irish. This isn't San Francisco and you can't take to your bed and indulge in your grief for months at a time. This is Alaska. Life goes on here, and damn fast. This place will kill you if you don't keep up."

He hadn't let anything about living get away from him in years.

"Are you complaining about my work?" She dared him with eyes that flashed the same coppery golden light as the whiskey in his hands.

Lucas stared at her without answering while his brain sorted through a thousand thoughts. He *couldn't* complain and she knew it. She worked like a demon at the exclusion of all else save sleeping. She didn't eat, not even when he had food brought in from Lottie's Restaurant down the street, and now that he stood this close to her, he could see a new gauntness to her cheeks and the circles beneath her eyes.

He hadn't thought much about the cleanliness of the place before Ashlynne had invented this job for herself. The Star of the North was a saloon—a place to make money, where men came to drink and gamble and spend a few hours in friendly conversation. Nobody wanted it neat and tidy, like a man's home—or did they?

As much as he hated to admit it, Lucas could see the difference since Ashlynne had started to work. Apparently so could his customers. They'd begun to make comments about how the Star was nicer than Clancy's or Jeff Smith's Parlor or any of the other saloons in town. Lucas could even tell a difference in the till.

Business was up.

"I'm not talking about your work," he confessed, though in a deliberately prickly voice. "I'm talking about *you*. You're as unhappy as I've ever seen a body. How long do you think you'll survive like this, crying yourself to sleep every night and moving through the days like a ghost?"

Her eyes widened, the surprise in them clear. Had she thought he didn't hear the sound of her tears or notice the aloof nonexistence she courted?

Well, he saw and heard, and he wasn't going to leave her to her own devices any longer. *She* was the one who'd insisted on staying in Skagway—and at his expense. Now, by God, she was going to start playing by *his* rules.

"You either wake up and start living again," he said flatly, "or you drink the whiskey." He smacked the shot glass down on her counter. "You choose—or I'll choose for you."

Chapter Eight

Excitement ran through the Star of the North like an avalanche heading downhill. Lucas had found a piano and he'd hired a crew of men to fetch it from the beach.

Ashlynne didn't want to share in the enthusiasm. She refused to allow it, in fact. It wouldn't be proper. Her brother had been dead only a week. It simply wouldn't be decent for her to be happy or excited about something.

Ian would never feel any of those things again.

Why, then, couldn't she seem to help this sudden, bubbling thrill of anticipation?

She remained in *her corner,* as she had come to think of her work area. She had found the most unobtrusive spot in the saloon and arranged a place where she could do as many of her chores as possible. Now, she stacked clean glasses on a tray so she could return them to Willie behind the bar…and she thought about Lucas's purchase.

A piano! Music. How she wished she could allow herself to smile, even laugh, with the delight that ached to burst free, but she held her reaction. She shouldn't—she couldn't. And yet she couldn't deny that she'd wished for something to help her forget…if only for a little while.

Music would do that; it had always done that for her. It was her special talent, one of the few interests she'd shared with her mother. When the Mackenzies had had the money, Ashlynne had gladly taken lessons. It was the one thing she could do that would please her parents. She had studied the classics, of course—Mozart, Beethoven, Bach—but she had also taught herself more popular tunes that her parents had favored. "There is A Tavern in The Town" and "The Sidewalks of New York" had been among their favorites. They had delighted when she'd played them, for once taking pleasure in her ability to entertain them.

But the Mackenzies' piano had been sold long ago and Ashlynne hadn't played in longer than she cared to remember. Still, just the thought of losing herself in the wonder of the music delighted her as little else could have.

Propriety, however, would not be silenced and Ashlynne stared down at her half-filled tray. She had learned to depend on her conscience for its quick and icy chastisement; it would keep her respectable, especially now, whenever she strayed from grief to more ordinary considerations. But this time, the memory of Lucas's earlier words answered. He seemed to think her grief was misplaced, that she should have put it behind her already and settled into this new life. She didn't deny that the idea had shocked her at first. If she'd been at home in San Francisco she would never have even considered such a thing. But she no longer had a home in San Francisco, and her time in Skagway had proved that Lucas Templeton was right about one thing.

Life here was different and the old rules didn't apply.

Could he be right about the rest of it? *Should* she start living again? Could she?

Dare she?

She hadn't spoken to Lucas since yesterday when he'd

tried to bully her with the whiskey, warning her to forget. His suggestion had infuriated her and she hadn't intended to break her self-imposed silence anytime soon. But sometime between then and now, she'd begun to have second thoughts.

What if he was right? She busied herself again, stacking the rest of the glasses onto the tray. Along with the other things she'd learned about life in Alaska, she hadn't seen where it tolerated much physical incapacity—and certainly nothing like emotional weakness. Grief and heartbreak and fear were patently unwelcome. If you had such emotions, you dealt with them privately, and then only when necessary. Otherwise, a person continued on with everyday life.

If you didn't, you might not survive.

In truth, she'd already proved the effectiveness of that very scheme. The night Ian had been murdered, her instincts had insisted that she think of nothing beyond each passing minute. She had indeed survived that first horrible night that way. And later, when she'd needed a job and a place to live, she'd put everything else from her mind…and she'd managed to achieve them, too.

Could she do the same thing again? For good?

Allowing herself to hesitate no longer, Ashlynne left her workspace. She delivered the glasses to Willie and then approached Lucas. As she neared his chair, a sudden attack of nerves threatened to rob her of her breath.

Swallowing, she bent to clean his table with a damp rag. "Where did you find the piano?" she asked.

She felt the weight of his gaze on her as she collected the dirty dishes to be returned to the restaurant after Lucas's dinner, but she didn't look up to see his eyes. She couldn't. Not yet.

"Another *cheechako*," he finally answered.

"Anyone you know?"

"No. He thought he was going to take the thing to Dawson and open a saloon there. Like you and your brother, he thought to come early and get a jump on the spring thaw. He changed his mind when he got a look at what it meant to pack a piano beyond Skagway."

"Is he going to work for you?" Still bent over the table, she peered up at him through the fan of her lashes.

Lucas was watching her, curiously, of course—and why wouldn't he after she'd become this sudden chatterbox? But he merely shook his head. "I bought the piano, not the man. He won't be in Skagway long. He's got gold fever."

She straightened, struggling to breathe as she forced herself to look into those glittering blue eyes. From somewhere deep inside, she found the courage to ask, "What are you going to do with the piano?"

He shrugged. "Find somebody to play it." He grinned suddenly in a deliberately wicked and sensual way that Ashlynne hated. "Maybe Candy's got a talent that I don't know about."

He wanted her to react. The calculated slant of his eyes and the knowing curve of his lips told her so. Just like when he called her Irish. And because she knew he wanted to upset her, she refused to allow it.

Just as she refused to acknowledge the lure of his handsomeness.

"Why don't you ask her?" Ashlynne suggested as a ruckus at the door erupted. She glanced past him and added, "It looks like your piano has arrived."

He turned away as the men he'd hired stumbled in through the door. There were five of them, one supporting each corner of the piano and one directing their progress. Big, burly men dressed in denim and flannel, they huffed and puffed and grunted as they manhandled the piano into the room.

"In the back, boys," Lucas called, and stood. He left Ashlynne standing by the table to cross the room. "The poker game moved up front."

A cheer rose up from the crowd and Lucas waved with a grin while Ashlynne glanced around the room. Sure enough, the table and chair arrangement that had occupied the far back corner had moved to the front of the saloon. And for the first time since she'd stumbled into the Star, no one seemed interested in cards. Instead, the men crowded around the space made empty for the piano.

She couldn't help smiling to herself, a soft expression she would never let anyone see. The collective reaction of these men fascinated her. Surely they couldn't all share her love for music. Who would have thought that something as simple as the arrival of a plain upright piano—and probably hopelessly out of tune—could so excite a group of rough, hard-drinking miners?

"Candy?" Lucas called, and Ashlynne found herself looking around the room. "Where are you, darlin'?"

An odd, indecipherable emotion settled low in the pit of her stomach and stole most of her breath. She swallowed. How could Lucas call Candy that? He'd called *her*—Ashlynne—darlin'. And honey. And Irish—but that wasn't the same at all.

Don't be silly! Ashlynne retreated behind a small frown. What did it matter? She wanted no part of Lucas and his meaningless endearments. He was her employer and not some man with whom she wanted to…dally.

You cannot trust men, she reminded herself sternly as she tried to look anywhere but at Lucas. *Not in that way—maybe not at all. Didn't Elliott prove everything you need to know about men and the lies they tell to get what they want?*

Yes, she *did* know. So why did she watch Lucas with more interest than she'd ever tendered for any other man? Including Elliott. And why did it prick at her that he shared his sweet nothings with other women? He hadn't used them as terms of endearment for her; he'd always said them with a certain amount of sarcasm. Worse, why did Lucas make her feel all odd and achy and breathless, as though she needed something that only he could provide?

"Are you looking for me, sugar?"

Candy's question interrupted Ashlynne's thoughts—and it was just as well. She'd been heading into dangerous territory, ground far better left uncovered. Permanently.

Dressed in a gown made of shocking yellow satin and decorated with strategically placed ruffles and bows that accented each of her very feminine curves, Candy extricated herself from the arms of an enthusiastic stampeder. Try as she might, Ashlynne couldn't help the bite of jealousy that kept her watching the other woman's every move.

The would-be miner, whom Ashlynne didn't recognize, growled his disappointment and Candy laughed with clear delight. She left the man behind, parading across the floor with a swing of her hips to show off shapely ankles and a glimpse of equally shapely calves.

"There you are, Sugar Candy." Lucas laughed at her antics, relaxing in a way Ashlynne would have never guessed he could. He looked suddenly younger, less debauched, and his handsome face became suddenly stunning.

Ashlynne caught a short, surprised breath, and a fine trembling started deep within her as she realized just how spectacular Lucas's looks really were. His fine broadcloth suits provided an effective disguise for his height and muscular build, or at least they encouraged her to forget about such things. His fine, aristocratic facial features, his piercing blue eyes and shaggy blond hair all gave him the dissolute look of handsome roguishness.

He made Elliott look like an untried schoolboy of little experience or consequence. The two were, quite literally, worlds apart.

Ashlynne should have enjoyed the comparison—and a part of her did, she realized with some dismay. But the heady danger that surrounded Lucas Templeton didn't reassure her one bit over the clear ineptness of Elliott Sanders.

A friend of Ian's, Elliot had turned Ashlynne's head with his attention and compliments. He had charmed her and made her care for him, and when he'd taken all her love, he'd tossed it back in her face like so much garbage. He had broken her heart.

Ashlynne had thought that Elliott's perfidy had cured her of any wanton tendencies. For good. Now, however, she was coming to realize he might have only heightened them. He'd educated her, given her a certain idea of the intimacies a woman could expect with a man. At one time, she had learned to be grateful for such lessons, believing they would save her in the future. Now she regretted it with all her being.

She had never imagined she would meet Lucas and be faced with the stirrings of desire such as she'd never known. And, worse, that Lucas would prove to be even less suitable for her than Elliott had been.

Across the room Candy's laugh caught Ashlynne's attention. "I've been waiting all night for you to ask after me, sugar," she said to Lucas, sidling up to him. She slipped her arm around his waist, as she did whenever she had the chance. Slim and curved, she reached to just below his shoulder and made a perfect foil for his blatant masculinity.

Ashlynne hadn't liked the sight of Lucas and Candy together the first time she'd seen them that way and she hated it now.

He laughed again, along with all the other men in the room. Ashlynne scowled.

"I want your *musical* talent, honey," Lucas said as he turned her toward the piano. The men he'd hired had turned to settling it into place and someone tinkled the high-octave keys.

Ashlynne had been right: it was out of tune. Not that anyone else seemed to notice—or care.

She forgot about the piano when Candy rubbed herself against Lucas and peered up at him. "One thing now, something else later, is that right, sugar?" she purred in a voice loud enough that Ashlynne could hear it clear across the room.

Ashlynne swallowed, though she couldn't tear her gaze away, not even when Candy slipped behind Lucas and wrapped her arms around his waist. The woman moved with agonizing slowness, her breasts against his back, her pelvis against his buttocks.

Ashlynne's mouth went dry and for a minute she thought she might throw up. Then Lucas laughed again, followed by a roar of amusement from the rest of the men in the Star. The noise drowned out any other sound.

Ashlynne sucked in a harsh, ragged breath and clutched the edge of the table. She swallowed and stumbled back until her legs found a chair.

These people were horrible—*horrible*—and this place was worse! It was as she'd first suspected. Men wasted themselves here, both their time and their bodies, and they did it day after day, night after night. They threw away their hard-earned money on cards and liquor and women. Fast women, easy women. Disgusting women.

A man's honor and his promises to family and loved ones mattered not at all.

The Star of the North was the scourge of society, and as frightening as that truth was, there was something worse.

She had nowhere else to go!

* * *

For chrissake, Candy was terrible!

Lucas didn't look around; he didn't need to. The same disappointment would show on every face in the Star. For a woman who had legs all the way to heaven and could hump like a mink, a man expected...more.

He had to give her credit, though; she gave it her best. The piano was undeniably out of tune after its arduous journey from Seattle to Skagway, but there was one hell of a lot more at fault than that. Candy hit as many wrong notes as she did right ones and her voice sounded like the caterwauling of a bitch cat in heat.

Damn, but he'd never heard anything so bad.

Knowing he couldn't put it off any longer, Lucas glanced around and saw the expected dismay on the faces of the other men. Even Willie, who had a known soft spot for Candy, looked horrified.

Now what was he going to do? Lucas glanced back at Candy who was perched on the edge of her chair as she pounded out...whatever it was she was supposed to be singing. He couldn't let her continue this way. She'd chase away more business than he'd have left.

Unable to watch any longer, he turned and saw Ashlynne seated at a table. She stared at Candy with the same wide expression of stunned disbelief that everyone else wore—and something more.

Satisfaction?

Hell, yes, Ashlynne would be satisfied. Happy, in fact, if this whole damn place fell to ruin, as it would if he provided *this* for entertainment. She hated saloons—and she didn't drink whiskey.

She was only here because she had nowhere else to go. And because he was a fool.

The woman was too damn stubborn for her own good. She wouldn't take his help without working for it, and she wouldn't go home. She was a goddamn martyr and he was stuck with her.

Unless...

"Ashlynne!" He strode across the room and grabbed her hand. "Come on, Irish." He pulled her to her feet. "It's your turn."

"I beg your pardon!" She twisted her arm and tried to extricate herself, but Lucas only tightened his grip.

"Come on," he said again, tossing the instruction over his shoulder. "You can play for us. It's sure as hell plain that Candy can't!"

"Well, I can't, either! I won't."

"You've got to. Do you have any idea what she's playing?" He glanced over his shoulder when Ashlynne didn't answer. She stumbled along behind him looking perfectly horrified. "Well?" he demanded. "Do you?"

She shook her head. "No, not for certain. It might be 'Roll Out the Barrel'?"

Lucas raised his eyebrows and let loose a bark of laughter. "Amazing. I'd have never guessed it."

He pulled Ashlynne to a stop just as Candy finished her rendition of whatever she'd been trying to play. She screeched out the last note and pounded the keys with a grand gesture...and then, mercifully, she was silent.

"Lordamercy, Candy, you were godawful!"

A sudden tension raked the air and even Ashlynne stiffened. Lucas coughed and glanced around. Oregon Charlie, who'd been so reluctant to let Candy go in the first place, grinned and pushed by them, swaggering up to her. She turned on him in a fury.

"What do you mean, I was awful?" She slapped his hands

away when he reached for her and stood, turning to glare first at Oregon Charlie, then Lucas, and finally the room in general.

"You do a much better job in my bed, Sugar Candy," wheedled Charlie as he reached for her again.

"Lucas?" She sidestepped her paramour and stared at him. "Are you going to let him talk to me that way?"

He didn't answer, debating with himself exactly what to say and how he could say it. He ran out of time to decide when Candy looked past him and narrowed her eyes.

He still held Ashlynne's arm.

Lucas shrugged and smiled with as much sheepish boyishness as he could manage. "I'm sorry, Candy, but singing and piano playing aren't among your best talents. You've got other attributes, though…"

Rather than finish his sentence, he tried to make his point by reaching for her with his free hand, tracing one finger over the low dip of her décolletage—and promptly had his hand knocked away. Ashlynne jerked her arm free of his grip at the very same time.

He frowned at them both, one after the other. "What's the matter with you women?"

Neither answered but both glared at him.

"You're talkin' about women, Templeton," called a voice from the crowd. "Don't bother tryin' to figure it out."

"Forget it." Lucas grabbed Ashlynne's arm again and made a wide swing around Candy to pull her forward. "Ashlynne's next."

The men in the saloon let out a collective cheer that drowned out any arguments from either woman. Oregon Charlie, meanwhile, pulled Candy into his arms and backed her up against the wall, cutting off anything she might have said by sealing her mouth with his.

Lucas dismissed the others and turned to Ashlynne. "Go on, Irish," he said in an admittedly arrogant tone. But—he had her this time. He knew it. *This time* she would agree to leave. "You *can* play, can't you?"

She stared at him for so long, the men began to shift uneasily. Then she closed her eyes slowly, deliberately, and when she looked at him again, her amazing whiskey eyes seemed to understand everything and nothing at once.

"Yes," she said softly. "I know how to play."

"You're not afraid to play in a saloon, are you?" he asked, keeping his voice heavy with the dare.

"Why would you ask something like that?"

He shrugged. "You don't seem real anxious to help us out."

She shook her head. "You don't know me at all, Lucas Templeton."

"I know you better than you think. I know you could walk away from this—" he swept his arm wide "—and I'd send you back to San Francisco on the next ship out of here."

She turned her back on him and sat down at the piano.

"Play 'Swanee River,'" called someone.

"No, play 'Little Brown Jug,'" called another.

"Do you know 'Silver Threads Among the Gold'?"

Ashlynne rested her hands on the keys, pressed them down to produce a discordant note or two. Then she turned to look at Lucas as if to dare him back.

"How about 'A Hot Time in The Old Town'?" he asked with a grin he was certain she would consider too wicked— and he was right. She frowned and turned back to the piano.

She played a few more notes, running her fingers up and down the keys, and the men quieted at the sound of *real* music being played by someone who obviously had some talent for it.

So she could play, Lucas thought with no real surprise. The satisfaction he should have felt at having pushed her into it instead felt…wrong. He couldn't say just what he felt and he wasn't sure that he wanted to know.

Ignoring them all, Ashlynne settled herself, readjusted her fingers on the keys and then softly, slowly, picked out the introduction of a song that sounded vaguely familiar. When she started to play in earnest and followed with the words, Lucas knew it for certain.

"'Mid pleasures and palaces though we may roam, be it ever so humble, there's no place like home! A charm from the skies seems to hallow us there, which seek through the world, is ne'er met with elsewhere. Home! Home! Sweet, sweet home! There's no place like home! There's no place like home!"

And with the sad, sweet melody echoing from the out-of-tune piano and in a voice like an angel, Ashlynne ruined the whole goddamned evening.

Chapter Nine

Ashlynne was playing the piano again.

A soft, haunting melody wafted up the stairs from the first floor, and with an uncanny certainty that made no sense at all, Lucas knew it was Ashlynne. It occurred to him that she'd been the only one to display any talent for music, but that didn't seem to explain his conviction.

No, it was more. She played for him. He knew it, and his certainty drew him from his bed.

He took his time coming down the stairs, planting each foot carefully as he descended each step. All around him darkness crowded close and yet he could see whatever he needed to, go where he wanted and with no difficulty. Vague thoughts left him curious as to why, for the first time since he'd built the place, the wood didn't creak beneath his feet when he walked, but he dismissed the oddity in his urgency to get down the stairs.

He was in such a hurry, in fact, that he'd dressed only in his trousers and his shirt, unbuttoned and untucked. Or had he slept in his clothes and simply gotten up when he heard the music? He couldn't remember, but it wasn't any more important than any of the other peculiarities such as the suspenders that dangled past his hips and his bare feet.

Lucas glanced down. Bare feet? Alaskans never went around in bare feet—not in winter—and he'd lived here long enough to know that.

But…it didn't matter enough to worry about and he dismissed the thought as unimportant. He had other concerns now that he'd reached the bottom of the stairs. He stepped down from the last step, into the music itself, it seemed, and then he saw her.

Ashlynne sat with her back to him, her hair loose and cascading down over her shoulders and the plane of her back. Nimbly she played the soft, enchanting melody that had called him from his bed.

Silently he moved closer, caught up in the rise and fall of the melancholy music and the sight of Ashlynne as she played. She wore a nightgown of pure white, primly styled. She was turned away from him, and though he hadn't seen her in her nightclothes before, Lucas was as certain of the details as he had been about everything else. How or why he knew such things eluded him, but he didn't waste time wondering about it. It wasn't important.

Nothing mattered save getting to Ashe.

The nickname came to him in a flash and he smiled. Yes, it suited her. Better than Irish, the nickname he'd used only to aggravate her. *Ashlynne* was too long, too proper-sounding. Oh, she wanted to be a good girl, all prim and respectable, but something about her didn't quite suit the image. It might have been her whiskey eyes or the hair that shimmered with the auburn-black-brown of mink, or even the lush womanly curves that defined her femininity.

Or it might have been all of them together.

Lucas crossed the room like a wraith, stopping when he

reached Ashe's side. Silently he laid one hand on her shoulder and she didn't seem the least bit startled. The music stopped and she looked up at him.

"I knew you'd come," she said with soft satisfaction.

"Were you waiting for me?" His voice cracked with a husky edge.

"No. But I knew you'd come."

"Why?"

"You couldn't resist the music."

That haunting melody. "The song sounded familiar. What is it?"

She smiled and turned back toward the piano. "It doesn't matter."

"I think it does. It...called to me."

"I called to you."

She turned to look over her shoulder and met his gaze with hers. It remained dark all around them, but Lucas could see her eyes sparkle in the darkness. How was it that he could see her as clearly as though every chandelier in the room was lit and yet shadow shrouded everything else?

Ashlynne—no, Ashe—smiled again, a sultry, knowing expression, and she scooted around to face him. The chair Lucas had last seen in front of the piano was gone, replaced by a long, rectangular bench.

Where had she found it? Did it matter?

"Why did you come down here, Lucas?" she asked, and he blinked. She looked—and sounded—so...patient.

"I heard you playing."

"And that's all?"

"No." He reached for her, drew her upward. "Because of this."

He hauled her tight against him and caught her mouth with

his. Her breath drew sharply inward and Lucas swallowed whatever she might have said.

Her lips were soft, her mouth hot and moist. She didn't try to pull away or keep him out. Her tongue awakened, encouraging his kiss and sending his blood on a fiery race through his veins. Suddenly, surely, he'd never felt so alive and his body responded with hard awareness.

Lucas groaned deep in his throat and dragged his tongue across the sharp ridges of her teeth, the fullness of her lips. It wasn't enough, not nearly so. He slid his arms around her waist and anchored her hips firmly against him. She must have felt the hard ridge of his erection against her belly, but he couldn't seem to stop himself and she didn't pull away.

He found her tongue, again and again, and flexed his hips against hers, hinting at more to come. Ashe wrapped one arm around his neck and gripped his shoulder with her free hand. Her heart pounded against his chest—or did his own heart drum with such heavy thudding?

The question ceased to matter as their tongues danced and parried. First they detailed the secrets of Ashe's mouth and then the recesses of his. She grew braver with each kiss, more demanding as she traced the edges of his teeth, his lips, then kissed him with the promise of more.

Unable to breathe, Lucas tore his mouth free. His breath wheezed in and out of his lungs with an agonized groan, and a matching, winded pant betrayed Ashe's reaction. He smiled to himself. He had brought her body to life, just as she had done to his.

"Lucas."

The brief moment of lucidity evaporated when Ashe said his name, uttered with the dull ache of desire. She pressed more closely against him and reached up to shove her fingers through his hair. Her breasts pushed against his chest and her nipples poked at him with hard urgency.

He dropped to his knees, a groan escaping from deep within him, and he pulled her down with him. She fell back onto the piano bench and he pulled her toward him, her legs spread wide enough to accommodate his hips as he knelt before her. Her nightgown rode high on her thighs and he pushed it up even higher, until it barely covered that feminine place that had him aching.

"Ashe."

He reached for her, cupping her shoulders from behind to hold her steady. With his mouth, he nuzzled her breasts, catching a whiff of the soft lavender scent that was such a part of her. And down low, where it counted, he tightened, grew heavy and hard and full to bursting.

God, how he wanted this woman.

He kissed her through the soft fabric of her gown, seeking out the rise of her breasts and the temptation of her nipples. Her skin would be soft, he thought somewhere in the back of his mind, and he ached to find out for certain.

Ashe moaned in a soft, husky voice and he laughed, exulting in the sound of her arousal. He pulled her head down for a quick kiss, trailing his tongue along her jaw, her throat, down even farther until he kissed her breasts through the cotton that hid them from his view. Ashe squirmed against him and he took her into his mouth, nightgown and all.

She stiffened, arching her back to thrust her breasts forward. Lucas kept one arm firmly around her, supporting her as best he could, and cupped her other breast with his free hand. She urged him on with a low cry that came from deep in her throat and her nipple tightened against his palm. He closed his fingers around her, finding the crest through the fabric and pinching, then rolling her nipple between his thumb and forefinger with rough gentleness.

Ashe cried out, a guttural moan that told him everything. Lucas increased the pressure of his fingers and caught her lips with his.

"Do you like that, baby?" he whispered against her mouth.

"I…yes…what…"

"Do you want me to stop?"

"No! Don't. Please. I—" Another moan cut off whatever else she had started to say.

He pulled back, but only as far as he had to before Ashe cried, "Lucas, please!"

"I want to see you."

"I-it's dark—and I want your hands on me."

Remarkably, he got harder, thicker, and he shifted, aching to be free of his trousers. But not quite yet.

"It's not too dark." He caught her bottom lip between his teeth and bit down, just hard enough to earn a soft cry from her. "And my hands are all over you, baby." He unfastened the first of the buttons that decorated the front of her nightgown, then the next and the next. "You see? I'm touching you. But I want more. I want to see and touch all of you."

"Yes." Somehow, her agreement surprised him, and then her hands were on his chest and he couldn't think.

She pushed his shirt from his shoulders, down his back and over his arms. Reluctantly he dropped his hands from her breasts and jerked his arms from the sleeves. Quickly, he thought to himself, and heard the fabric tear. He didn't care. He needed to be free, to touch Ashe again, skin to skin, and to remind himself that she was still there with him. His.

"I want to touch you, too," she said, her voice half soft and half rough and completely betraying her arousal. Instinctively he flexed his hips against the hidden juncture of her thighs.

She slid her hands up his arms, from his elbows and over his shoulders, then down his chest. Her skin felt as soft as silk against him. She splayed her fingers wide, and he sucked in a betraying breath when her palms found his nipples. They puckered as stiff as hers had.

"You like that, too." She made it sound like a wondrous discovery that satisfied her on some deep and fundamental level. Leaning forward, she circled her arms around his back and took one nipple into her mouth. Her tongue swirled 'round and 'round, over the tip and then around again.

"Jesus, baby." He groaned and pulled away. One touch, one kiss, and it would be over. He'd come before he even got his pants open. "You're making me insane."

She laughed, a sound full of approval. "Isn't that good?"

Lucas couldn't concentrate enough to smile. "Maybe so." He flexed his hips again. "But let me make you insane first."

He pushed her nightgown down over her breasts until it caught at her nipples. The fabric dragged roughly over the stiff peaks and earned a half gasp, half groan from Ashe. This time Lucas did smile, and he tugged until the nightgown fell to her waist, revealing her to his hungry gaze.

She freed her arms from the sleeves with wild, jerky movements and reached for him, as though she couldn't bear to be separated from his touch. He caught her hands with his and spread her arms wide.

"You're beautiful," he breathed. "I knew you would be."

Her nipples puckered even tighter and peaked a flushed coral color. The darkness didn't keep Lucas from seeing and knowing everything about her…except for the way she would taste without her nightgown between her skin and his tongue.

He took her breast in his mouth once more, laving it with his tongue and raising her arousal a notch higher with the

scrape of his teeth over her nipple. She tasted...perfect. Just
as he would have dreamed. Ashe moaned and arched against
him.

"Oh, God, Lucas. I want you."

"Do you?" He pushed her back onto the bench and she
turned as she moved until she could stretch lengthwise across
the seat. "And do you know how much I want you?"

She didn't answer but merely watched as he unfastened his
trousers and shoved them down to his ankles. His penis
sprang forward as he kicked them free and he placed one knee
on the bench between her legs. He ached to do more.

"Lift your legs and open for me, baby," he whispered, and
moved closer. She complied with a soft sound that might have
been "Yes."

He grasped her hips in his hands and brought her closer.
Once there, she wrapped her legs around his waist and held
him there. He could smell the musky scent of her arousal, feel
her silky dampness against the aching tip of his penis.

He couldn't wait any longer. He thrust his hips forward,
feeling suddenly as though he had no say over his body. He
slipped into the tight moistness of her and she closed around
him as though made for only him.

"Jesus," he muttered through clenched teeth, but he
couldn't stop. He pushed himself into her warmth, as far as
he could go, and then pulled back until he almost left her.

"No!" she cried, and tightened her legs around him.

"Don't worry, baby." He laughed a rough scrape of sound
and flexed forward until he was buried in her to the hilt. "I'm
not going anywhere."

And he wasn't. He couldn't. Not now, when he'd tasted her,
felt her touch, smelled her scent and found the core of her very
essence.

Lucas moved again, thrusting over and over, and Ashe

moved with him. She cried out his name in a sharp, broken voice, and his climax rolled over him. And then he spilled himself into her.

Lucas awoke panting with an inexplicable fear that all but choked him…and a hard-on the likes of which he hadn't had since before he'd first known a woman. He lay stiffly, his breath wheezing in and out as it would if he really had just pumped himself dry in Ashlynne's body. He tried to ignore the trembling in his arms and legs but with only marginal success.

It was a dream. Only a dream, he reminded himself with more urgency than should have been necessary. But…he'd spilled himself in her. Lost control and given her his seed.

It was against every belief he had, the very heart of his existence.

Dream or no, how could he have lost himself that way? And where had the goddamned thing come from in the first place?

Disgusted, Lucas rose from his pallet and stalked naked across the room to the curtainless window that faced out over the street. He'd been bedding down on the second floor of the Star since Ashlynne had moved in, using the room he'd set aside as the parlor of his living quarters…if he ever got around to finishing them off. A man alone didn't have much need for home and hearth.

Right now, he needed the distraction of whatever activity Skagway could offer when it was still hours before dawn. There were those who claimed it was a town that never slept. Lucas decided to see if it was true.

He wasn't surprised to see a fully loaded wagon rolling down Broadway. Or a group of people—a couple of dance hall girls and their *gentlemen friends* for the evening—roaming the boardwalk amid giggles and shouts of laughter. None seemed to have a care in the world.

None except Lucas, whose shoulders suddenly ached with the weight of his thoughts.

Why had he done it? Dreamed of Ashlynne? Of touching and kissing and losing himself in the soft heat of her? So much so that he was compelled to stand next to the window and pretend to watch the night sky, when he remained as hard as he'd been in the fantasies of his mind.

The room should have been cool enough to douse his body's heat; it was the middle of winter and he'd banked the fire in the potbellied stove hours ago. And yet sweat beaded his skin and dampened his hairline.

Trying to pretend that he didn't feel the least bit desperate, Lucas opened the window and let a blast of frigid air waft into the room and over him. Especially the part of him that needed cooling the most.

It didn't do any good.

He remained by the window, his eyes closed and his body as relaxed as he could make it. He took the brunt of the brisk breeze against himself…and still it did nothing.

Lucas hadn't made love to a woman in more than four years. Oh, he'd had women—a number of them, in fact. And it hadn't been that long since he'd eased his occasional ache with Candy and been glad of it.

But he hadn't made love to a woman since Emily's death. And he wouldn't, ever again. He couldn't. He hadn't the softness or tenderness left within himself for something as intimate as lovemaking.

And he never—ever—touched a woman without the security of one of Mr. Goodyear's condoms. Thank God he'd known how to get one before he'd come to Alaska. No child of his would ever distort a woman's body, wreaking its infantile havoc as it tried to enter the world.

So what had happened tonight? How could he have been cursed by a dream such as this one?

Ashlynne Mackenzie was a beautiful woman, that much was true. Even desirable. But she was trouble, as he'd known from the very start. He hadn't wanted to help her, had tried not to—and yet couldn't seem to stop himself.

Now this?

Dreams about making love to her, about throwing his usual cautions to the wind and giving her every bit of himself, scared him as nothing else in this world.

Lucas shivered as the icy wind whipped through the open window, but the cold air did nothing to appease his arousal. His body wanted sex—and with Ashlynne. Just as his dream had promised.

Disgusted with himself and the world in general, Lucas closed the window and turned back to the empty room. It satisfied him on some deep and elemental level that he'd never finished the upstairs of the Star. He didn't *want* it finished; he didn't want a home.

He only wanted…what he could never have again.

Lucas shook his head, if only to remind himself of who and where he was. No, if there was anything he wanted at the moment, it was Ashlynne gone from his life. He wanted things as they had been before she'd gotten herself stranded here and dependent on him.

And no more goddamn dreams about her, sexual or otherwise.

Then you'd better do what you can to forget this one. Because you never had better sex than you did with Ashe in that dream. Not even with Emily.

"Shut up."

The words echoed across the room, harsh and rude and satisfying something within him, so he spoke again. "*Nothing* is better than it was with Emily. She was my wife. I loved her. Ashlynne Mackenzie is just…a nuisance."

But she was more than that. She was trouble…and he was going to have to do something about it. Soon. He couldn't afford to have her around at all, especially not if she was going to invade his dreams with the promise of how it felt to sheath himself with the softness of her.

"Goddammit!" he snapped, louder and sharper this time.

Hell, yes, he was going to have to do something about this unnatural hold that Ashe—no, *Ashlynne*—seemed to exert over him. Starting tomorrow.

But right now he had something else to take care of.

Lucas allowed himself to remember the soft noises of passion that Ashe had made in his dream, to remember the feel and taste of her, and then he gave himself the relief that he could never take from her.

Chapter Ten

Midmorning was quiet at the Star, much as Ashlynne had come to expect. Like many of the patrons who played cards and drank their fill during the evening hours, Lucas generally slept late. Willie arrived before midday and Candy put in her first appearance later in the afternoon.

Ashlynne had come to appreciate the quiet of these mornings. She liked the aloneness of the time; it's when she did many of her heavier—and less glamorous—chores, like scrubbing the floors, shaking out the thick velvet curtains that covered the front windows and collecting empty bottles and other trash. Today, she left all of those things to wait.

Today she needed the fresh air and freedom of the outdoors. Today she needed to get away from the Star.

She slipped silently out the back door and picked her way down the frozen dirt pathway that some called an alley. There were no boardwalks here to keep the ground from being as badly churned up as the main roads from the horses and wagons that moved so frequently over them. The alley saw little traffic.

Coming out onto the street where it intersected the alleyway, Ashlynne slipped into the crowd, merging easily with the foot traffic all around her. It came as something of a surprise that no one paid her any attention, considering Skagway's wicked reputation—and Ashlynne's own experience with the place. But no one seemed the least bit interested in a woman alone. Rather, they all seemed to be in such a rush. The gold was waiting; what interest had they in someone they didn't know?

She skirted a group of men who laughed and teased each other over their exploits of the night before, then bypassed another pair whose argument sounded like the end of a friendship. Neither group noticed her, nor did they surprise her. Sadly she had begun to think nothing ever would again.

Not after all she'd lived through. After all she'd seen— and done.

She had made her own selfish wish come true last night. She'd wanted to play the piano, to forget about her grief and Ian's loss and the way he had left her forsaken—and so she had done it. She'd played for a room filled with people…and lost her self-respect in the bargain.

An empty space hollowed itself out in the pit of her stomach and she caught a sharp little breath, hoping to fill it. How could she have given in to Lucas's urging? And though she longed for answers, her conscience only asked other questions. Had she allowed herself to be coerced because she was pouting after Lucas had called Candy *honey* and *darlin'*? Or had she simply wanted to show off when Candy's performance had been so terrible?

Ashlynne swallowed a sigh and made her way through the center of town. Shops, saloons and businesses of all manner did a brisk business, no matter the day or time. The heavenly smell of freshly baked bread wafted out of the Sourdough Bakery and she dallied just long enough to fortify herself with a warm, yeasty bun.

Returning to her original course, the durable boardwalk beneath her feet enabled her to move quickly, without awkwardness. She glanced around with fresh curiosity to watch the bustle of the street. Horses pulled loaded wagons out of town, toward the trailhead, and returned empty. Men carried packs as big as they were, trudging through the churned-up mud to make their way north to the foothills of the Coast Mountains and the arduous White Pass that marked the beginning of their passage into Canada. Others hurried to and fro, conducting business of all sorts, and all intent on their own situation.

Ashlynne felt almost invisible and the notion tempted her to smile. It relieved some of the tightness in her chest, the trembling in her hands, and she blinked as she tried to concentrate on the elements around her.

The sun shone with a thin if welcome brightness and the day felt warmer than she had expected for the middle of winter, perhaps because the wind had died down to almost nothing. Still, Ashlynne kept her cloak securely around her and her hands tucked into her pockets. She might feel safe enough on the crowded streets, even unseen, but she wasn't foolish.

Or she wouldn't be again. She hadn't been smart last night, that much was certain. She'd allowed herself to be goaded into playing the piano and singing for a crowd of drunken miners, and what could be wise—or safe—about that?

At least they hadn't liked it much, her sense of fair play pointed out.

Lucas had hated her choice of songs. He'd wanted something bright and cheerful, something to encourage the men to spend their money foolishly on drinks and gambling.

Instead she'd played "Home! Sweet Home!"

The crowd had lost its zest after that. It had been the one and only song she'd played, and that's all it had taken. Many of the men had left the saloon after that, and the Star had remained nearly empty for most of the night.

She hadn't consciously planned it; she hadn't even realized her success at first. But as the night had dragged on without the frenetic, boisterous mood that usually inhabited the Star, she'd begun to understand precisely what she'd accomplished.

She'd made them remember.

She'd made them homesick.

A part of her wanted to smile with satisfaction, but the rest of her couldn't seem to rally from the disappointment she felt in herself. She might have made them remember things they'd rather have forgotten, but at what cost? She could have only felt worse if she'd actually played "A Hot Time in The Old Town," as Lucas had requested.

She stepped down into the road and hurried across the intersection to the boardwalk on the other side of the street. *Don't be so hard on yourself.* The voice of encouragement that she'd learned could see her through so much gave her comfort now. *This is about more than your own convictions. Those men needed to remember the homes and families they left behind. That was more important than Lucas's desire to earn more money.*

But…what would happen if he didn't earn that money? How many unprofitable nights could he endure before he was no longer able to stay in business? She had no idea how secure his financial situation could be in a place like Skagway, but if he was forced to close down, what would happen to her?

It was selfish, she knew it, just as she knew she couldn't let it matter. Reality put her very survival at stake, and that meant keeping her job. She meant to stay in Skagway, and she must earn a living to do so. Putting Lucas out of business would allow her to do neither.

A familiar tension began to seep up into her neck, her shoulders. Why did it always seem as though any choice she made damned her, no matter what she did? If she listened to her heart, she felt too much and it became a struggle to survive each day. But if she kept her feelings at bay, she felt too little. She'd compromised nearly everything about herself to stay in Skagway and to work at the Star. Did that mean she must compromise her soul, too? And did she really have a choice? But was it such a high price to pay if it meant she could find justice for her brother?

Ashlynne let out a soft breath and glanced around, realizing she'd almost reached the edge of town. Despite her weighty thoughts, she allowed herself a pleased little smile. Ian had loved the adventure of coming to Alaska. He might have been a weak and selfish man, even childish at times, but he'd never been deliberately evil. Unthinking, even unkind perhaps, but never wicked. He had been, simply, a man. A mortal like all others.

Her brother. The only family she'd had left.

The time was coming—and soon—when she would have to find a way to avenge him. The need was never far from her heart and mind, but her confrontation with Deputy Taylor had, if nothing else, taught her caution. Lucas had warned her not to storm off and demand satisfaction—and he'd been right. And so, for the moment, she would wait and learn and plan and prepare. And when the time came that she was ready, when the opportunity was right, she wouldn't tip her hand to Lucas or to Taylor or to Soapy or to anyone else.

She would be shrewd and clever and smart.

But not today.

Ashlynne let out a weary breath. She left the last of the boardwalk behind her and now had a choice. Go toward the beach and Taiya Inlet that provided Skagway's harbor or take the tree-lined path that headed toward the mountains? The inlet contained a frenzy of activity as men unloaded boats or ferried themselves across the water to Dyea, Skagway's sister settlement and the gateway to the treacherous Chilkoot Pass. And while the road to the mountains was laden with traffic, the pathway headed off into the trees and promised a welcome solitude.

No, today she wanted these moments of privacy. Today she needed to clear her head and to consent to the inevitable.

Today she must learn to accept this new life she'd chosen for herself.

Lucas sat at his usual table and nursed his usual whiskey. Without the coffee this time, though it was his first of the day. He didn't want anything to interfere with the stinging bite of the liquor as it curled through his gut.

He needed the edge he could only get from alcohol.

The Star was quiet at the moment, maybe a half dozen men around. All were occupied, either at cards or in conversation. Nobody but Lucas paid a bit of attention to the piano—or the floors that hadn't been swept, the scattered table arrangement and the glasses that hadn't been washed.

Where the hell had Ashlynne disappeared to? Lucas took some pleasure in his frown. He hadn't seen her today and, frown or not, he told himself that pleased him just fine. The last thing he wanted was to come face-to-face with the seductress of his dreams.

And yet he couldn't help wondering where she'd gotten off to. It wasn't the first time she'd left the Star, but she'd always told him where she was going. Today she seemed to be simply…gone.

Maybe she's in her room pouting, he thought with a spurt of admittedly childish satisfaction. Or hiding. Or maybe her little trick last night made her wary of facing him again today. At least she couldn't have any idea about last night's dream.

Where the hell had the damn thing come from? He'd asked himself the same thing repeatedly during the long, sleepless hours of the night and he'd arrived at no clear answers. He'd fallen asleep just before dawn, which meant little. Daylight came at midmorning this time of year and he'd been awake again after no more than an hour's sleep.

Now, sitting here in the same room where he'd had her in his dream, he could almost taste her again and feel her soft skin beneath his touch. He grew hard just thinking about it.

"Oh, stop it, for chrissake!" His teeth gritted, he uttered the words just under his breath.

What a stupid thing to do. The last thing he could afford was to relive that dream during waking hours—and particularly here, in the middle of the Star, when Ashlynne could come around at any moment. The erection he'd awoken with, hard enough to rival a randy miner who hadn't left his claim during the long months of winter, should have taught him that.

Lucas finished his drink and considered signaling for another. But…no. It was too early to start drinking in earnest. He had a long time to go before the Star closed down, and he'd had too few hours of sleep.

No, he'd have to distract himself on his own. Try something else—anything else. Think of something to occupy his attention. Lucas shifted, mostly to ease the tightness of his trousers over his erection. Damn his body for betraying him. He couldn't trust anyone anymore.

Not even himself.

A bit of a ruckus at the door drew his attention and Lucas glanced across the room in time to see Candy stroll in. A group of stampeders followed her inside.

"Hello, boys," she called with a wave to the room in general. "You can start the party. Sugar Candy is here!"

A welcoming cheer and a round of applause followed, and Lucas found himself smiling, despite his mood. Candy always livened up a place. She was pretty, fun-loving, friendly—and just what the Star needed.

Just what he needed.

"Candy, come over here, darlin'," he called.

She turned to him, her smile bright enough to tell him that he'd sounded more enthusiastic than he would have liked. But he couldn't do anything about it now. He tried to bluster his way through it with a deliberately seductive smile even though it felt all…wrong.

"Mornin', sugar." She sashayed over to him with a broad swing of her hips and a come-hither smile if he'd ever seen one. "Or is it 'good afternoon'?"

He shrugged and tried to work up a flirty grin. "Why'd you come around so early?"

She lifted one shoulder, mostly bared by the thin strap of her sapphire-blue gown, and raised the opposite eyebrow. She grinned, sidling up next to Lucas as she ran one hand over his shoulder and down his chest. "Oregon Charlie snores."

"You let him spend the night?"

He'd meant it only curiously; Candy wasn't known to tolerate a man after his business was completed. But her broad smile left little doubt that she thought he was jealous. Still, Lucas didn't explain. Any protest would only further the wrong idea.

"He paid me enough for the whole night," she declared with a saucy smile. "And I won't make that mistake again, no matter how much he offers. I wouldn't have to worry about that if *you* were spending the night in my bed, sugar."

Lucas laughed, a genuine sound. Candy might be outrageous, but she was also entertaining. And she could make a man forget the things he needed to.

"I might not snore, but I can't afford to spend the night in your bed, honey. You're too expensive."

"Don't you know you wouldn't have to pay, sugar?" She batted her eyes like the practiced flirt she was—but did he catch a flicker of something more in her gaze? The possibility made him distinctly uneasy.

"For you—" she ran a graceful hand down her body, illustrating her charms from neck to hip and effectively recapturing his full attention "—it's free."

"And how are you going to make a living that way?"

"I'll charge all the other men double."

Lucas laughed again, dismissing his second thoughts and reminding himself that she wasn't such a bad girl. True, she'd hinted that she wanted exclusivity between them, but that didn't mean anything. People in hell wanted ice water but that didn't mean they were going to get it.

And what difference did it make if he *didn't* feel any real emotion for Candy? He hadn't felt anything for a woman since Emily had died, and nothing about that would ever change. Now that he thought about it, he saw how very safe that made Candy. He had no deep emotions for her, didn't think about her when they were apart and he didn't dream about her, either.

"Get yourself a drink, Sugar Candy." The invitation sounded like more of a command, but he made no attempt to soften it. "Then sit down here with me. We've got some catching up to do."

"Catching up?" She pretended to pout.

"Catching up," he repeated, and tried to lend the idea some encouragement with a seductive wink. "I've left you alone for too long, girl." He patted his leg. "It's time we got to know one another again."

* * *

Ashlynne spent too long walking and it was early afternoon before she returned to the Star. She had become caught up in her thoughts, some good and some painful, but the time alone had proved to be utterly valuable. Even necessary. She'd needed to think, to come to terms with her life…and to consider what came next. It hadn't been easy, but she realized now that she should have done it days ago.

She hadn't spent the entire time consumed by such weighty thoughts. She'd also paid some attention to the magnificent scenery that surrounded her. How could she not?

Ashlynne had never given much thought to the landscape this far north until she'd actually arrived in Alaska. Oh, she'd heard about its notorious and rugged treacherousness as much as its grand beauty, but Ian had been so overcome with excitement, she'd given up her concerns. It had been so easy to believe his praise for the frontier lifestyle and he'd convinced her the stories were completely overblown.

Now she saw yet another truth. They'd spent their entire lives in San Francisco; how were they to know what it meant to live thousands of miles from civilization, with the cold, ice and snow?

Ashlynne was learning fast.

Strangely enough, except for saloon life, she thought she could like it in Alaska. Oh, she didn't appreciate the hardships so much, but the grandeur that surrounded Skagway was like a gift from God and, despite everything, she couldn't help but marvel at it.

The mountains—the Coast Mountain range, she had been told—presented themselves as the most spectacular sight. Snowcapped and looming above the landscape like a great castle wall, they looked both forbidding and comforting at once. She loved the sight of them—and the thought of traversing them frightened the wits out of her.

Guarding the foothills was a ragged growth of trees, mostly spruce and aspen. Ashlynne didn't know much about the outdoors, but she'd spent a bit of time with her grandfather as he'd talked about his gold-mining days in California. He'd even taken her to the mountains once, which might explain her fascination with them now, she thought with a ripple of warmth for her grandfather's memory.

The rumble of a loaded wagon and the soft nicker of a horse as it trudged past brought her thoughts back to the present. She sent a quick look of sympathy toward the horse, which had probably made the trip dozens of times already today. She'd gone only one way—and now she was late getting back.

Not that she intended to answer to Lucas Templeton for it.

She swallowed and ignored the slight trembling in her hands, then pulled open the door to the Star and boldly strolled in through the front entrance as though she belonged there.

A round of laughter greeted Ashlynne as she stepped into the saloon, and she stumbled to a halt as her eyes adjusted from the bright outdoors to the dark interior. As her eyesight adjusted, Ashlynne blinked and glanced around the room— and then she blanched. Candy sat with pretty pride on Lucas's lap, his arm hooked securely around her waist. Everyone in the Star seemed to approve of the match, if she could believe their delighted laughter.

An awful breathlessness settled low in Ashlynne's chest and she lost a gasp of surprise. She searched anxiously for a trace of air, but when it refused to come, it left her heart pounding uncontrollably. Only Lucas had ever produced this odd, winded feeling within her, and though she had never liked it, she knew full well what it meant.

Attraction. Desire. Lust. She wanted to be with him, as a woman wanted a man. As wrong as it might be, she wanted to touch him, to have him touch her…and she knew what kind of woman that made her.

But then, she hadn't had any illusions about herself since Elliott had shown her the truth.

Oh, God. Ashlynne struggled for a full, deep breath. It had been years since Elliott and his lessons; she had been immune to any man's charms since then. So where did these feelings come from now—and for *Lucas Templeton?*

She wished suddenly, fervently, that she had never met him or any of the other horrible people here. She wished she'd never found the Star of the North that first night, never taken Lucas's help…and certainly never asked—let alone convinced—him to hire her. He kept doing things that hurt her. Things he knew she would object to. Deliberately.

But he didn't care, and her standing here now like a heartbroken lover could only show him how very successful he'd been.

She knew she should move, escape to the privacy of her bedroom for at least long enough to compose herself, but she couldn't seem to do it. Her arms and legs refused to cooperate and she could only stand immobile and stare at the crowd around Lucas's table. He—or was it Candy?—held the audience captivated by some tale of adventure that apparently took them both to tell. He did most of the talking, while Candy inserted a comment now and then and waved her hands generously in the air whenever she spoke. The crowd burst into another round of delighted laughter, this time accompanied by applause, and for a moment, Ashlynne thought she would be sick.

She swallowed, dragging her gaze away from the sight of Lucas and his little party. What had happened to her plans, her idea of the future?

*Don't be such a...*cheechako, she told herself with a shot of very real impatience. She'd known from the very beginning what kind of man Lucas Templeton was, and Candy's behavior was no surprise, either. What they did—or didn't do—had no bearing on Ashlynne's grand plan for her future, and she was foolish to become so upset by them. All that mattered was that Lucas kept his word—and she kept her job.

And if the meaning behind the words seemed hollow, Ashlynne pretended otherwise.

Chapter Eleven

Feigning more confidence than she could claim in truth, Ashlynne left the entrance for her room. No one seemed to notice, not even Willie. He, too, stared at Lucas and Candy, though his expression allowed for none of the excitement that delighted so many of the others. He looked rather pained, almost... pining.

Could Willie be in love with Candy?

The idea saddened Ashlynne as much as it surprised her. What chance did he have if it was true? Releasing a small breath, she glanced among Willie, Lucas and Candy. If Lucas truly meant Candy to be his, Willie didn't stand a chance.

Weariness settled over her like a second cloak and Ashlynne turned from the sight of Candy still perched on Lucas's lap with such blatant sauciness. She waved to Willie as she passed, just a casual hello that revealed nothing of her suspicions, and he nodded in return. It seemed worse, somehow, that his usual smile had gone missing.

Ashlynne unlocked her door with the key Lucas had given her and a moment of relief washed over her. She had made it back to *her place.* To others it might be a small, cluttered storage room, but Ashlynne felt safe here. She knew it clear through to her soul.

At the moment, however, she hadn't the luxury of remaining in her sanctuary. As much as she hated the idea of going back into the saloon, she had work to do and no need to give Lucas an excuse to fire her. Besides, she wasn't going to let him and his alley cat morals chase her into hiding.

Ashlynne shed her cloak and replaced it with an apron tied at her waist. Normally she tried to wear the thing before any customers arrived—purely for vanity's sake, she admitted as her cheeks flushed with warmth. The truth was she didn't want to look frumpy and entirely unattractive—too much like a maid—while Candy dressed in her flamboyant silks and satins. Today, however, it couldn't be helped.

Ashlynne turned to gather her supplies and stumbled back with a gasp when she caught sight of Lucas. He stood just inside the doorway, his blue eyes glittering as he stared at her. Other than disapproval, his expression reflected little else. His shoulders filled the width of the opening, while his head reached almost to the very top of the door frame.

"What are you doing here?" She didn't even try to sound welcoming.

"Where have you been?"

She dropped her gaze, but only, she told herself, to keep from responding to the sudden dare in his. "I went for a walk."

"A walk?" He sounded disbelieving enough that she looked back at him. He shook his head and hair tumbled over his forehead in that boyish way that didn't suit him at all. He brushed it back with typical impatience.

"A two-hour walk?" he clarified.

She shrugged with whatever casual unconcern she could muster. "I lost track of time."

"You lost track of time?" Lucas repeated, turning it into a question. He stepped all the way into the room and shoved the door closed behind him. Ashlynne flinched when it slammed. "Do you realize what a stupid thing that was to do, Irish?"

"I beg your pardon?" She drew herself up and glared at him. How dare he! "I know that I usually have most of the cleaning done before the Star gets busy, but changing my routine one time does not make me stupid. I'm only a little late."

"I don't give a damn about the Star." Lucas flung one hand wide, indicating all that lay beyond the door. "It survived months without being cleaned at all. A couple of hours—or days—aren't going to matter. I'm talking about *you* going off on your own and not telling anyone where you went."

She refused to concede that she'd already reached a similar conclusion. "No one was here," she insisted stubbornly.

"*I* was here." He opened his mouth as though to say something more, but then he closed it again and settled his gaze on her with unblinking steadiness. "You know where to find me," he said after another moment.

"Ye-es." She dragged the word out, not quite sure how to answer. Surely he understood how awkward—and inappropriate—it would have been for her to approach him when he was still in bed. "It didn't seem important enough to wake you," she added carefully. "I only wanted a walk, but then…I stayed gone longer than I meant to."

"A walk." He shook his head again, with perhaps a trace of resignation this time. "Don't you understand, Ashlynne? Walking alone is not a good idea. Not in Skagway, not now—and especially not for you."

"Especially not for me?" The idea that she should be singled out for any reason outraged Ashlynne. She would have advanced on Lucas, even shaken her finger at him, but the room was too small. She dared not reduce the distance between them.

"What difference does it make if I walk alone or not?" she demanded when he said nothing more.

"Did you ever think about Soapy Smith?"

"What about him?" she snapped. "Oh, yes, I've heard all about him. You've even told me some of it. And I admit I believe he's probably responsible for Ian's death and my—" she paused, searching for a word she could tolerate "—situation. But I'm beginning to think he's a figment of everyone's imagination. I have yet to meet the man or see any sign of him!"

That didn't seem to please Lucas as much as she might have expected. His eyes narrowed and his brow furrowed with his frown. "You can thank your lucky stars for that, Irish. The last thing you want is to meet him when you're not prepared—like when you're out walking. Alone."

"And why is that?"

"Taylor knows who you are, and he knows how you feel about what happened to your brother—and how you feel about Soapy. He knows you're out for *justice*." Lucas spat the word like a curse. "If either of them sees you out there alone…" It seemed deliberate, the way he let the words trail off, and then shook his head. "Well, they just might decide to do something about it."

"What do you mean?"

He shrugged. "I wouldn't want to venture a guess. But I will say that your brother isn't the first to die."

A different breathlessness, shot through with a new kind of fear, settled over Ashlynne and she swallowed. She stared at Lucas, but she didn't really see him. Rather, she remembered the many strange men who'd milled about her as she'd been out on the street.

Yes, the idea had crossed her mind that someone might try

to stop her—or even to accost her—but she hadn't taken the concern with any real seriousness. It had been broad daylight! She had never considered the possibility that she should fear for her life.

"He wouldn't...kill me." She tried to sound certain, even emphatic, but she couldn't quite manage it. "Would he?"

"Why not?"

"I haven't done anything to him."

Yet. The word echoed between them as clearly as if she'd said it aloud.

"You know how things stand, Irish," Lucas pointed out, his voice relentlessly insistent. "You asked around and you didn't hide the fact that you meant to make trouble." He kept her gaze trapped with a serious one of his own. "It's good that you've backed off from that—for the time being at least—" he inserted when she would have interrupted "—but Soapy isn't the kind of man to wait until trouble finds him. He takes care of things before they become problems, and Taylor does what Soapy says. That could mean trouble. Hell—" he laughed without humor "—it *does* mean trouble."

He was trying to scare her. Ashlynne stared at Lucas and searched for a different truth in his eyes—that it wasn't really as bad as he made it sound—but she couldn't tell anything for certain. That damned bleak expression he used to such effectiveness revealed only what he wanted her to see.

Damn him.

Shocked, Ashlynne blinked and dropped her gaze to the toes of her sturdy boots. He had her cursing now. Before that, he'd gotten her drunk. And his mere presence teased her with the promise of a sensual delight about which a well-bred young woman should never even consider. He had helped her in many ways, that much was true, but he had also proved to be a terrible personal influence on her.

She raised her gaze and glared at him. He probably just wanted to upset her enough that she'd turn tail and run back to San Francisco on the next ship out. Hadn't he been trying to force her to do that very thing since the day they'd met?

Well, it wasn't going to work.

"Wouldn't you like that?" She stalked across the room, pretending to ignore him as she collected the broom, dustpan and a few other assorted supplies. "If Deputy Taylor and Soapy would—how did you say it?—*take care of me,* then you wouldn't have anything to worry about, would you?"

"Goddammit, Ashlynne!"

Despite her brave words, she flinched at his harsh, over-loud curse. Still, she forced herself to turn and face him. "Don't concern yourself with me, Lucas. You've told me everything I need to know. Anything that happens from now on isn't your fault. I absolve you of all responsibility."

"Irish—"

"Let me pass." She refused to allow him to say anything more and she didn't meet his gaze. "I have work to do and I'm already behind."

He remained in place and stared at her. The tension in the room mounted with each breath, but Ashlynne did her best to pretend that she didn't notice. Finally, Lucas turned away with a frustrated snarl and flung the door wide. He stalked from the room without a backward glance and, Ashlynne told herself, she was glad.

If only she could make herself believe it.

Lucas had made a mistake—and a damn big one. He could no longer pretend it wasn't true. Worse, he was going to have a hell of a lot harder time getting himself back out of this mess than he had getting into it.

He lounged at the same table where he sat every damn day

and pretended to stare at the various scrapes and gouges and other marks that scarred the wooden tabletop. He'd memorized them long ago, but the pretense allowed him to slant a series of careful glances around the room. He could easily retreat behind the fan of his lashes so that no one—and most especially Candy—would know where he looked.

Thank God, Ashlynne had retired for the night. He didn't want to have to worry about her—though any idea of why she should concern him remained elusive. She had all but ignored him for the past few days, ever since he'd confronted her about her walking alone. He'd kept himself busy enough with Candy, which had seemed like the perfect solution to his dilemma of driving Ashlynne from his thoughts—and dreams. It had worked, too, though not quite in the way that he had hoped. Oregon Charlie had left Skagway to wait out the rest of the winter in Sheep Camp. He wanted Candy or no woman, he'd claimed, and she'd bid him goodbye without the blink of an eye. Lucas, on the other hand, hadn't forgotten Ashlynne for a moment.

There had been another weakness to his plan that Lucas hadn't considered and now it was too late. He'd spent more time with Candy than he'd ever meant to, and that had worked to encourage the appearance of a closeness that he'd never intended. She'd shown a perception he'd never expected from her, almost seeming to recognize the ambivalence he usually tried to hide with women. He disguised it by flirting, even allowing a certain amount of physical closeness when others—Candy—had pushed for more. But this time, she'd always let him go whenever he pulled back. Even when that meant she went home alone at night.

He hadn't gone back to her room with her and he hadn't taken her upstairs, either.

He'd meant to; he'd told himself that he wanted to. Nor did

he doubt that Candy wanted more, as well, even if she hadn't insisted. She'd never hidden her desire from him and he had to admit that that had soothed something very male within him—pride or ego or some other such useless emotion. His every look, every kiss, every caress had made promises that he'd told himself he would keep. Each morning he decided that today would be the day, tonight the night.

But he couldn't bring himself to do it.

Her kisses left him cold and her touch did nothing to arouse him. The overpowering stench of her favorite rosewater had begun to turn his stomach and she was just too damn forward. Simply put, he didn't want to be with her.

"So what the hell *do* you want?" he muttered to himself, though not expecting much by way of a reply. He'd been asking himself the question all week and had yet to come up with a satisfactory answer.

At least not an answer he could stomach.

Erotic dreams or not, he couldn't allow himself to want Ashlynne Mackenzie.

At the moment, however, he still had Candy to worry about—and the one concern he dared not overlook. She hadn't pushed to get him in her bed—yet…but she wasn't going to wait much longer. She grew bolder each day.

The cloying scent of roses warned of her approach. "Here you are, sugar." Candy handed him a glass that shimmered with the amber elixir of whiskey.

"Thanks."

Her smile left no doubt about the direction of her thoughts. "Willie said you could use it."

Lucas glanced across the room at the bartender. Willie looked back.

"So…" Candy began as she slipped into the chair next to him. She leaned forward to rest her arms on the table—and display a generous view of her cleavage. Her favorite emerald-green dress couldn't have been cut with any more daring. "I've planned something special for tonight."

Lucas looked away from the curve of her breasts and eyed the shimmering alcohol in his glass instead. Uneasiness and appreciation vied for dominance. "And what's that?" he asked carefully.

"It's a secret." She laid her hand over his and drew his gaze back to hers. "I'll tell you—no, I'll *show* you—later." She winked.

Here it was, the moment of truth. Candy had been patient; he couldn't deny it. He hadn't known how he would respond when she demanded more—until now.

What's wrong with you? he asked, giving himself one last chance. *A beautiful woman wants you in her bed. You've been there before. So why not take her up on her offer?*

He delayed the moment by sipping the whiskey, then he placed the glass on the table. Finally he peered across the table at her. She stared back expectantly.

"Not tonight, Candy."

Her eyes narrowed. "What do you mean, *not tonight?*"

Fairness demanded that he opt for honesty. "Not tonight," he repeated with a shrug. "Maybe not ever."

"What's wrong with you, Lucas?" She leveled a narrow, distrustful gaze over him. "What has this week been about? I thought you were teasing. That you were working us up to some real…fun."

"I thought I was, too. But I was wrong."

Candy sat back in her chair and stared at him for the longest time. She didn't speak, didn't blink, merely looked at him as though trying to see clear through him.

"It's *her,* isn't it?"

"Her?" He fought the urge to glance toward Ashlynne's

corner and aimed for an expression of innocence instead. "I don't know what you mean."

"Yes, you do." Candy sat straight with sudden impatience. "Your new little *housekeeper.*"

He shook his head. "This isn't about Ashlynne." And he realized with surprising if unwelcome clarity, it *wasn't* about Ashe. At least not completely. "It's about me," he admitted. "What I want—and what I don't want."

"And you *don't* want me."

"Candy—"

"I was good enough before." She surged to her feet and sent her chair skittering back. "But you don't need Candy anymore, do you?" She glared at him. "Not since you've found your Irish whore to diddle."

He, too, stood and even stepped around the table toward her. "Isn't that a little like the pot calling the kettle black?" he snapped, the words hard with sarcasm, just as he'd meant them to be. "Ashlynne isn't a whore."

Candy stepped back and kicked the chair out of her way. "That's the way of it, then. Your precious Ashlynne is what's important to you. Well, Sugar Candy doesn't stay around where she's not wanted."

"You can still work for me."

"Wouldn't you like that? To have us both here at your beck and call? Well, you can't have it both ways, Lucas." She shook her head with a pride he hadn't expected of her. "This is the way it is. You don't want me in your bed? You don't get me at all."

She stalked away, then suddenly swung back to him. "We'll just see how well the Star of the North does without me. Maybe you can find yourself a piano player to liven things up. Oh, that's right! You've got one. Looks like your Ashlynne will have to do more than just clean up after you.

Maybe she can play another song and take care of *all* the men around here."

With that, Candy stormed from the saloon.

Chapter Twelve

The weather in Skagway turned bitter. The temperature dropped, the wind blew with renewed strength and the clouds moved in, bringing with them several days of sleet and snow. The already long nights now seemed longer, with daylight revealing little more than a mere lightening of the sky. Only the very hardy ventured out—or those so hopelessly bored they found themselves in desperate need of companionship.

Lucas called it cabin fever, and as much as the term suited Ashlynne's mood, it only seemed worse knowing that Alaskans had a name for it. She already suffered from acute loneliness—and now she was anxious and irritable. Worse, the ongoing storm had kept her from doing anything to investigate Soapy Smith's or Deputy Taylor's part in Ian's death.

It had been days since she and Lucas had argued, and they had hardly spoken since. That was just fine with Ashlynne; she had been angry enough at first that she hadn't wanted to talk to him. As it turned out, he'd been too preoccupied with Candy to pay much attention to anyone else. And Ashlynne was, after all, nothing more than his hired help.

An employee he'd never wanted to hire.

Still, that knowledge didn't keep her from becoming increasingly disgruntled as the days wore on. She tried to pretend otherwise, for her own peace of mind—and because she could do nothing about it. She could only linger in her work corner as she did now and watch the mostly restrained activity all around her. Men sat at tables and talked quietly among themselves or played cards, although strangely without their typical enthusiasm. Everyone appeared to be out of sorts and yet they all behaved in an oddly restrained way, as though no one quite trusted his temper.

Everyone except Candy, that is.

Rumor had it that Lucas and Candy had argued and she'd stormed out of the Star in a huff. Ashlynne hadn't witnessed any such thing and she wasn't so sure she believed the gossip, even if Candy had been conspicuously absent all day. On the other hand, if it *had* happened, it was probably nothing more than a lover's quarrel. Once Lucas agreed to whatever Candy wanted, she would be quick enough to forgive her lover.

Ashlynne frowned. She'd come to hate that word. It didn't make sense, it wasn't right, but still she hated using the word to describe whatever Lucas and Candy felt for each other. It was no surprise; Ashlynne had known the truth of their *association* from the very beginning. How could she not understand when Candy had rubbed herself against Lucas and touched him whenever she had the chance? He'd never seemed to mind and, in return, had made his own interest equally clear.

The days had forced Ashlynne to face a few painful truths about herself. She was as wanton and wicked as she accused the others of being. She had a secret desire to be as brave as Candy, to offer herself to Lucas with the same openness—and beg him to take her. It didn't seem to matter whether or not she approved of the way he made his living or the things he said and did. There was an undeniable physical attraction between them and she couldn't pretend otherwise.

There was something else about him, as well, and that held the key to her worst defeat of all. Lucas might be a very questionable knight in shining armor—or, more accurately, tarnished armor—but he had a certain morality, a sense of right and wrong. He didn't cross that certain line and he didn't allow others to trample it, either.

Integrity proved to be a lure she couldn't deny…and that led her to a truth about herself—and Lucas—that cut as deep as any other. She had to accept that she was a hypocrite, while he was entirely honest about who and what he was. He never pretended to be anything different than the owner of the Star of the North—and her unwilling rescuer. She, on the other hand, behaved as though it was all right for her to take money from Lucas for the work she did, but it was wrong of him to earn it in the first place.

Ashlynne blinked and shifted from one foot to the other, troubled by the direction of her thoughts. A certain amount of self-righteousness may have made her life more tolerable over the past week, but that didn't make it any less dishonest. She couldn't claim one set of rules for herself and another set entirely for Lucas.

Wasn't that exactly the kind of thing she was accusing Soapy Smith and Deputy Taylor of doing?

The question twisted something inside of Ashlynne, something she didn't quite recognize and nothing she was willing to investigate at the moment. She grabbed a rag instead and began scrubbing her makeshift counter. There wasn't much need; she kept the area spotless at all times. But it kept her hands and mind occupied, however briefly.

She hadn't had enough to do since the snowfall had begun,

she admitted to herself with a quick glance around. She'd all but given up cleaning the floor; as soon as she mopped or swept it, someone new decided to brave the elements and tracked in more mud and snow. But her lightened workload left her anxious for a distraction.

Anything was better than allowing her thoughts to roam at will.

Ashlynne glanced around the room again. Willie occupied his regular place behind the bar, and Lucas sat at his usual table, dressed in his customary elegant suit. He always looked so refined—and so out of place in this territory where civilization hadn't yet found a toehold.

He usually came downstairs each morning shortly after Ashlynne had begun to do the first of her chores. They ignored each other while she worked and he sat at his table, drinking coffee and handling whatever paperwork he might have for the day. Today had been no different. He'd settled in with several cups of coffee and thumbed through a sheaf of papers, making notations with a pencil—and eventually he'd changed his drink to whiskey.

Yes, Ashlynne kept her distance from him, just as she'd taken to avoiding the piano with equal care. It had remained silent since the one night she'd played. Either Lucas hadn't looked, or he hadn't been able to find a piano player in all of Skagway. Neither would surprise her; everyone, it seemed, was on the way to Dawson, overcome with gold fever.

Everyone except her. And Lucas.

So why hadn't he asked her to play again?

Ashlynne couldn't decide if she was angry or relieved. Granted, it saved her having to decide whether or not she could—or *would*—play "A Hot Time in The Old Town" or "Roll Out the Barrel." But there was also a part of her that would have liked the chance to say no to him. Just because she could.

How childish could she be?

"Ashlynne."

She glanced around at the sound of her name. Willie motioned to her from behind the bar. She swallowed a weary groan, suddenly tired of washing glasses, whether or not she had enough to do. But she dropped her rag and approached him.

As much as she might have preferred otherwise, she could admit it now: she liked Willie. He was friendly and jovial, blond and attractive. He deserved more than to be serving drinks in a saloon and pining away after a woman who hardly noticed him, but he didn't seem to be of the same mind and Ashlynne had never found the right moment to approach him about it.

"What is it, Willie?"

"Here." He slid a shot glass across the bar. A full shot glass. "Take this to Lucas. He wants to talk to you."

She eyed the glass, then slowly peered over her shoulder at Lucas. He sat with his back to her and didn't notice.

She turned back to Willie. "Take…this?" He'd never asked such a thing of her before. "It's whiskey."

He nodded. "Yeah. Lucas wants a drink and he wants to talk to you. You might as well take it with you."

Yes, she might as well. The suggestion sounded practical enough, but…serve whiskey? To Lucas? He drank too much as it was. Maybe not as much as some of the men who frequented the Star, but still more than he should. As tempting as it was to provide Mr. Lucas Templeton with some aggravation by not taking him the whiskey, it would achieve nothing.

"All right." She picked up the glass. "But I want you to know that I don't approve of this."

Willie stared at her without blinking and without revealing anything of what he was thinking. Finally he nodded. "I know. But your temperance won't do you any good, Ashlynne. This is Alaska and things are different here. And Lucas is…Lucas."

"Yes." She flicked a quick glance at the bar that separated them—and represented so much. "So I'm learning."

She approached Lucas with some trepidation, mostly due to the fact that she'd been so studiously avoiding him. She'd known that it couldn't last forever, but she'd been grateful enough for whatever reprieve she could manage. Now it was over.

Ashlynne skirted the table, circling around to place the glass in front of Lucas. "Willie said you wanted to talk to me."

He looked up, ignoring the whiskey and staring at her instead. He said nothing but simply watched her with that deep, all-consuming gaze. She fought against the urge to squirm under his stare. That would reveal too much, and she simply couldn't allow it.

She blinked instead and tried to glare back at him, as though his look meant little to her. She didn't think she did a very good job; her expression seemed to have little impact on him. Lucas, it was clear, was much better at maintaining an attitude of remote disinterest.

"I want you to work in the Star tonight," he announced suddenly. It wasn't at all what she expected.

"What do you think I'm doing?" She pointed toward her work area in the far corner.

"I don't want you to hide out in the corner. I want you to get to know the men. Circulate through the room, serve drinks—talk to them. Maybe…" He paused with a frown and slowly angled his head as though pointing. "Maybe play the piano."

An uneasy breathlessness filled her chest and started a

fine trembling somewhere deep inside her. Her fingers curled tightly into fists, though she couldn't imagine what good she thought that would do. Hadn't she anticipated something like this, after all?

"Like a…dance hall girl?" she asked, her voice sadly weak with disbelief.

He stared at her without answering but his gaze said enough.

She shook her head. "Why would you ask such a thing of me, Lucas? That was never part of our bargain."

Her claim didn't seem to move him. He continued to stare silently at her, and that, as much as anything else, frightened her.

"Things change," he finally said.

"But…" She looked around, as though seeking an escape—and the idea didn't seem so farfetched. But the same question that had haunted her since Ian's death returned once more. Where would she go and what would she do? Especially now, in the middle of a snowstorm.

She couldn't leave now any more than she could have before.

"I…can't do something like that, Lucas—and you shouldn't ask me! I never agreed to any such thing. I-it's not fair!"

"Who ever said life was fair?" Lucas lost any pretense of disinterest when he laughed, though admittedly the harsh bark contained little amusement. He snatched up the whiskey and tossed half of it back. "There's nothing about life that's fair," he insisted as he banged the glass back on the table. "It never has been, and you're a fool if you think differently. Haven't you learned that by now?"

"Yes, I *have* learned it." She remained unyielding. "Very well, as a matter of fact. But these things you're asking me to do…" Though she hated the sound of it, she couldn't hold back the plaintive question. "How can you?"

He leveled another austere gaze on her. "I told you. Things change." He shrugged as though it was of little consequence. "Candy walked out last night and it doesn't look like she'll be back. I need you to work until—*if*—I hire another girl."

Ashlynne stared. Didn't Lucas realize how difficult this request—this *demand*—was for her even to consider? Of course he did! Just as he knew she wouldn't—or couldn't—agree to such a thing.

"I suppose you don't have to do it," he said, slanting a careful look in her direction. She didn't miss the calculating tone in his voice. "I can put you on the next ship to San Francisco, just as soon as this storm lets up."

There it was again. That same old threat he trotted out every time she opposed him. The very same threat that she couldn't fight him on. She wouldn't leave—*couldn't* leave— and he knew it very well.

She took a deep breath. "Why can't you understand? *If* I did this—" she stressed the word just as he had "—it would be like condoning what these men are doing. Encouraging them to indulge their whims, their vices, while they forget about the homes and families they left behind."

Lucas straightened and pointed to the chair across from him. "Sit down."

"But I—"

"Sit down," he said again, his voice clear in its impatience, and he stared pointedly until she moved.

"All right." She sat stiffly on the edge of the chair, her spine straight enough to make her grandmother Mackenzie proud. "I'm sitting. Is that what you wanted?"

"I've listened to your narrow-minded opinions about saloons and *men like me*." Lucas ignored her question and smiled a wolfish grin that disappeared almost as quickly as it had come. "And I'm tired of it. You're wrong, and you're too blind to see it."

"Wrong?" She might have scoffed at him, if not for something else he'd said. "Narrow-minded?"

"Narrow-minded," he repeated, his voice stiff with disapproval this time. "And you prove it every time you say something stupid, like these men are here because they've forgotten their families."

"Does the truth surprise you so much?" she demanded hotly. "It doesn't me. I know the kind of people who frequent a place like this, and I refuse to encourage their behavior."

Lucas settled back in his chair and stared at her. "There's nothing in this world quite like the righteous, is there?"

"Righteous?" she repeated. "I might be, but what's wrong with that?"

"Nothing—if you understood anything in life at all. But you don't have the faintest idea about me or these men or a place like the Star."

She frowned and stared at him through narrowed eyes. She understood plenty, more than he might want to admit. But if he wanted to pretend ignorance, she could do the same. "All right. What is it that I don't understand?" she asked, relying on her tone to make it clear that she didn't believe he could tell her anything new.

"Why these men are here. Why they left their homes and families behind to put themselves through the hardships of getting to Dawson."

"Gold fever. Wanderlust. Excitement," she answered immediately, shortly. "Because they were bored at home."

Lucas glanced around the room and Ashlynne did the same. Nothing had changed; the men still talked and drank and gambled.

"I suppose that's true for some of them," Lucas agreed as he looked back at Ashlynne. "Maybe even all of them, to a degree. But it's impossible to paint all these men with a brush that simple."

She thought about her own family, about the days—and nights—when her parents had left to follow their own pursuits and hadn't come home. She remembered Ian and how he'd thrown away their money—and their very last chance— in a place like the Star of the North. The roll of the dice, the turn of a card, and it had all been over.

"How much more difficult can it be?" she asked as the memories hardened her heart.

"What brought you and your brother here?"

"You know why we came," she answered carefully. "I told you already."

"So you did." He nodded. "It was your second chance, you said. What was it, exactly? A sign from God?"

Ashlynne's heart sank. Leave it to Lucas to throw her words back at her. "Yes." She wet her lips with her tongue and took as deep a breath as she could find. "That's what I said."

"And why can't that be true for anyone else?"

"I…what?" She shook her head. "What do you mean?"

"These last years have been difficult for most people. Surely you've heard talk of the depression."

"Well, yes." And she had. It just hadn't meant that much to her. She'd had her own difficulties, her own family's financial problems to consider. In truth, she hadn't given much thought to the rest of the country's struggles.

"Then why can't you see that many of these men are not that much different from you and your brother? They're desperate to provide for their wives, their families. If it takes months of separation and hardship, they're willing to do that for the chance of a better future."

Lucas paused, pinned a sharp, deliberate gaze on her and added, "If it was right for you and Ian, why is it so wrong for others to take whatever chances they have to?"

"Ian and I didn't come to the Klondike to spend our days and nights in a *saloon*." She didn't realize how defensive—or disdainful—the words would sound until it was too late.

"But you found yourself here, anyway," Lucas pointed out inexorably.

And he was right. Ashlynne couldn't argue with the truth. She slid back in her chair until the wooden slats against her spine stopped her from moving any farther. She gripped the chair arms on either side of her and stared at Lucas almost as though she'd never seen him before, contemplating his words.

Could what he said be true? Could others here see the gold as their chance for a fresh start, just as she and Ian had believed? Could they have seen it as an opportunity to provide for their families and not simply as an excuse to turn their backs on their responsibilities?

"I suppose that might explain why they came north." She was forced to agree, at least in part. "But why are they *here*? In the Star? They shouldn't be wasting their time and money on liquor and cards and—women."

Lucas laughed suddenly, surprising Ashlynne with the sound of genuine amusement. He shook his head. "I don't know why I waste my time trying to make you understand. You're nothing more than a prejudiced little Puritan."

She stiffened at the implied insult. "I beg your pardon!"

"You blame these men for being selfish fools and nothing more," he said without sounding the least bit apologetic. "You accuse them of forgetting their families, of failing to remember their wives and sweethearts. What if you're wrong? Did it ever occur to you that they're here for a very simple reason?"

"And what would that be?"

"They're lonely." He said it baldly, almost impatiently, certainly impertinently. "They haven't forgotten what they left behind. They just miss it." He pinned her once more with that hard gaze. "They can't find it in Alaska, so they look for a way to forget."

"And you make a living from their loneliness." She didn't phrase it as a question.

Lucas shrugged. "If I don't, then who? Someone will, whether or not it's me. You can be sure of that. Do you really think they're better off without a place like the Star?"

The explanation resounded in Ashlynne's head. Could it be possible? Her family's decadences certainly had never been about loneliness; they had indulged themselves for far more selfish reasons. But could she really tar everyone else with her parents' and Ian's behavior?

"All right. Why are *you* here?"

"What?" He seemed genuinely puzzled.

"You," she repeated. "Why are you the one to operate a place like the Star? Is this your second chance, as well?"

Sudden and unquestionable tension sent a crackle through the air and Lucas stiffened as though she'd gravely insulted him—or worse. Uneasiness crawled up her spine and Ashlynne shivered. What had she said that was so wrong?

"Lucas?"

"No. I'm not a man for second chances."

"What about your…family? Do you…miss them?"

Her breathing stumbled and she swallowed a sharp gasp that would reveal too much. *Family.* Lucas could have a wife, a sweetheart, someone special he'd left behind.

A wife. Why had the possibility never occurred to her before? Not once in the weeks she'd been in Skagway. Until this moment she'd blithely assumed that Lucas's interest in Candy meant there was no other woman in his life. Was it because that's the way she'd *wanted* it to be? Or because she hadn't wanted to admit she was interested enough to care? Thinking about it now, Ashlynne realized that the same notions she'd had about the other men could be true for Lucas, as well. The idea twisted something deep within her like the painful turn of a knife.

"I have no family, no one to miss and no one to miss me." His voice sounded cold enough to rival the iciest outdoor temperatures. "I'm alone, just as I should be."

"I see." She didn't, but her instincts—and his reaction—warned her away with clear emphasis.

Lucas tossed back his whiskey and signaled for another. Ashlynne swallowed a sigh and averted her gaze. She didn't want to think about Lucas and another woman any more than she wanted to see him drink any more whiskey. Willie took one of the decisions from her when he arrived with a fresh drink.

"Do you want anything, Ashlynne?" he asked with his usual smile.

"Thanks, Willie, but no."

Lucas snatched up his glass and took a long, slow sip, clearly brooding as he drank. He watched Willie's departure silently, then turned to Ashlynne with a bleak expression she didn't recognize at all. She fought the urge to squirm with uneasiness.

"What about you, Irish? Are you one of *those women* you look down on with such disdain?"

The question wasn't completely unexpected, but still the words struck like a blow. "No. I'm not."

"You're not?" His disbelief made him sound so arrogant. "You work in the Star, don't you? And the men here are glad to see you. Hell, they're glad to see any woman, even if you don't speak to them."

"I speak to them." She said it softly, knowing it was a lie. "I—" She broke off the words, uncertain how she wanted to continue. "I don't…go with them. Or drink with them."

Lucas straightened in his chair, then leaned forward and gathered up his papers into a tidy pile. He tossed back the remainder of the whiskey and finally looked at her once more.

"There are always special circumstances for you, aren't there, Irish? Reasons that make things all right for you and no one else?"

Ashlynne's stomach churned, filling the space she needed to breathe. She made an odd, gasping noise and tried to arrange her thoughts well enough to argue with him, but no explanation came to her under his unblinking, defiant stare. She needed time to think, to reevaluate—to reconsider.

Everything she'd thought about Skagway, the Klondike and the Star of the North suddenly seemed…wrong. Or was it her? And what could she do about it, especially now?

She didn't want to agree; she wanted to escape to her little back room, to be alone to consider all the things that Lucas had just said. She had no choice, however, and she knew it. Either she helped Lucas now or he'd ship her back to San Francisco before Ian's killer faced any justice at all.

"All right." She said the words softly—as though that would make her less responsible? "I'll help you out."

She stood then and pushed in her chair, forcing herself to meet Lucas's gaze once more. "But it's not for you and it's not for the men here. It's for the others—the loved ones they left behind."

Chapter Thirteen

Ashlynne had done it!

The night had passed in a blur, but she had the satisfaction—however dubious—of knowing that she'd acted as Lucas had asked and she'd handled it well.

She didn't remember everything about the night or even most of the men's names. She'd spent time with so many, listening as they talked about their wives, their mothers, their homes, their sweethearts.

"I knew the minute I saw her that she was the one for me."

"No one can bake an apple pie like my mother."

"I promised we'd marry as soon as I make enough money to set us up in a fine house, right there where we grew up."

There were other men who said different things, sourdoughs who'd come north years before and had ceased to look back or *cheechakos* who meant to stay in the Klondike forever.

"After I lost the last of my family I decided I might as well head out for someplace new, so I come north."

"There was one gal I was fond of, but her daddy didn't think I was right for her. Said I wouldn't amount to much, and

I guess he was right. I come north when he married her off to another fella. It's been ten years or more, and I ain't been back since."

It hadn't seemed to matter that Ashlynne wasn't dressed in low-cut, provocative silk gowns, that her face wasn't painted or her hair done up in an elaborate coiffure. Her plain, dark skirt and demure white blouse hadn't elicited a bit of notice as the men had displayed remarkable eagerness simply to talk with her, to tell her their stories.

And maybe that had been the difference. With Candy, they'd joked and flirted in the same way that she had. Ashlynne had only wanted to listen. She'd smiled and nodded as they talked and gradually she'd come to realize that Lucas had been at least partly right.

They hadn't all been nice and friendly and open like that, but many had. She couldn't deny that most of the men seemed only lonely, just as Lucas had said. That still didn't explain their gambling or drinking to her satisfaction, but she supposed complete understanding in one night was asking too much. And so, while the men had drunk their whiskey, she'd sipped the tea that Willie had provided for her.

Even now, the next morning, Ashlynne couldn't resist a small smile when thinking about the tea. It had been a decided improvement over the dark, bitter coffee. Where Willie had found *tea leaves* in Skagway, she couldn't guess. Maybe it had been on the last ship. Willie wasn't saying and Ashlynne could only appreciate the delightful surprise.

He, at least, listened when she said that she didn't drink spirits.

This morning she had gotten up early. She hadn't been able to sleep. She'd awoken and lain in bed long enough to be certain that the blowing wind meant that the storm still raged, then she'd dressed in her work clothes and vowed, storm or not, she would do all her chores today. Even the floors.

Maybe it would keep her from thinking too much, she hoped as she fastened the last button on her blouse. She didn't want to remember the things Lucas had said last night—and how the men with whom she'd visited had seemed to prove him right. Oh, she knew she couldn't avoid it forever, but for these moments, she wanted to enjoy her moments of success.

She could always rethink her long-held beliefs later.

Ashlynne left her room, apron in hand as she moved into the Star's main room. She carried a lantern to light her way, planning to light the lamps and chandelier later. For now, the shadowy room comforted her, made her feel warm and cozy and even secure. If she couldn't see all the trappings of a saloon, then she didn't have to think about the kind of place the Star really was.

The time was coming when she could no longer pretend or ignore the changes that seemed to be forcing their way into her life. But for now she would think about the friendly respectfulness of so many of the men and how it had warmed her to cheer them up. She didn't try to delude herself by thinking that the Star of the North attracted only men who were morally respectable and law abiding; she'd been here long enough to know that wasn't true at all. But for that one evening, most of them had treated her well.

Maybe it had been the uniqueness of it—for all of them. She'd never thought that talking with a few lonely men was such a bad thing. She tightened her grip on her apron, crushing the cotton fabric between her fingers. It was the rest of it that continued to trouble her.

She'd served liquor to those men and sat at their tables with them as they'd drunk. She'd done it and she'd survived. Now she must accept what she'd done and move on.

She could at least take solace in knowing that she hadn't further entertained them by playing the piano.

Lucas hadn't mentioned it again and Ashlynne hadn't offered. Several of the men had hinted about their interest in music, but she'd demurred. "Maybe later," she'd said, but later had never come. Now, in the light of day, she recalled how disappointed they had looked by her refusal.

Would it really have been so bad if she'd played a song or two? Her parents' favorites would have done well enough. A simple song like "The Sidewalks of New York" surely wouldn't have been too risqué, even if she *did* play it in a saloon.

Despite herself, Ashlynne's thoughts drew her across the room to the piano. Cautiously she ran her fingers up and down the keys, playing a scale or two and trying not to wince at the tinny, out-of-tune sound. It was a shame, of course. But if Lucas couldn't find a piano player in all of Skagway, he surely wasn't going to find himself a piano tuner.

Out of tune or not, Ashlynne was unable to completely resist, now that she'd given in to the least impulse. She retrieved a chair from a nearby table and placed it square in front of the piano. She perched on its edge, not intending to get comfortable or to sit for long. She only wanted to feel the keys beneath her fingers and to hear the soft sound of the music she felt in her heart. She might even play "Roll Out the Barrel," just because Candy had done it so badly.

You needn't prove you're better than Candy at anything, her sense of annoyance insisted, and Ashlynne felt childish for even thinking such a thing. Instead she picked out the first notes of another song, the one Lucas had asked her to play.

Concentrating, she tried to recall the words. She'd only played it a few times, at Ian's request, and he'd always started her out. She hummed as she played, until a few of the words came to her. "You're all mine and I love you best of all, and you must be my man, or I'll have no man at all," she whispered under her breath. "There'll be a hot time in the old town tonight, my baby."

Oh, my!

Ashlynne gasped and jerked her hands from the keyboard. No wonder she hadn't wanted to play that song. She must have remembered, somewhere in the back of her mind, how suggestive the words were. It was—

"Awk!" she croaked, the sound garbled and guttural as cruel, hard talons squeezed her shoulder and jerked her from her seat.

It was the dream that woke him.

Dream? Lucas shifted on his pallet as he narrowed his eyes and squinted into the darkness around him. Was that what it was? Had he been asleep and dreaming?

He couldn't say for sure, but the idea of a dream seemed…right. Thank God, it hadn't been about Ashlynne this time; his body allowed him to be certain of it. No awareness of her thrummed through him, no sense of her lingered to heat his blood, no faint scent of lavender to remind him.

He released a breath he hadn't realized he'd been holding and curled onto his side to stare out the window. It was still snowing. The still-dark sky kept him from seeing for sure, but the odd lightness told him all he needed to know. Only when it snowed did the darkness seem strangely white.

White. He lived in Alaska, surrounded by ice and snow, and the color still reminded him of Emily. She'd been a vision in white on their wedding day and then again that night as they'd entered the marriage bed.

The evening had been a disaster.

Lucas had dreamed of making love with Emily from the

time he was thirteen and had stolen his first kiss from her. Oh, he hadn't known much of what lovemaking was all about at that age, but he'd known it was…something.

Something special. Something he wanted to share with Emily.

She hadn't been so sure, and that hadn't changed with their marriage. Nor by the time they'd celebrated their first anniversary. The physical side of marriage was as distasteful to her as it was splendid for him, but as his loving wife, she'd learned to…tolerate it.

"Why are you thinking about this now?" Lucas muttered with more than a little irritation. Had he dreamed about Emily? Was that what this was about? But…why would he?

He rolled onto his back and stared through the darkness at the ceiling he knew was there. If he concentrated hard enough, he could almost see her face in the shadows above him.

He hadn't dreamed of her in so very long. There had been a time when she'd come to him so often in his dreams, he'd begun to look forward to the nights. He'd ached to see her again, to touch her, to hold her—and he could…in his dreams. And there, in that fantasy world, she had touched him back, held him, burned him with a passion she'd never shown in life.

But the years had passed, more than four of them now, and she'd come to him less and less often. He'd learned to take his physical release in temporary liaisons that meant little or nothing, and by the time he'd opened the Star, he'd ceased to dream of her altogether.

Now he dreamed of another. Of Ashlynne and a sexual joining like nothing he'd ever known or could hope to experience in real life.

It seemed significant somehow.

How hard is it to understand? scoffed a rude voice that tolerated no self-denial. *Ashlynne is here—and Emily isn't.* Not only that, but his wife would never be here again. She was dead as surely as Ashlynne was alive. Nothing would change that.

He'd tried, spending that first year mourning her, wishing he had been the one to die, waiting to join her at any opportunity. And then, when he could no longer hope for the impossible, he'd set about punishing himself for daring to survive.

Lucas sat up and ran a hand through his unruly hair, shoving it back from his face. Where had that damned idea come from? Punishing himself? He wasn't so self-destructive as to do something like that.

Was he?

What had he told Ashlynne? *You can't afford to be in mourning… This is Alaska. Life goes on here, and damn fast. This place will kill you if you don't keep up.*

Well, he'd kept up and it hadn't killed him, but that didn't mean the life he led now meant anything, either. It didn't. It was only a way to mark time. What did it matter if he did that here, in a saloon in Alaska or in his old life in Minnesota? And as for—

A scream tore through the silence and Lucas surged to his feet before he even realized that he'd begun to move. The faint brightness that seeped in through the window spared enough light for him to race from the room, down the hall and to the stairs. Plunging downward into the dimly lit saloon, he cursed the winter darkness.

Near the bottom of the stairs, Lucas made out faint movement within the shadows. Two figures struggled against each other, a man of considerable size—and Ashlynne. He didn't doubt his eyes or his instincts. He leaped down the last of the stairs and tore across the room, reaching the others just as the man gave a low grunt.

"Let…me…go," panted Ashlynne.

Even moving, Lucas could tell he was taller than the other man, though perhaps not as heavy. Relying on the element of surprise, he jerked the man away from Ashlynne and spun him around at just the right angle for Lucas's fist to connect with the other man's jaw. The intruder's head jolted back and he stumbled away…and then he came back for more.

Movement blurred as Lucas struggled with the man, pushing and shoving and landing as many blows as he got. Neither seemed to have much for technique; Lucas's only advantage was his fury that this man had dared to put his hands on Ashlynne that way.

With as much of a conscious plan as he could form, Lucas tried to work them across the room and away from Ashlynne. He shoved the intruder more than once, until the man pushed back hard enough that Lucas stumbled against a table and almost lost his footing. The attacker laughed and lunged forward—just as a chair came smashing down over his head.

Pieces of wood flew all around them and the intruder stumbled back. "Son of a bitch!" he bellowed, and he swung around to catch himself on the edge of a table.

Lucas righted himself and advanced with a growl, driven by his growing rage, and the intruder stepped forward as though to meet him. Movement flickered at the edge of Lucas's vision, but he dismissed it as he concentrated on the fight at hand. It was the other man who paused suddenly, blinking and muttering something low that Lucas couldn't quite make out. Before any of it made sense, the man turned and raced for the entrance. The door banged wide and stayed open behind him.

Confused but no less angry, Lucas took off after the man, skirting pieces of broken chair as he ran.

"Lucas!"

The sound of his name riddled with strident fear stopped him and he turned to glance over his shoulder. Ashlynne stood wild-eyed and panting, a pistol pointed straight at him. Willie's pistol. The one he kept behind the bar…just in case. As far as Lucas knew, no one had ever used it.

"Ashe?" Breath heaved in and out of his lungs, but he managed to say her name with some distinction. And softness. She stared back at him and he started to back away, toward the entrance and the man who was escaping. "Are you all right? Put the gun down."

"No." She shook her head and he caught the sheen of tears in her eyes. "Where are you going?"

"After him." He flicked a quick glance over his shoulder.

"No," she repeated. "Don't go, Lucas. Please!"

"I have to! The son of a bitch is getting away."

"I don't care." The gun didn't waver. "You can't go. You…you're barefoot—and you don't have a shirt on." She swallowed. "You can't go out that way. It's still snowing."

Lucas spared a cautious glance for himself. She was right. He wore his trousers—he'd slept in them because of the frigid temperatures—and nothing else. Even his feet were bare.

He jerked his gaze back up and stared at Ashlynne. She was right; he couldn't go out in the middle of a snowstorm half-dressed. He hadn't even thought about putting his clothes on when he'd heard her scream; he'd simply raced from the room to investigate.

Besides, he couldn't go off and leave her, holding a gun.

"He's gone," she added as though to further convince him, "and that's all that matters. Just…don't leave me here alone." She dropped her gaze from his but still clutched the pistol. "Please."

Lucas stared at her for another minute. She looked so damn vulnerable, even with that gun held at the ready. Her blouse was pulled from her skirt and tendrils of hair fell all around her face, loosened from her once-tidy hairstyle.

It took another moment, but gradually his breathing steadied and his thoughts slowed enough to make sense. Considering the strength and resilience he'd witnessed in Ashlynne over the past weeks, he could only imagine what it had cost her to ask him to stay.

He slammed shut the Star's front door and locked it, something he'd never done before, then turned back to her. "All right," he said softly. "I won't go. Now, why don't you put Willie's gun down. That man won't be back." Lucas would make certain of it.

Ashlynne blinked and glanced down, as though just remembering that she still held the pistol. She blinked again and slowly lowered her arms.

"Here." He took the gun from her and carefully placed it on the nearest table. It made a hollow thud that sounded too loud, and Ashlynne jumped.

"Are you hurt?" he asked softly, and moved closer.

She shook her head. "No. He just…frightened me."

"What happened?"

"I don't know." She swallowed and closed her eyes as though trying to remember.

Lucas glanced around him, taking in the mess of tables and chairs shoved all around and the clutter of broken wood from the chair that Ashlynne had smashed over her assailant's head. He almost smiled to himself until her apron, crumpled on the floor, reminded him of what might have happened.

"I was playing the piano," she said, recapturing his attention. She stood straight, her shoulders stiff and her hands fisted at her sides. Even from a distance, he detected a fine trembling in her. "I was thinking, trying to remember—a song. And then…he was there."

"What did he want?"

She pressed her lips together and shrugged, though the movement was awkward and jerky. "I don't know. He said something like, 'I heard you were here.'" She shook her head and raised her eyes to meet Lucas's. Confusion darkened the whiskey-gold to near ebony. "What do you suppose he meant by that, Lucas?"

"I don't know." It was a simple answer and one he hoped she would accept for now. He had his suspicions, something that had begun to occur to him once he'd started thinking instead of reacting, but Ashe needn't think of such things now. If she did, she might reach the same conclusion he had.

Soapy Smith. Worse, it was Lucas's own damn fault. If he hadn't forced Ashlynne out into the public view by insisting she mingle with the men, Soapy might have never discovered where she was staying. Or even if she remained in Skagway. Lucas swallowed a sour taste at the back of his throat. As sick as it made him feel, he couldn't deny his own guilt.

"He tried to kiss me, to…touch me," she was saying in a faint voice of disgust. She shuddered and it was everything Lucas could do to shove the rage back down inside himself.

"I didn't want him to," she continued before he could say anything. Her gaze roamed the room, seeming to land anywhere but on Lucas. "He didn't like it when I refused."

Lucas shoved back a hank of hair from his face. "It's a good thing you screamed."

Finally, almost shyly, she glanced at him. "I didn't know if you'd hear me."

He scrubbed a hand over his face, thinking of how he'd been doing nothing more than lying there, thinking of Emily…feeling sorry for himself, while Ashlynne had been fighting for her life. Thank God, he hadn't lost all his instincts.

A tenderness beneath one eye made him wince, but he ignored it. "I was—"

"Lucas, you're hurt!"

"What?" He blinked and glanced down at himself. Shirtless and barefoot, he couldn't see anything wrong.

"Your knuckles—and your face." She took a step closer, bringing her less than an arm's length from him. "You might even have a black eye."

He couldn't see his face without a mirror, so he glanced down at his hand instead. Indeed his knuckles were scraped and bleeding, but not enough to worry about. Somehow, seeing that made him realize that his jaw throbbed, as well. "It's all right."

"No, it isn't." She took his hand in hers before he realized her intent and bent her head over his injury. Her hair, thick and shining with its mink-brown color, fell over her shoulder where it had pulled from her neat braid.

"Here," she said as her fingers brushed carefully around the wound. "Let me clean it up for you."

"There's nothing to clean." He spoke with casual indifference, as though unmoved by both his injury and her touch, but his voice came out with unmistakable roughness all the same. Even so, he didn't pull away; he couldn't seem to make himself move at all. It felt good to have her smaller, softer hands cradle his with apparent caring.

"Of course there is! Look, your knuckles are bleeding. You don't want them to become infected."

Lucas couldn't help it; he smiled softly. When was the last time a woman—or anyone, for that matter—cared whether or not he was injured or needed any sort of attention? "I don't think you have anything to worry about. It's just a scrape."

Why, then, did his hand come up to cover hers? He never meant it to.

Ashlynne raised her gaze to his, but she didn't say a word. She merely looked at him, her hand cradled between his.

"Please?" she finally said. Uncertainty and something more flickered in the golden depths of her eyes. She swallowed. "I'm… It's my fault. I want to make it up to you. I want to…do something."

Lucas nodded, understanding but knowing that nothing that would put them in such close proximity seemed like a good idea. Not now.

"It's all right. You don't have to."

"Yes." She nodded and, though she tried to smile, it wasn't much of an effort. "I do." She pulled her hand from his and raced from the room.

"Don't be stupid," Lucas muttered to himself as he stood there waiting. He flexed his fingers into fists, then splayed them wide again. His knuckles continued to bleed—just as he deserved, he thought with some disgust. He had no business letting Ashlynne dress his wounds—or anything else. If he were smart at all, he'd hightail it back up the stairs before she came back. He could take care of his damned scraped knuckles on his own.

She returned before he managed to take even a step, carrying a damp rag and a jar of…something. "Here." She took his hand gently in hers and dabbed the rag carefully over his scraped skin. "I think it will stop bleeding soon."

He'd never doubted it; it wasn't much of an injury. Still, he stood quietly as she did her utmost to clean every speck of blood and dirt from his skin. She was being conscientious, he told himself…and his body didn't care. It only knew that Ashlynne stood close and warm, her lavender scent clean and sweet. The line of her neck looked soft and vulnerable, and it took everything within Lucas to keep from raising his free hand to stroke his fingers over the softness there. His awakening body urged him to do it.

"Here." Her voice flowed around him like soothing liquid

and he blinked, watching as she stuck her fingers into the jar. She smoothed a salve of some sort over his torn knuckles and it stung.

"What is that?" he asked in a hoarse voice that he was almost beginning to expect. It dogged him whenever he stood so close to Ashlynne.

"Pond's Extract. It's witch hazel ointment, good for healing. I brought it from San Francisco with me." She paused and peered up at him. "Knuckles are awkward for a bandage. Do you want one?"

He shook his head and swallowed. "No." He should just jerk his hand from hers, he thought, but he couldn't quite make himself do it. "It'll heal just as quickly without."

"Are you sure?"

Lucas stared at her. "Yes."

Ashlynne raised her head and her gaze stumbled across his. Their eyes caught and locked, and he couldn't have looked away if an avalanche had suddenly swept through the room. His body noticed everything about her and his blood pooled low, making him fully and firmly erect in the space of a heartbeat.

"Ashe."

He knew better than to allow himself the use of the shortened version of her name, but he did it, anyway. *Stick to calling her Irish,* he told himself. *It's safer.* It put a distance between them that he desperately needed right now, but suddenly he couldn't seem to do anything good or safe.

She blinked, and when she looked at him, her eyes were bigger and wider than he had ever seen them. "Lucas," she said, her voice soft and maybe a bit choked, and then she dropped her gaze. "I was so frightened."

"Of course you were." Without thinking, he slipped his arms around her and pulled her close.

"It was Soapy, wasn't it?" she whispered against him, her voice suddenly thick with unshed tears.

"Not Soapy himself." He couldn't lie to her, but at least that much was true.

She shuddered. "But it was someone he sent."

Lucas hesitated, then wondered why. Ashlynne wasn't a stupid woman and he'd already spent a good deal of effort warning her away from Smith.

"It could have been."

"By why? Why now?"

"I don't know, baby." He smoothed his hand—the injured one—over the silken strands of her hair and down to her shoulders. With his other arm wrapped securely about her waist, he held her close—and noticed every inch of her body against his bare chest. And lower.

She moved her head against him, a nuzzling movement that sent the blood pooling low, just where he didn't need it. "I haven't made any more trouble," she insisted, sounding a bit fractious. "I haven't done anything to draw his attention. I'm sure of it."

Lucas knew better, he knew what he'd done, but he couldn't concentrate at the moment. Not with Ashlynne so warm and soft and available in his arms. "Shh…" he murmured against her hair. "Don't think about it now. I'll find out more later."

"No! Don't! I don't care. I never want to see that man again."

"Then I'll make sure you never do." He spoke against her forehead, whispering to keep his tone soft and soothing, and he pressed his lips softly against her skin. She seemed to inch closer and he expanded the feathery caress until it became more.

Ashlynne sighed and dropped her head back, as though to look up at him. And then, before he quite realized it, Lucas had taken her mouth in a kiss.

Chapter Fourteen

Ashlynne hadn't expected Lucas to kiss her, and yet, once his lips touched hers, she couldn't imagine why not. It seemed exactly…right.

Other thoughts lurked at the back of her consciousness, things she knew should concern her. Things she should consider before encouraging Lucas's kiss or allowing this closeness to go any further. She didn't pay attention to any of them; she didn't *want* to pay attention to them.

She only wanted Lucas.

If there was a price to be paid for being with him this way, she would worry about it later. Right now, it only mattered that she felt warm and safe and needed. Right now, she only wanted to be in his arms.

Right now, she could admit that she'd yearned for something like this for almost as long as she'd known him.

His skin was hot—more than she would have thought. The room remained cool, a combined result of the frigid outside temperature and the still-cold stove. Perhaps his struggle with the intruder was to blame.

A bit of hysteria caught at the back of her throat and would have choked her had Lucas not been holding her…kissing her. Struggle? He'd fought to protect her.

Nothing could have elated—or relieved—Ashlynne more than the sight of Lucas bounding down the staircase after she'd screamed. Shirtless and barefoot, he'd waded into the fight without pause and with a strength and energy she'd never expected. He'd ignored his own safety and put himself between Ashlynne and her attacker.

He'd taken more than one blow because of it.

Her heart ached that he'd been hurt and yet she thanked God that he'd saved her. She'd been so very frightened. Then. Now Lucas held her close against him. A fine trembling started somewhere deep within her—a reaction to her ordeal? Or were Lucas's kisses to blame?

Ashlynne's mouth softened under the increased pressure of his lips and she shivered. She parted her lips and he took advantage of the moment. His tongue, his mouth, took control of the kiss and she knew, undeniably, that nothing could matter more.

They had been destined to be together.

Ashlynne's nipples tightened while a new breathlessness spread through her abdomen. It carried a fiery heat that had nothing to do with the temperature inside or out but everything to do with Lucas and his closeness. She sighed and gave him free access to take the kiss wherever he chose.

Lucas seemed to recognize her invitation for exactly what it was. His tongue surged forward, carrying with it a new fire, and he warmed her blood almost to boiling. He traced a line over the arch of her top lip, the fullness of the bottom and she couldn't hold back a soft moan of submission. Answering with a growl of his own, he thrust his tongue forward to the depths of her mouth.

Ashlynne welcomed him with a boldness that should have

shocked her. It didn't. Instead she could only wonder at how right it felt to be so close to him. He was very much a man; she had always known that. And at this moment, with his arms around her and his lips on hers, she felt very much a woman.

"I want you, Ashe." He said the words against her mouth, his voice as hoarse and agonized as any she'd ever heard. "I've wanted you for weeks. I tried to pretend I didn't—" he laughed with an odd, hopeless groan "—but I was only fooling myself."

He kissed her again, before she could answer or even think about what his words meant. His tongue plunged forward, seeking the furthest recesses of her mouth and she parted her lips to welcome him. His arms tightened around her, pulling her firmly against him from breast to hip…and revealing unmistakably the hard ridge that proved how badly he wanted her.

Lucas Templeton, as handsome as sin and as self-assured and worldly as the devil, wanted her.

Desire flooded through Ashlynne, startling her with the force of its power. She could hardly think, could hardly breathe under the lure of Lucas's kiss. She was no green girl who'd never known passion, but she had never experienced anything like the weakness, the excitement, the *fever* that ignited in her now.

Lucas wanted her—and she wanted him. It seemed so very clear, so very right. Why hadn't she seen it before, recognized her awareness of him for exactly what it was meant to be?

He was the one.

The knowledge had come to her in various forms over the past few weeks. How many times had he been the only one for her? Though she saw the truth now through a haze of sensation, she understood it in a very different way. He had saved her, helped her, consoled her. More than once. He was the one she turned to, the one she relied on. The one she trusted, even when she knew better.

And now…he was the one she wanted to make love to her.

Ashlynne tore her mouth from Lucas's and gasped for air. Her heart pounded in her chest, her mind swam with thoughts and ideas and feelings that all seemed to flood through her at once. But she could only say the word that she prayed he wanted to hear.

"Yes."

"Yes?" Lucas pulled back enough to look at her with bright, fevered eyes. His lips were heavy from their kiss and his chest heaved more than she would have expected.

"Yes," she repeated. She would have liked to have smiled with a sultry, come-hither expression that would tell him everything he needed to know, but she could never carry it off. She wasn't a seductress; she had no vast experience with such things. She could only stare and try to nod.

She swallowed. "I want…to be—with you."

Lucas blinked and shook his head, a quick movement from side to side. Ashlynne's heart sank and a fearful breathlessness settled over her like a snowy blanket. Had he changed his mind? Didn't he want her anymore?

She shifted, stepping back and away from him. With enough space between them, she could run—escape this humiliation—and then it was too late. He swept her up into his arms and strode across the room.

"Lucas!" She caught another breath, this one more of a gasp.

"What?" But the sharp intensity in his eyes told her what she needed to know: he hadn't changed his mind at all.

"Put me down," she amended. "I'm too heavy for you to carry."

"You're perfect. Hardly more than a mite."

It wasn't true, but she hadn't the time to argue the point with him. She swallowed a soft cry as he started up the stairs.

"Lucas?"

"What?"

"Where are we going?"

"I don't want to be downstairs." He spared her a quick if undoubtedly implacable gaze. "I want to be away from everyone and everything. I want to be alone with you." One corner of his mouth kicked up, but the seriousness in his eyes didn't diminish. "I want to take my time and get to know you the way I've imagined."

Heat, bright and fiery, pooled low in her belly and Ashlynne's response grew within her. Her breasts felt heavy, her nipples ached and lower, in the heart of her femininity, sensations she'd never known had suddenly begun to shudder awake.

They reached the top of the stairs before she could find a breath and Lucas lowered her to her feet. She'd never been up to the second floor and she had little interest in investigating it now. She knew all she needed to from the vague description that Lucas had offered before: unfinished rooms with no adornment or comforts.

She forgot her surroundings altogether when he kissed her again. As she had before, Ashlynne opened herself up to Lucas's kiss; she parted her lips and welcomed his tongue, and after a moment or two, she followed his seductive dance. Forward, he urged her and she pursued him, daring to bring her own tongue into play. She tested the soft fullness of his lips, the sharp ridges of his teeth and then she sank home, in the moist heat of his mouth.

Lucas pulled her close enough that she could feel the beat of his heart pounding in his chest. Or was it hers? She couldn't be sure but couldn't see that it mattered, either. She brought her arms up to circle around his back and test the smooth warmth of his skin. The hard strength of his muscles rippled under her touch and she splayed her hands wide to hold him close.

Ashlynne sighed with a low moan over which she had no control. It must have meant something to Lucas, because he immediately changed the kiss. His lips softened, gentled, and he became more tender. It was, she thought with dim amazement, as though he'd been desperate for a taste of her, and now that he'd had it, he could relax and enjoy their kisses to his satisfaction. She shivered.

"Are you cold?" His lips moved softly against hers.

"No," she breathed, all she could manage. "It's just… I—" She couldn't seem to think well enough to finish the sentence. But how could she put into words what she could only *feel?*

"It's all right. I'll make sure you're warm enough."

"Yes."

She kissed him because she couldn't stop herself, just a quick touch of her lips to his, but it proved to be enough to bring him closer. He shoved his hands into her hair and she swallowed a murmur of pain as his fingers tangled in what remained of her braid. She didn't care.

Lucas traced a slow, leisurely path from her mouth, her jaw, her ear. He caught her earlobe with his teeth, worrying it gently, and then he moved on, trailing soft butterfly kisses over her cheek, her nose, her eyes. All the while, he massaged his fingers in her hair and when he lifted his head, it was to fan the dark length over her shoulders.

"I've wanted to see your hair down like this." His expression might have been a smile, if it hadn't had such a fierceness to it.

"It's too thick. Too long. It gets in the way."

"It's perfect."

He followed the words with another kiss and Ashlynne wondered if she would ever be able to breathe on her own again. It had begun to seem as though their shared breath was all that kept her alive.

His hands nestled between them and she knew his familiarity should concern her. It didn't. It warmed her, satisfied her…excited her. Only when a faint coolness drifted over her skin did she notice the first stirrings of alarm and she struggled for coherent thought. Her skin? Lucas must have unfastened the buttons of her blouse.

Before she quite knew how it had happened, he'd pulled from her embrace and stripped the garment from her. Then she stood before him wearing only her camisole and skirt.

Lucas's eyes darkened to a heavy, piercing royal blue and Ashlynne shivered. The blatant desire on his face gave her a moment's pause—and then he reached for her again.

Oh, God.

Feminine skittishness raced up her spine and she grabbed his hands, clutching them between both of hers. A rush of uncertainty pulled her from the fog of emotion—the fog of utter *feeling*. What did she think she was doing? She stood in this man's bedroom, half-dressed! If she allowed him—and herself—to continue this way…well, she knew what would come next. She would be naked before long—and she had no illusions about what followed that.

Was that what she really wanted?

"Lucas?" She swallowed and raised her gaze to his. Her voice wavered with the insecurity that betrayed far more than she would have liked.

He didn't answer but went completely still, as though he had suddenly become frozen in ice. Slowly, as though in great pain, he closed his eyes. Reopening them, he pulled his hands from hers. "What?"

"I…" She hesitated. "I don't know. Is this…should I…we—"

He reached for the waistband of his trousers and her words fell off with a gasp. His movements were practiced enough and yet terse and jerky. Then, before Ashlynne quite knew what to expect, he had rid himself of his pants and undergarments.

He stood before her, gloriously and marvelously naked. He spread his arms wide and leveled a clear if serious look on her.

"I'm just a man, Ashe. A man who wants you. I won't hurt you."

She couldn't help it; she stared at him. As she had suspected, he was splendidly made. Earlier she'd noticed his chest, his shoulders and arms, and she knew he was toned and muscular. Now she saw that his hips were slim, his legs firm and solid…and the very elemental part of him—the most masculine part—jutted forward with a certain male pride.

Ashlynne tried to swallow, but she'd lost her breath and couldn't seem to do anything more than stare. Lucas wasn't the first man she'd seen naked, true, but he was certainly the—finest.

The largest.

The very literal truth of who they were—who she was— and what they were about hit her then, and slowly she raised her gaze to his. "Lucas." She tried to take a breath and managed to swallow a hiccup of air. "I…have to tell you something."

"What?" His voice sounded almost strangled.

"I…didn't plan for this to happen." She fluttered a trembling hand behind her toward the doorway, the staircase. "That we would be…together this way."

"Neither did I."

"But now that we are…" Realizing that he stared at her breasts, she lost the words. Her nipples tightened anew, poking against her camisole in the sauciest of ways.

"Ashe?"

She swallowed and started again. "If we're going to do this, you should know the truth first. You deserve to know the truth. You aren't—" she stumbled over the words "—the first."

"The first…" He shook his head. "The first what?"

"The first man I've been with. I'm…not a virgin."

"You're not a virgin." He repeated the words slowly.

"No." Did her admission appall him? Disgust him? Would he hate her for it, as most men would?

"I'm not a virgin, either." He stepped closer. "In fact, I don't think there's a virgin left in all of Skagway—except maybe for Henry Clifford's boy. And that won't last."

A nervous half laugh escaped her. "Well, no, I didn't expect you were…inexperienced." The word *virgin* had begun to make her feel a bit flustered. "You…and Candy—"

"I haven't been with Candy since before I met you."

He had been with the other woman; Ashlynne didn't miss the admission. But still…

"You haven't?" She knew better than to ask the question, but it came out anyway. "Why not?"

"I wanted you."

He said it so directly, so plainly. As though that explained everything. And she supposed in some ways it did. And yet it explained nothing.

"Do you want me, Ashe?" He stepped closer still.

She blinked, glanced away and found herself looking at his erection in spite of her nerves. "Yes. You know I do."

He reached for her, settled his hands at her waist. "Then we won't waste any more time." And he divested her of her remaining clothes with skilled deftness.

She breathed, stepped, turned, aided him however he requested and her skirt, petticoat, camisole, drawers, stockings, shoes—all disappeared. She accepted a fleeting moment of relief that she didn't wear a corset when she worked in the Star. And then a heartbeat later, she stood before him as blatantly naked as he was.

"You're beautiful." His voice sounded hushed, almost awed. But that couldn't be. Everything about Ashlynne was ordinary; her parents had made certain that she understood her shortcomings. And hadn't she proved to be a complete disappointment to Elliott?

"No." She answered Lucas with a tender smile. "But you are sweet for saying so."

"Shall I prove it to you?" he asked as he reached for her. He placed the pad of one index finger on her collarbone and began a lazy pattern that traced down and around to the middle of her chest—and then to her breast. He circled one stiffened nipple, then the other, and smiled wickedly when her breath caught on a sharp sigh.

"Come here," he said, and pulled her tight against him. One of his legs slipped ingeniously between hers and she had no choice but to straddle his thigh. Excitement shot through her as his hair-roughened skin brushed against the softness of her inner leg and then an avalanche of other sensations followed, rolling over her, one after the other.

Her bare breasts pressed against Lucas's naked chest, smooth and muscular. Her nipples nudged against him, while the hard ridge of his manhood pressed boldly against her belly. They stood so deliciously close…and she longed for more.

"Lucas." His name came out as a low moan that revealed the jagged edge of her desire. Ashlynne couldn't help herself; she sagged against the length of him, and Lucas caught her close. A moment later he captured her mouth in a full, deep kiss.

"Come with me," he muttered against her lips, and pulled her down to his pallet on the floor. "I'll take you to heaven."

Ashlynne believed him. She was already halfway there.

She found herself stretched out on her back with Lucas next to her. The scent of him enveloped her, familiar though she couldn't say when she'd noticed it before. It was bold like the man—clean and masculine and distinctive, and with perhaps a touch of bay rum.

He touched her and she forgot about such ephemeral things. His hands moved over her, broad and warm and certain. He explored her from shoulder to hip and back again. He fondled her breasts and plucked her nipples to aching each time he passed. Gooseflesh pebbled her skin and a heated moistness that she'd never known gathered between her legs. Embarrassed, Ashlynne pressed her thighs together.

"Lucas." She whispered his name again, all she could manage, though she felt the need to say something.

He pushed up on one elbow. "What is it, Ashe?" He punctuated the question with a kiss.

"I…don't know." She swallowed and reached for him, threading her fingers through his hair. It felt soft as silk. "Nothing has ever been like this."

"Is that good?"

She thought she smiled, but she couldn't be sure. "Oh, yes. It's very good."

He kissed her again. "There's more."

"Yes," she breathed. "But that—" Her voice broke off and she shivered as a wave of awareness washed over her when he leaned forward and placed his mouth at her collarbone. He had touched her there with his one wandering finger and now his lips followed the same leisurely path.

Breathlessly she tried again. "But *more* can't be anything…like this."

He laughed, a knowing sound of appreciation. "You might be surprised." He peered up at her through the fan of hair that had tumbled over his forehead. "I'll show you."

His mouth closed over her breast and she lost any chance to answer. He suckled, nipping with his teeth, and Ashlynne arched against him. She held him tenderly to her as his deft fingers massaged her other breast, rolled her nipple between them, plucked it to an aching point. He caressed her until she had become nothing more than a trembling bundle of sensation and nerves.

"Lucas." She twisted against his hands but it was too late. He pulled away and left her on the edge of tears. She said his name again, a plaintive demand this time, and she didn't care how it sounded.

"Shh, baby. It's all right."

Ashlynne accepted the rough encouragement of his voice, searching the shadows for him until she found him kneeling between her thighs. "Lucas, what—" she began, but then he bent down and pressed his lips against the curve of her hip. She jumped as her overheated skin reacted to his soft, taunting touch.

"Do you like that?" She couldn't mistake the satisfaction in his voice and he kissed her there again. "I'm just getting started." And then he proved his word by placing a trail of kisses that wandered from one hip to the other. He even came dangerously close to the nest of curls that protected her femininity—and for a moment she thought she'd lost her mind when he touched her there.

It was a soft kiss, a gentle kiss, a kiss that promised more than she could begin to imagine. A kiss he repeated, that became increasingly intimate.

A kiss that panicked her as nothing else he'd done.

"Lucas." She squirmed against him and clutched at his shoulders. "Please. I'm…I don't…what…"

Slowly, almost languidly, he moved upward, dragging himself over her so that she felt every inch of his body against hers. "What is it, darlin'?" he asked as he reached her, face-to-face, and calmed her with a kiss.

"I…that…" She tried to catch her breath but couldn't. Not when Lucas lay against her, his chest crushing her breasts and the wholly male part of him pressing dangerously close to her most feminine place.

"Is that too daring for you?" She could have sworn he chuckled, but then he traced her bottom lip with his tongue and she couldn't think clearly enough to be sure. "After everything else?" He bit her lip with just enough pressure to make her squirm against him. "My fierce little warrior." He smoothed the bite with a kiss. "All right, baby. Don't worry. We've got plenty of other things we can do."

"We do?"

Was that thin, reedy voice hers? And why ask that silly question? She knew very well what would come next. In truth, it should have been over with already. Elliott had never dallied with her this way.

But Elliott had never come close to arousing her the way Lucas did. And Lucas hadn't even *finished* things yet.

"If my touch makes you nervous," Lucas whispered as he took her hand in his, "then *you* can touch *me*."

He wanted *her* to touch *him*? Ashlynne's panic returned twofold, but he merely placed the palm of her hand against the plane of his chest. If she concentrated very hard, she could feel his heart beating a steady, reassuring rhythm.

He was just a man, he'd said. A man who wanted her.

As she wanted him.

Encouraged by her thoughts, Ashlynne gave in to his urging and allowed her fingers to discover the warm firmness of his shoulders, his chest, his belly. And lower?

She hesitated. Could she? Should she?

Lucas seized the decision when he took her hand in his and placed it exactly where he chose. "You can touch me everywhere, Ashe. I won't break."

He felt hot—incredibly so—and thick, his skin surprisingly soft. Ashlynne released an amazed breath. She spread her fingers to curl around him and rested her palm against the length of his shaft, not caring that it exposed her as a complete wanton. She tested the size, the length of him, moving her hand, her fingers, and Lucas groaned deep in his throat.

"You like it," she asked hesitantly, "when I touch you?"

"Oh, yeah." He might have laughed, but it sounded more as though he was in pain. "I like it, baby. I like it too much."

"Too much?" She flexed her fingers. "How can that be true?"

He swallowed a guttural groan and pulled her hand from him. "It's true. Trust me." And he twisted away from her.

"Lucas?"

He didn't answer. Instead she heard odd sounds, like that of items shifting, of things tossed and discarded. Vaguely she recalled a crate that had stood next to the pallet. Was Lucas fumbling around in there? And if so, why?

She shifted, turning toward him, and whispered his name again. If only she could see through the shadowy darkness or think with some clarity and not just react to physical need. With her skin so hot, so sensitized, and the room so cold without Lucas's touch, it seemed all but impossible.

"It's all right, Ashe." More odd noises accompanied the reassurance, but then Lucas returned to her and it didn't seem so important anymore.

"Come here, baby." He caught her mouth in a sudden, fierce kiss that somehow surprised her as much as it delighted her. He knelt between her thighs and pulled her close, his hands lingering at her waist.

"I need you now, Ashe." His fingers tightened over her hipbones and the words sounded torn from him. "Are you…sure?"

"Yes." She answered immediately, though in a soft and ragged voice. "But, Lucas, what—"

"Open up for me, baby." He released her waist and leaned forward. His hands came down on either side of her, near her shoulders, and she felt him seeking entrance at her most feminine core.

Ashlynne had lost her control to the drive of instinct before Lucas ever carried her up the stairs, and she proved it now by flexing her hips in a natural invitation. He reciprocated as he pressed inside of her and stretched her in a way she'd never felt. Uneasy, she stiffened, but he murmured soft, reassuring little noises that made no sense at all, and she found her muscles relaxing. He pressed himself home, and with a gasp of pleasure, she forgot everything else.

Lucas retreated, pulling away, and then he returned, filling and stretching her in the most delicious way. The wetness that had embarrassed her now seemed to aid him and the fit between them seemed…perfect.

"Oh!" She could say nothing else, could only follow wherever Lucas and these stunning sensations would lead. Nothing she'd ever felt before approached this odd mix of pleasure so delightful it bordered on pain, and she breathed out a small, shuddering sigh.

Lucas set up a steady pace that left Ashlynne gasping. He slipped almost from her, then joined her again completely, and again. She didn't have to think about moving her hips in rhythm with his; they followed his lead without hesitation.

"That's right, baby. Move with me."

Lucas slipped his hands beneath her hips, lifted her, and then she felt him go deeper. She gasped as a world of sensation began to build within her, teasing her, taunting her with more to come.

"Yes," she breathed, because it was right and she knew Lucas would understand. He must.

Ashlynne shifted, flexing her hips as he seemed to demand, and Lucas moved faster, harder. She tried to say his name, but the words seemed torn from her and she couldn't think how to call them back.

Lucas took her mouth in a deep, soul-searching kiss. "What is it, baby?"

"I…" She gasped as he pressed himself as deep as her body would take him, withdrew and then thrust again. "Oh, Lucas…I don't…know. I can't…I just…" Again, the words failed her.

He didn't seem to care, didn't hesitate. "Move with me, Ashe. Come on, baby."

And she did. She could do nothing else. Something wonderful had begun to build—between them? Within her? She couldn't be sure, and yet instinct recognized that Lucas held the key.

Ashlynne followed where Lucas led. He moved harder, faster, left her panting and on the edge of tears. And then with no warning at all, the world exploded around her.

She cried out—his name, and perhaps more—as her body surged against his. Lucas drove himself into her with utter abandon and she welcomed every thrust. And then, from a distance, his agonized groan shuddered all around them.

Wave after wave of ecstasy rolled over her and Ashlynne lost awareness of anything else.

Chapter Fifteen

Lucas took his time descending to the saloon proper, scanning the room for any sign of Ashlynne. After they'd made love, he'd fallen asleep, sprawled over her like a human blanket, and later when he'd awoken, she was gone.

Made love.

Was it true? Could that describe what had happened between them? It hadn't been merely sex; he couldn't quite make himself believe that. But he wasn't so sure that they'd actually *made love,* either.

It had been nothing—and everything—like his dream.

The truth of what they'd done—and the resulting questions—haunted him and had since he'd first opened his eyes and remembered.

He'd…*been with* Ashlynne—wasn't that how she'd termed it? The one woman he'd known from the very first that he should avoid at all costs. The woman who'd been trouble since the moment he'd met her. The woman he recognized as being dangerous to him on so many different levels, he didn't even try to understand what they were.

The woman who, for the first time in four years, had

made him think about all the things he'd lost when Emily had died.

And now? What happened next?

Ashlynne wasn't in the saloon; the Star, in fact, was deserted except for Willie, who stood in the middle of the mess left over from Lucas's earlier fight and was sweeping debris and broken wood into a cluttered pile.

"Morning," Lucas said with as much indifference as he could muster.

Willie looked up and stared at him. "Almost afternoon," he said.

Lucas shrugged. "I slept late."

Willie nodded, angling his head toward the entrance. "The front door was locked, so I came around back."

"I locked it earlier."

"What happened?" Willie gestured to the splintered chair and pile of rubble he'd collected thus far.

Lucas frowned at the reminder. "We had a visitor."

"What kind of visitor?"

Lucas eyed the splintered pieces of wood that had once been a chair. "An intruder. He was after Ashlynne. She screamed..." Lucas paused, deciding how much to say. He shrugged. "Between the two of us, we got rid of him."

"An intruder?" Willie's eyes widened. "Who was it?"

"I don't know." Lucas took a quick peek around him to make sure the Star remained deserted. "I'd never seen him before. But I have an idea he was one of Soapy's men."

"Ashlynne still thinks Soapy had a hand in her brother's murder." Willie didn't form it as a question.

Lucas nodded. "That or one of his men."

Willie propped his broom against a nearby table. "Well, it might be true, but Ashlynne would be better off to let it go."

"I figured she'd be safe here," Lucas admitted. "And I suppose she was—for a while. But it's changed now."

"What are you going to do?"

Lucas glanced around him with a shrug. They could clean up the broken furniture, erase the physical evidence, even take turns guarding Ashlynne from further harm. It wouldn't be enough and he knew it. Not against Soapy or Taylor—and it wouldn't do nearly enough for Lucas's peace of mind.

But then, he'd shot that all to hell the instant he'd touched Ashlynne.

"I don't know," he answered Willie shortly.

But he had an idea.

Lucas turned away on the chance that his expression might betray something of his thoughts. Willie was too damn perceptive for his own good and Lucas knew well the risks he could be taking with his scheme. But if he could make it work, he might have found a solution to all his problems. All of *their* problems. If anything went wrong…well, either way, it would solve things once and for all.

He stalked over to the bar, fighting a kind of hopelessness he hadn't known since the first days after Emily's death. He grabbed a bottle of whiskey—the good stuff—and a glass and carried them both to his table. He pulled the cork from the bottle before he even sat down.

Lucas could no longer pretend; he'd known the truth for some time now and it was time he accepted it. He'd flirted with the idea when he'd first faced Ashlynne and her stubbornness about leaving Skagway. It had seemed like too much of an overreaction then. Surely, he'd thought, if he waited and watched and was very, very careful, he could find another way.

Now he was out of time and he knew there was no other way. Too much had happened.

An intruder attacking Ashlynne complicated matters

enough by itself. Lucas didn't doubt that the man—or some-one like him—would be back. The final blow, of course, had nothing to do with that and everything to do with Lucas making love to Ashe. It was the one thing that could force him to take drastic measures.

It changed nothing—and everything.

Thank God, he'd had the control to use his condom. His hand steady, Lucas poured himself a drink, overwhelmingly relieved that he didn't have to face the added worry of a baby in their future. Why then, did a sudden image flood his mind…that of Ashlynne pregnant and swollen with his child?

With a grunt more panicked than Lucas would like to admit, he tossed back the whiskey without a second thought. The liquor scalded down his throat and he appreciated every fiery moment. Ashlynne pregnant? With his child?

No. Lucas shook his head. Just the possibility scared the hell out of him. And though the idea alone should have been enough to keep him from having another erection in this life-time, it didn't seem to be. His body stirred with his thoughts, his memories. Worse, he remembered how difficult it had been to find the control he'd needed to protect them with Mr. Goodyear's prophylactic.

No, if he was going to do anything to protect Ashlynne—and himself—the time was now. It would be the final solu-tion and he would have to take care of it himself.

Willie approached the table. "I put the gun away."

"Gun?" Lucas scrubbed a weary hand over his face as he remembered. "Jesus, Willie. We—I left the gun on the table, didn't I?"

"Yeah, you did." Willie stared at him with more insight than Lucas might have liked. "How did it all happen? The gun, the broken chair?"

"I'm not sure myself," Lucas admitted with a laugh. It

was a rough sound of disgust that made him feel no better and only reminded him of the choice he didn't want to have to make. "I heard Ashe scream and I came downstairs. She was struggling with a stranger, I pulled him off and we fought. The next thing I knew, she smashed a chair over his head." The memory tempted him to smile, but the urge flitted away before it became a reality.

"Where'd the gun come into it?"

"The chair didn't stop him." Lucas shook his head. "Ashe must have known you keep a gun behind the bar, because the next thing I knew, she had it in her hands."

"A woman with fire power'll scare damn near any man."

"Any man who's smart."

"Is Ashlynne all right?"

Lucas glanced in the direction of her room despite knowing he shouldn't. He wasn't prepared to see her yet—but somehow he couldn't get her out of his mind.

"Yeah." What else could he say? How did he know how she was? She had been damn fine when she'd come apart in his arms.

But how did she feel now?

"She'll be all right," he added because Willie's expression seemed to expect more. "She was scared, but she'll get over it."

"What about you?"

Lucas dropped his gaze to the bottle on his table and his empty glass. Damn Willie and his keen eye. He saw too much, heard too much, understood too much. It didn't usually matter; Lucas rarely had secrets to keep. Now, suddenly, his whole life seemed based on the damn things.

"I'm fine." He poured himself another drink. "Couldn't be better."

Willie hesitated, but Lucas didn't look at him again. Instead he swallowed the whiskey and kept his gaze trained determinedly on the scarred tabletop. Finally, Willie left, but only after Lucas had poured himself yet another drink.

He could never let his bartender suspect a thing. Oh, Willie might guess that something had happened between Ashe and Lucas, but that's all it would ever be. As for the rest of it, Willie could never have reason to even speculate. He would try to stop Lucas—and that was out of the question.

Ashlynne must be safe and Lucas himself must be free; he'd wanted that from the very beginning. If he did anything else in this life, he was going to finish things between them. She would go back to her life in San Francisco where she would never again have to face the kinds of things that Ian had left her to in Skagway.

And he…?

Lucas had a life to endure and penance to pay. Ashlynne wasn't—and couldn't be—a part of it. And now that he had held her in his arms and made love to her, he could no longer delay. He could no longer pretend that he had a choice. He didn't and probably never had.

Lucas must kill Soapy Smith.

Ashlynne dressed carefully. She chose a royal-blue dress with long sleeves and a stand-up collar. Well-made, it was cut in a clever design that accented her bustline and nipped tight at the waist. The bodice, hem and sleeves were decorated by a simple embroidered pattern that gave the fabric an added richness. It looked nothing like the seductive silk gowns that Candy wore, but it was one of Ashlynne's favorites.

Wearing it now for the first time since she'd come to Alaska, Ashlynne was surprised to discover that she'd lost enough weight to make a corset unnecessary. She smiled, picturing Lucas untrussing her from the constrictions of such a thing. Butterflies fluttered through her stomach as she remembered the deft way he'd undressed her earlier. Might he want to do the same thing again?

She stood before the crooked piece of mirror that Lucas had tacked to the wall and pinched her cheeks. They flushed a dusky pink, as much as she could do without cosmetics like those that Candy wore. Ashlynne had never used such things, had never wanted to. Suddenly, though, a string of uncertainties left her wishing she could do…something.

Would Lucas find her pretty enough?

She smoothed the stray hairs away from her forehead and turned from side to side, looking for any imperfections in the upswept hairstyle she'd fashioned. It was different from her usual coiffure, softer and less severe. She wasn't sure how much she liked the look, but what mattered was that she wanted Lucas to like it. She wanted him to find her attractive.

She wanted him to love her, as she loved him.

Love. The word resounded in her head with all the subtlety of a cascading avalanche.

Ashlynne could hardly believe it, but it was true; an innate certainty left her with no doubt. She was in love for the first time in her life, and with Lucas. In comparison, her feelings for Elliott had been nothing more than infatuation. A shallow amusement that would have never become more.

Her feelings for Lucas had been building since the night she'd met him; she realized that now. They had grown and changed until she had glimpsed the truth in Lucas's arms as he'd made love to her and wave after wave of ecstasy had rolled over her.

Frightened once the passion had faded, she had slipped away once he'd fallen asleep. She loved him? How could she?

But how could she not? After everything else, it seemed like the most natural thing in the world.

No, it didn't! She chastised herself again now, adding a frown to make her point. Nothing about her situation could be termed the least bit *natural*, nor did Lucas's life in a saloon seem so. But he had a good heart—though he tried desperately to keep others from seeing it—and *that* had been her downfall. He treated people well. He didn't lie and he didn't cheat. And as difficult as it seemed to believe at times, he had a certain moral line over which he never crossed.

More than that, he made her feel things she'd never felt before.

The butterflies made another circle through her stomach and Ashlynne knew she couldn't hide out in her room any longer. She'd make herself sick with nerves if she did. It was time to face the truth—and Lucas—for good.

She took a deep breath, smoothed the wrinkles from her bodice, her waist, brushed her hands over her skirt and left the room before she could find an excuse not to go.

Lucas sat at his usual table, his back to her.

"Are you the girl I been hearin' about?"

Ashlynne turned toward the voice and saw a big, burly man staring at her from the bar. Willie was there in his usual place, taking care of other customers. The stranger was dressed in denim and flannel, like so many other would-be miners. His eyes glittered with unquestioning clarity and his dark hair had a touch of gray at the temples. He watched her with decided interest.

"Excuse me?" She forced herself to stop, rather than hurry over to Lucas.

"I heard there was a girl workin' here. You must be her."

"Well…yes." She considered the possibility. Could he mean Candy? Ashlynne had spent only one evening visiting with the men, though she'd played and sung the one song—but that had been weeks ago.

"You're as pretty as they said you were."

Ashlynne gave in to a small laugh and approached the man, despite her urgency to see Lucas. "You must be talking about Candy. She was here before me—the pretty one."

"She got dark hair like you?"

"No. Her hair is red."

"Then it was you I heard about." He nodded decisively. "Unless there's another dark-haired gal around here."

"No. I'm the only one."

The man smiled then, an expression so unexpected and so charming, it changed everything about him. It softened the gravel in his voice, dimmed the hard light in his shrewd eyes and gave him a gentleness she would have never thought possible.

"Then it's you."

She stopped a few feet from him, marveling at the acute differences in this man. Clearly there was more than met the eye and the inconsistencies intrigued her. It put her in mind of her discoveries about the men in the saloon, once she'd gotten to know them.

"What's your name?" she asked the man.

"Jim." He grinned, the same uncharacteristic smile that had surprised her before. "Lucky Jimmy."

"Lucky Jimmy?" Ashlynne couldn't help smiling back.

"I got God's own luck. I never lose. Cards, dice, women." He winked at her. "And prospecting."

"You're heading for Dawson, then?"

Jim nodded. "I'm headed over the pass come spring breakup. I wanna get there quick and stake a claim. My gal's takin' the St. Michael route and she'll meet me in Dawson come summer."

"You're taking…a woman?"

"Meeting," he corrected with a genuine laugh that surprised her as much as had his smile. "She can take care of herself and she doesn't wanna miss anything. Why? Does that surprise you?"

"Well…yes."

Ashlynne dropped her gaze, wondering how she'd lost sight of a woman's right to adventure, to security—or whatever reasons called to any one of them. Just like a man's, though likely for different reasons, none of which made the trip any less worthy. Hadn't she made that very claim—and more than once—before she and Ian had ever left San Francisco? And even to Lucas, once she found herself stranded?

Or had she thought she was the only one, as Lucas had accused her about so much else?

"I haven't seen that many other women who wanted to come north," she admitted a bit shamefacedly.

"At least not many women who aren't…workin' women?" he asked with a grin. "Well, my Aggie isn't a soiled dove, but she isn't one to listen to what others think she needs to do, either. She couldn't leave when I did on account of some family business, but she'll be there. She isn't gonna let me go by myself and her miss out on all the fun."

"Can I ask you something, Jim?"

"I guess so."

Ashlynne bit the inside of her lip as she reconsidered her question. But she had to ask. "Why are you here, in the Star?"

He shrugged as though it was of little consequence. "I was lookin' for some conversation. You hear a lot of stories in a boomtown like Skagway, and you keep listenin' and askin' until you figure out the truth for yourself. Word's gettin' out about some of the other places not treatin' fellers right. 'Specially Jeff Smith's Parlor."

He slanted her a new gaze that was just as shrewd as any other. "'Sides, I told you. I heard there was a pretty girl at the Star of the North. It's still winter, gal, and after travelin' this far with a gang of men who don't smell too good anymore, a feller'd have to be half-dead not to appreciate the chance for some different scenery."

So Lucas had been right. It wasn't that she'd suspected him of lying; it had been more a case that she hadn't believed he'd truly understood the motives of these men. After spending an evening with them and hearing their stories, she'd begun to see something of the truth—and yet it had still been so difficult to believe.

Could it be possible…had she been wrong about so many things?

Chapter Sixteen

Lucas was drunk.

He knew it and reveled in it. He'd had more than the few whiskeys he might toss back in the course of a day, and he'd deserved every damn one of them—without the limits he normally set on himself. Today had changed everything.

A man never forgot a day like today, no matter how long he lived. It wasn't often when anyone went through the emotional highs and lows that Lucas had experienced in just one day. From the sensual delights of lovemaking in the morning to the hard coldness of deciding to become a killer in the afternoon. If a man didn't deserve to get drunk after a shot from that double barrel, Lucas didn't know when he did.

He dragged a leisurely gaze around the mostly quiet room. He'd been sitting here so damn long, the place had filled up and then emptied again. Ashlynne had made a first, tentative appearance, but he'd ignored her—or pretended to—while he drank his whiskey and tried to think about nothing. And when she'd approached him, finally, nervously, he'd held himself aloof. His body might be hard as stone and ready to drag her upstairs to the comfort of his bed, but he didn't have to give in to it.

Instead he'd watched beneath half-closed eyes as she'd visited with the ever-changing round of customers. The hours had passed, sometimes slowly and sometimes at an alarming rate, and somehow the afternoon had turned into evening. Now it was late into the night.

Ashe had stopped coming to the table hours ago, after the whiskey had turned him surly. Lucas smiled to himself. He'd known it would happen; he'd even counted on it helping him to keep her at a distance. Too much whiskey always made him a bad-tempered ass, which was one of the reasons he'd always limited himself and his drinking.

But tonight was different, and the hell with Ashlynne Mackenzie. And while he was at it, the hell with her damn dead brother, who'd gotten them all into this mess to begin with. And the hell with Soapy Smith for making it all necessary.

The hell with them all.

Lucas squinted at the shot glass he'd left sitting on the table. His vision had gone all fuzzy and wavering and was damned inconvenient. Maybe that's what it meant when people said you were blind drunk, he thought with a chuckle. Still, he didn't look away from the glass.

It was full. To-the-very-top full. As full as it could get with the one thing that could make him forget. And that was exactly what he wanted.

For tonight.

Tomorrow would come soon enough and then he'd have to remember again. And worse. Tomorrow he'd have to do the deed he'd set up for himself.

Tomorrow he would take a life.

Lucas made short work of the whiskey in his glass and poured himself another. He didn't drink this one but left it waiting on the table, as had become his habit. He stared at it, entranced.

There had been a time when he would have never given himself over to liquor. When he drank only on rare occasions. Celebrations, like the day he'd married Emily.

But that had been a lifetime ago.

"A man has to do what a man has to do," he muttered to himself, and found surprising satisfaction in the words. There was no denying it, no pretending or crying over it. Life was what it was. Emily's death had proved once and for all that a man didn't always get the choices he craved. When they were there, you took advantage, but the time would always come when you had to pay up.

Sometimes for a lifetime.

Lucas had thought he'd paid; he'd been naive enough to believe that losing Emily had been the ultimate price. Now he knew better. Her death had only been the cost of his failures. For his arrogance in believing he'd had a *gift,* as Emily had always called it.

They had both been wrong.

No, now he understood the truth of it. He could never completely erase his debts. When he killed Soapy Smith, he would simply pay another price—one for everything he'd done since Emily had died and he'd turned his back on her and her memory.

Lucas reached for his glass and swallowed the whiskey. And now, he reminded himself, it was time to get drunk. He couldn't do what he needed to if he didn't.

The smile faded and then died altogether. He touched his tongue to his lips, then pressed them together in a tight line. Either he was far drunker than he thought or the whiskey didn't taste as good as what he'd been drinking earlier. He leaned forward and squinted at the bottle.

Damn, but the thing was almost empty! How the hell had that happened? It couldn't be the same bottle he'd started with. There would have been more left—wouldn't there? Some varmint must have switched bottles on him, stealing the good stuff and leaving him with a half-empty bottle of rotgut instead.

"Willie!" He peered around the room. "Where are you, Willie?"

"Lucas."

It was Ashlynne who came to him. He recognized her soft, seductive voice and the faint, clean scent of lavender. She came up behind him and rested her hand lightly on his shoulder. His body surged to immediate life and he tried to ignore his reaction. He couldn't.

"Ashe." He twisted around to see her. Her eyes shimmered with concern, her cheeks flushed and her hair looked all soft and touchable. She was so damn pretty it made him ache. Everywhere. Especially the unruly masculine places on his body that had begun to resist every effort at discipline and never listened worth a damn where Ashe was concerned. The loss of control angered him beyond measure, but Lucas hadn't a clue how to overcome it.

He frowned at her. "Where's Willie?"

"He's busy." She dropped her hand as she circled around him and sat down. "What's wrong?"

She sounded more concerned than critical, much to Lucas's disappointment. Her disapproval would have given him an excuse to explode, to chase her away once more. Without it, he could only work up enough irritation to sound...cross.

"The whiskey," he growled, and pointed at the nearly empty bottle. "Somebody stole mine and left this one in its place."

Even in his present state, Lucas recognized her uneasy

pause. But she steeled herself and picked up the bottle. She inspected it, even sniffed at the narrow opening before wrinkling her nose as a small rigor shook her. Gingerly she placed the bottle back on the table and leveled him with an indecipherable gaze. "It's the same bottle, Lucas."

He glared between Ashlynne and the bottle. "It can't be. It's almost empty."

"I think…" she began, then paused, taking a breath deep enough that he noticed the rise and fall of her breasts concealed by the dark blue fabric of her dress. "I think you've had quite a bit to drink tonight."

"I haven't seen that dress before."

"What?"

"Your dress." He pointed, and the sight of his hand distracted him. Still steady. Lucas smiled to himself. Even after all that whiskey.

"Er, no," Ashlynne said. "You haven't."

He squinted at her. "What?"

"You haven't seen this dress before. I haven't worn it since I've been here."

He shrugged, having lost interest in her clothing as quickly as it had developed. He stared at her face instead. "Did you know your eyes are the same color as whiskey?"

"What?" Her eyes widened and she blinked.

"I noticed it that first night," he admitted, but his mood turned sour when he recalled how he had noticed *everything* about her that night. He should have recognized the danger from the beginning, but he'd been too full of himself. Stupidly arrogant, he thought now.

Indulging his frustration, he pressed on. "I knew you'd hate it if I told you, so I didn't." He found a grin he figured she'd hate just as much. "I thought about it a lot, though." He shrugged. "But I s'pose you might as well know."

"Lucas…" Ashlynne paused and ran her tongue quickly over her lips before she started again. "What do—"

"Damn woman!" He shot straight in his chair and glared at her, the lazy, daring persona gone. In its place returned the edgy drunk. "What the hell do you think you're doing? You make me want you all over again when you lick your lips that way!"

She stared at him, her mouth gaping and eyes wide, then abruptly she put one finger to her lips. "*Lucas.* Shh." She glanced around the room, looking all too furtive to suit him. "You shouldn't say things like that. Not here."

"Why not?" Something told him he didn't have to be so argumentative, that in a better frame of mind he might agree with her. But he didn't want to listen to reason at the moment. "Are you surprised that I want you again?"

Her initial expression of stunned surprise softened. "No, I suppose not." She opened her mouth and the tip of her tongue peeked out before she seemed to think better of it. "I…hoped you would. I just didn't expect you to announce it to the room."

Lucas glanced around, squinting as he turned his head from one side to the other. He looked carefully, then turned back to Ashe and imitated her with one finger in front of his lips. "Shh," he said sternly. "Somebody might hear, and we don't them to know. It's…" He paused and wrinkled his brow as he searched for the right word. "Secret. Yeah. It's a secret."

"Well, it might have been." Ashlynne gave him an oddly soft smile. "But I don't think it is anymore."

"Well, it ought to be." He frowned. "I told you that Skagway is no place for secrets."

"Yes, you did."

Satisfied that she'd agreed with him, Lucas poured himself another whiskey and this time drank it. It tasted better…so maybe nobody had stolen his whiskey, after all.

"Lucas?"

"Yeah?"

"It's late. Nearly everyone else is gone." She gestured to the nearly empty room. "I'm sure Willie can finish up here. Why don't you let me help you upstairs to bed?"

"Bed?" He raised an eyebrow and gave her the best wicked smile he knew. "Sure, honey. Let's go to *bed.*"

"Lucas."

"What?" He tried to push himself to his feet.

"Never mind."

Ashlynne swallowed a resigned sigh and stood. She waved to Willie so he'd know what she was about, then slipped her arm around Lucas's waist to steady him. "Come on. Let's go."

He followed with surprising acquiescence, for which Ashlynne was grateful. She wasn't in the mood for any other commotion; the night had been difficult enough already.

It shamed her to admit it, but she'd avoided him once she'd realized his condition. She had expected something…more, something wonderful. Certainly something different, though she couldn't say exactly what. He'd been so gallant when he'd saved her earlier, and then he'd made love to her with such exquisite care.

She'd hoped it had meant as much to him as it had to her…and then she'd discovered he was drunk.

Why? And why tonight, after all they'd been through? All they'd shared.

Isn't that the way of a drunk? demanded an impatient voice from within her. *To disappoint you whenever you needed them most?*

She couldn't argue with the truth. It didn't matter how

good a drunk was most of the time, it never lasted. Her father had proved it time after time, year after year. And hadn't Ian done so from the moment they'd arrived in Skagway?

In her heart of hearts, Ashlynne admitted to herself now, she had always held out the hope that Lucas wasn't truly an alcoholic. Had she allowed desperation to fool her into ignoring the truth?

Troubled by the question, she adjusted her hold around him and urged him up the stairs. He complied with a broad, foolish smile that fell away the moment he took the challenge of the first step. Slowly, one by one, she guided him up the stairs.

She'd watched her parents go through a similar routine, night after night, though it had often been hard to tell whether her mother or father had had the most to drink. And Ian had been so proud to follow in their parents' footsteps. Only Ashlynne had been the one uneasy—and at times frightened—by their behavior. She had always insisted she would never love a man who drank.

Now what had she done? She'd made love with Lucas and the first thing afterward he'd gotten drunk.

Did she love him?

Could she put herself back into the kind of life she'd known growing up? She'd come to Alaska for a fresh start and almost immediately found herself living a life filled with all the things she'd grown to fear. She perhaps had learned they weren't always as dreadful as she'd once believed, but did she have the strength to love a man who embraced drinking and gambling and the nightlife of a saloon?

Ashlynne had no answers by the time they reached the top of the stairs. Her heart tripped with the uncertainty of knowing the solution wouldn't come easily. Lucas had given her back her life, but she had no confidence that she could now become a part of his, no matter how her heart embraced him.

"Come on," she murmured quietly as they stepped up to the second-floor landing. "Let's get you into bed."

"Bed," Lucas repeated. He didn't turn toward her, but still she could feel the force of his gaze as he slanted a look in her direction. "Good. I'm ready for bed."

"Yes," she agreed with a dry smile. "I'm sure you are."

"And you with me."

A shiver of reaction ran through her, tightening her nipples and awakening all her feminine instincts. She kept her reactions to herself, however, unwilling for Lucas to know how he could affect her with nothing more than his words.

"We'll see," she said quietly. She met his gaze a heartbeat later and he stared back, his eyes dark in the second-floor shadows. The sensual heaviness around his mouth, his face, destroyed her last semblance of normal breathing.

"Lucas," she whispered because she had to.

He pulled away and led her into the room he'd taken as his own. He wasn't as unbalanced as she had expected and Ashlynne followed willingly enough, shivering as the cool upstairs air enveloped her. Though the storm had abated as the day and night had aged, the temperature remained frigid.

Or was Lucas the cause of her gooseflesh?

"Here, let me stoke the fire." She escaped him and hurried to the room's potbellied stove. The fire had been banked from earlier, but she managed to coax the flames back to life, then added another log.

"I need you, baby."

He had come up behind her; she could feel him there. Ashlynne adjusted the grate to allow for an even flow of heat into the room, closed the little door and slowly straightened.

Lucas slid his arms around her waist, pulling her back against his chest. She crossed her arms over his to hold him there and laid her head back against his shoulder. Almost immediately, he bent to nuzzle her neck, her throat. She shivered again, certain this time that Lucas was responsible. She whispered his name and he nipped her skin.

"I've never wanted a woman the way I want you." He licked the spot where his teeth had staked their claim, kissed her there, bit again. The pleasure of his mouth warmed Ashlynne all the way through, from the inside out, and a broken little sigh gave her away.

He lifted his head and turned her to face him. The fire revealed just enough that she could see the utter seriousness—and the sheer desire—in his expression. "I never even wanted Emily this badly."

"Emily?" Every bit of warmth fell away and an icy coldness spread through Ashlynne's veins. She shivered and stepped back, away from him but away from the fire, too. "Who's Emily?"

Lucas reached for her. "My wife."

"Your…wife?"

The words seemed to come from Ashlynne, but how had she managed to say them? Her throat felt so very dry, her lungs so very empty. She gasped for breath, or tried to, and commanded herself to remain standing. "I thought you said…you had no family. No one waiting for you."

Lucas blinked and shook his head, grumbling under his breath at the hair that fell over his forehead. He shoved it back. "I don't."

"But…you have a—a wife." It took everything within Ashlynne to choke out the word. She had asked him about his family and he had claimed he had no one waiting for him. Oh, God. Had she fallen in love with a married man?

He frowned. "Had. Not anymore."

"I don't understand."

"Why are we talking about Emily?" Lucas turned and

stalked away until he reached his pallet. "I don't want to think about her anymore. She's dead." Lucas dropped down to the bedroll and blankets he'd appropriated and began pulling off his boots. "Forever and ever. Amen."

"I—I'm sorry." The words sounded so…feeble. They weren't nearly articulate enough, and the part of her that could think about polite propriety scrambled to find something more suitable. The rest of her knew only a great rush of relief, a wild, tangled whirlwind of emotion that kept her immobile.

"You don't have anything to be sorry for," Lucas snapped as he dropped his boot to the floor. "You didn't kill her."

"Well, no, of course not."

"I did."

"You—what?" A bewildered, crazy screech bubbled up at the back of Ashlynne's throat and she coughed. The sorrow, the elation, the fear all crowded inside her until her head began to pound and she thought her heart might stop beating.

"What did you say?" she asked when he didn't answer.

"I killed her," he repeated irritably and scowled up at her. "I suppose you could just say it was my fault, but it's the same thing."

"Your fault?" She couldn't withhold the question; his declaration made no sense. He was a very capable man, certainly not careless with others or their safety. He might not always like what he had to do, but she had yet to see him do something that wasn't…honorable.

He didn't answer and so she approached him on the pallet and dropped to her knees before him. "Lucas? What happened?"

"I killed her." He said it again, his frown impatient. "I told you that. Her and the baby. My baby." He said the words shortly, a little too precisely, as though it took more than a little effort to repeat them. "When her time came…" His explanation trailed away and he shrugged. "There were problems. Complications. The baby was turned wrong. Emily was too small. Everything went wrong. And I couldn't save them."

"Of course you couldn't save them," Ashlynne murmured with soft soothing. "You shouldn't think that way," she added as she reached for him. "I'm sure no one could have saved them. Not even a doctor."

He drew back as though she'd slapped him and scooted away from her. "Jesus, Ashe," he snapped, and she couldn't remember ever hearing a more agonized sound. "Don't you understand? I *am* a doctor.

"I *was* a doctor," he amended as he dropped his gaze to the floor. "A doctor who couldn't save his own wife and child."

Chapter Seventeen

Lucas found consciousness slowly, not quite awake and not really asleep, either. Liking the pitch-black darkness for a change, he accepted the awareness that came in sketchy bits and pieces. That seemed to be enough.

He shifted for a different, more comfortable position—and then he stopped. Something—someone—was next to him. He stiffened and turned his head.

A certain warmth and the soft sound of breathing told him all he needed to know. A dream. It must be, for he hadn't slept the night with a woman since Emily's death.

Lucas relaxed, perhaps even frowned, but it drifted away before he could be sure. These damned dreams. He'd had more than his share lately and he'd come to hate some of them. There were others that he didn't mind so much, reminders of better times gone by or hints of the life he might find for himself someday, but they came less often than the difficult ones.

Then there were the ones where he made love to Ashlynne. He smiled to himself. He liked those best. They made things possible that could never be in real life. He blew out a soft sigh of pleasure and then it hit him: lavender. He could smell her soft scent, a mix of her toilet water and something more that was just Ashe. Exactly as he remembered her.

Just as he would always remember her.

Lucas blinked against the darkness. Making love to Ashe was better than any dream; he'd found that out for certain. He wanted her as he'd never wanted another woman.

Even Emily.

A frown turned down the corners of his mouth. He knew damn well he shouldn't feel that way, but knowing the truth and changing the way he felt were two different things. His desire for Ashe threatened his carefully arranged life—his very self-control—and was dangerous to him in every way. And yet, whether it was for real or in his dreams, he wanted her again as he'd never wanted anything in his life.

He didn't care if it was a dream. It put her right here next to him.

"Ashe."

Her name came as a low groan and he inched closer to nuzzle his mouth against her neck. Her skin was warm and soft, the taste of her sweeter than it should be. Lucas pushed himself up on one elbow, realizing then that he'd lost his shirt somewhere along the way. Ashlynne, too, was more or less undressed. She wore only her soft, thin underclothes.

Dreams were nice that way. He smiled again. Satisfying. They made things simple. If clothes needed to be gone, they just…were. Everything was more difficult when a body was awake. *This* was better.

Lucas kissed Ashe's throat, trailing his tongue around to the column of her neck where he gave her a quick, biting kiss. It was the kind of kiss that left a bruise, he thought distantly. He had rarely allowed himself that kind of kiss. Emily hadn't liked it and he'd since refused to leave his mark on any other woman.

Except Ashlynne.

Besides, he could do anything he wanted to in a dream.

She murmured in her sleep and Lucas increased the pressure of his mouth. She shifted—not closer but not away, either—and he could feel the change in her as she gradually came awake.

"Lucas?"

"I'm here, baby." He licked the spot where he'd been nibbling and kissed his way long her jawline.

"Is something wrong?" Her voice sounded husky with sleep and a bit broken. He liked the combination; he felt exactly the same way.

"No. Did I wake you?" he asked, even knowing what the answer would be.

"I…yes."

She stretched, and though he couldn't see her all that well, he felt the slow, languid movements of her body against his. It reminded him suddenly of just how hard he was—and how much he wanted her. How much he had wanted her for weeks now. Having her earlier had only made him hungrier.

"I should have let you sleep," he admitted, but he wasn't really sorry and didn't sound it. "I couldn't help it. I wanted you."

Her sharp intake of breath satisfied him on some deep, elemental level, reminding him of one of the best things about dream lovers. They never left you alone and wanting; they always pleased you.

He took her mouth in a full, deep kiss, using his tongue to tease her lips apart. Ashlynne sighed her approval as he gained entrance to the moist heat of her mouth. He reminded her, again and again, of the delight his mouth could offer, and she picked up his rhythm almost immediately. His body responded, as well, hardening with an erection that felt almost painful.

Growing suddenly frantic, Lucas fumbled with the ribbons that tied her chemise, her petticoats. He slipped his fingers beneath the barrier of her garments, caressing the warm, soft skin and aching to touch more.

Slow down, he cautioned himself, *or you'll never make it through to the end.* Yes... If he could manage it, the wait would be worth it.

Only when his breath ran out did he tear his mouth from hers. Her labored breathing rent the quiet night, a clear accompaniment to his own heavy panting. She wanted him, Lucas thought with a profound satisfaction that would have made him uneasy outside his dreamworld. For this moment, however, it was good that she wanted him so badly.

He wanted her exactly the same way.

He pulled back, whispering a soft, "Shh," when Ashlynne protested with a soft moan. He couldn't wait, though. He needed to touch her, skin-to-skin, and he bent to the task of divesting her of her few remaining undergarments, ridding himself of his trousers. The darkness didn't seem to hinder his movements much—or did Ashlynne help more than he realized?

It didn't matter. He only cared that finally he was naked and so was she.

"Lucas." She muttered his name and he recognized the heavy need in her voice. If it hadn't been a dream, the depth of her passion might have surprised him. Ashlynne had always held herself mostly aloof—unless, of course, she was giving him hell. He smiled to himself with wicked understanding. How often had he done something just to get the reaction he sought from her?

At the moment he was only pleased to languish in this hazy world of his dreams. Here it was safe for them both to show the depth of their desire—and anything else.

"I know, baby. I know," he murmured under his breath, and

kissed her. His mouth opened against hers and her tongue surged to life in a familiar greeting. They kissed that way until he simply couldn't breathe anymore, and even then, he didn't want to release her.

He tore his mouth free with a gasp and nuzzled his way down her body. To her neck, her throat, the plane of her chest, her breasts. He kissed each of them and drew her pebbled nipples into his mouth, one at a time, while his hands sought out her waist, her hips, lower.

"Please, Lucas. I want you." Her voice broke on a pained wheeze and she arched against him.

His control slipped a notch and he knew he hadn't much time left to him. Sharing her need, he parted her legs. "Open for me, will you, Ashe?"

"Yes…I…please, Lucas. Hurry!"

He inched forward and the tip of his penis found her moist opening with unerring precision. She sucked in a sharp breath at the contact, but then she lost it again when he flexed his hips and buried himself in her with one thrust. She wrapped her legs around him, drawing him deep, and met his thrusts with a demand of her own. Her passion drove his excitement to a new high.

Each movement built the sensual tension between them and gradually Lucas understood he was powerless against it. His desire caught him, bound him to Ashlynne, and she didn't hesitate to follow his lead with equal ardor. The moments, the movements, went on and on…and when the world exploded around him, Lucas lost himself in Ashlynne.

Ashlynne woke late in the morning. Finally, after the endless days of snow, the sun had come out.

She smiled to herself and stretched with an almost feline contentment. The patchwork quilt slipped down, exposing her bare breasts and she tugged it back into place with a soft laugh. Her nipples puckered with the cold and she shivered, snuggling back under the warmth of her cocoon.

Fortunately, Lucas seemed to have blankets and quilts in abundance. He'd gotten them along with the many other things he'd purchased from would-be miners who, faced with the only trail to the Klondike, sold or abandoned everything that wasn't absolutely necessary. Lucas had enough to furnish the upstairs of the Star, if he'd ever been so inclined.

Thus far, he hadn't.

Would he ever consider it? Ashlynne wondered dreamily. They could make a real living area upstairs. A sitting parlor, a kitchen, a bedroom of their own.

Stop right there. She caught her breath and forced herself back to reality. *Don't get carried away with any silly ideas. It's not that simple and you know it.*

No, nothing between Lucas and her seemed simple.

Ashlynne blinked against the sunlight that streamed in through the uncurtained window and glanced around the room, seeing it for the first time in full light. It was as bare and unfinished as Lucas had warned, with only the stove, a crate that he used as a dresser and his sleeping pallet. Lucas was nowhere around.

Disappointment swamped her, while a more practical side reminded Ashlynne it was just as well. She gave up her snug position under the covers and sat up with a sigh, clutching the quilt to her chest. In truth, she needed this time alone. The last few days had been…hectic. Difficult and amazing. Awful and wondrous. All that and more, she thought, and Lucas resided at the heart of it all.

She hadn't planned to spend the night with him, not after his night of drinking. But his stunning confession had changed things between them yet again and she simply hadn't been able to leave him. Rather, she'd helped him off with his shirt and tucked him in like a child, then undressed down to her underclothes and snuggled next to him.

It had seemed so…right. And later, when he'd awakened her in the middle of the night, that had seemed right, as well. Ashlynne flushed, remembering his urgency and how it had ignited her own desire. She'd responded to him with a passion unlike anything she'd ever known.

Where had it come from and how had Lucas known the ways in which to draw it out? He'd made her want him in ways she still didn't understand.

And now what?

Ashlynne swallowed an uneasy sigh and wrapped her arms around herself. Suddenly she wished Lucas hadn't left her. Just seeing him would reassure her, allow her to believe that everything would be all right. Somehow.

Wouldn't it?

She closed her eyes and faced the truth her innate honesty wouldn't allow her to avoid. There was no guarantee that their lovemaking had changed anything for Lucas. He had been a man in pain for a long time. Now that she understood his anguish…she couldn't be sure of anything except that she had misjudged him unforgivably. She owed him an apology—and so much more. But would he find it in his heart to forgive her?

Anxious now that she'd let her thoughts get the better of her, Ashlynne scrambled from the covers. She dressed quickly in defense of the chill morning air, uncaring that her clothes were wrinkled after a night piled on the floor. She could change later, after she found Lucas.

Pray God, he hadn't started drinking again. If only all the alcohol could be gone.

Heedless of her disheveled look with her hair loose about her shoulders, Ashlynne clattered down the stairs.

"Morning."

Willie stood in his customary position behind the bar. She reached the bottom step and tried to smile in an ordinary way, as though she came down the stairs from Lucas's bedroom every morning.

"Good morning," she said. "Where's Lucas?"

Willie shrugged. "I thought he was upstairs with you."

Her cheeks flushed with the heat of embarrassment, but she tried to brazen it out. "I...he was gone when I woke up."

Willie glanced back to his morning inventory of the bar area, and Ashlynne let out a breath of relief. Lucas's bartender saw too much—more than she wanted him to—and understood more. She counted herself lucky that he rarely said anything unless pressed for an opinion.

"It stopped snowing," Willie said after a moment.

"I noticed the sun came out."

"Maybe Lucas had a touch of cabin fever and wanted to get away for a while."

"Maybe," she agreed, but the suggestion made her distinctly uneasy. No matter how she felt about the place, Lucas loved the Star. He *liked* being there and never seemed to want to get away from it.

You might want to remember that, she told herself firmly, *instead of dreaming up silly plans. You're here only by necessity, but Lucas chooses to live here.*

Ashlynne started across the room, reminding herself of all the things she'd learned since Lucas had taken her in. Really, the Star of the North wasn't such a bad place. The men—the customers—had been nice and respectful for the most part. Except for that first misunderstanding with the Irish coffee, no one had forced her—or anyone else—to drink liquor. It had been just as Lucas described it: a place where lonely men spent a few hours forgetting their troubles. Could she really begrudge them that, with all the hardships they had yet to face between Skagway and Dawson?

But what about Lucas—and all the others—who drank too much? Men who couldn't—or wouldn't—stop? A place like the Star only made it possible for them to continue their roguish ways.

Wait, soothed a calm voice of reason. *Talk to Lucas.* And Ashlynne knew it was only fair. But…where was he?

"I'm glad the storm is over," she said as she reached the bar, more to have something to say than for any other reason. "The wind and the cold grew a little tiring day after day. The sun is nice for a change."

Willie glanced up, his expression more serious than she had expected from her casual comments. Ashlynne fought the uncertainty that urged her to look away.

"I know you don't like it here," he said.

"Like it?" She did her best to sound lively, perhaps even amused. "I haven't seen enough of Alaska to know if I like it or not."

"Winter's not the time to decide if you like Alaska," he said with unmistakable emphasis. "You have to go through a whole season—especially the summer—before you can decide. By then you know for sure." He nodded. "By then you've learned that summers make the winters tolerable."

He smiled then, a kinder smile than she might have expected. "But that's not all I meant, Ashlynne. You might like Alaska, but you don't like being in the Star."

They both knew she couldn't argue with him. Even so, she tried to sidestep the truth, if just a bit. "I'm not…fond of saloon life, that much is true. I've never pretended otherwise. Before Ian died, I never imagined I'd ever step foot inside a place like this, let alone live and work here."

Willie nodded but didn't reply. After a moment she added

with a shrug, "Sometimes it seems like the only part of Alaska I've seen is the inside of the Star of the North." She gestured to the room behind her but smiled, hoping to take any sting from the words. "But I'd like to stay in Skagway and see what else Alaska has to offer."

"The Star is Lucas's life, you know."

"I…" Ashlynne paused as her heart suddenly seemed to hammer at the back of her throat. How could Willie recognize her fears so clearly? And yet, how could he not know? She'd never made any secret of her feelings about saloon life.

He also knew she'd just spent the night in Lucas's bed.

She swallowed. "What are you saying, Willie?"

He shook his head. "Not that much. Just what I said before. Lucas is who he is. You can't change him, and it's not fair to expect him to be a man any different than the one you already know he is."

"Willie—"

"I know you're lovers." He talked over whatever else she might have said, and his pronouncement produced a blazing heat that shot up her neck and over her cheeks. "You're a nice girl, Ashlynne," he continued, "and I like you. But you don't belong here. Not in Skagway and not in a place like the Star. And you know as well as I do, this is the only place where a man like Lucas *does* belong. So I just want to warn you not to get any romantic ideas about a future with Lucas. At best you'll be disappointed, and he could break your heart."

Her insides went cold. Hadn't she feared the very same thing? How much worse it sounded coming from another. But she'd vowed to wait, to talk to Lucas first, and so she would.

She had to.

She couldn't find a smile, but she couldn't be angry with Willie, either. "I know you're trying to do the right thing,

Willie. For me and for Lucas. But there are things you don't know. Things—"

"Things that Lucas kept to himself. I know that. Every man in Alaska has something in his past he doesn't want known. It's why we're all here. But that doesn't change anything. You're still a good girl—a teetotaler. And Lucas is still a man who owns a saloon and drinks more than his share of whiskey. *He* knows the truth about how life works, even if you don't want to see it. Why do you think he's tried so hard to get you to go back to where you came from?"

Ashlynne swallowed back a sick feeling that shuddered to life within her. How many times and in how many ways had Lucas tried to send her back to San Francisco? She'd always refused—for Ian, she'd claimed, and it had been true. But now that she and Lucas had made love, it felt as though everything had changed. Forever.

"Willie?" Slowly she forced her gaze up to his. "Are you sure you don't know where Lucas is?"

"No." He turned back to counting bottles under the counter. "I haven't seen him this morning."

"All right." She said nothing more but remained standing at the bar. Where could Lucas have gone and why would he have left without a word?

"Son of a bitch."

"Willie?" She straightened and stared at him. "What is it?" He had never cursed in front of her before.

He straightened slowly, his eyes downcast as though he refused to look at her. He didn't answer, either.

"Willie, what's wrong?"

Finally, slowly, he held up a piece of paper that had been folded in two. "This."

"What is it?" she asked again.

"A note. From Lucas. I recognize his handwriting."

Relief spread through her. "What does it say? Where did he go?"

"I haven't read it yet."

"Well, why not?"

"Ashe…" He paused and the shortened version of her name trailed away. He'd never called her that before. Only Lucas had.

Her relief died a sudden, certain death. Something was wrong. Very, very wrong. Willie's expression, and a new instinct born the moment Lucas had taken her in his arms, assured her of it.

"What's wrong, Willie?" she asked quietly.

"He left the note where I keep my gun. And the gun is gone."

Chapter Eighteen

Lucas sat at a table in Jeff Smith's Parlor, the saloon owned by Jefferson Randolph "Soapy" Smith. He'd been forced to cool his heels waiting for the man, and impatience crowded over him.

Jeff Smith's Parlor was smaller than the Star, about half the size, and had none of the few amenities the Star could boast. The place was empty except for the bartender and a couple of drunks seated in the back.

Ashlynne would have hated it there.

No, not simply hated it, Lucas corrected himself. She would have hated it *worse* than she hated the Star. It was a distinction worth noting, and he would be wise not to forget it.

He shifted and tried to restrain the edgy impatience that made it so difficult to sit still. Soapy was a notorious figure in Skagway, known to spend a fair part of his day in the Parlor. Today didn't seem to be a typical day for Smith—or, for that matter, Lucas himself. He'd been waiting for an hour now and Smith still hadn't come around. It was the one contingency for which Lucas hadn't planned.

What plan? he demanded with very real irritation. *You drunkenly decided how to solve your problem—and Ashlynne's—and now you're disappointed when things don't simply fall into place around you?*

Lucas didn't bother to try to defend the observation, except to remind himself it wasn't entirely true. He hadn't been drunk when he'd concocted this scheme; he had, in fact, been perfectly sober. He'd simply realized the need…and the only solution possible. It was later when he'd gotten drunk and then he'd stayed drunk long enough to do the one thing he'd vowed that he never would again.

He'd made love to a woman without using a condom.

And it hadn't been simply *any* woman, either. It had been *Ashlynne*.

He'd thought it was a dream, like the first one. That alone should have warned him not to trust his self-control, but he'd been so hard, so hot…and he'd wanted Ashe so damn bad. And then he'd taken her.

Lucas swallowed a frustrated growl. He couldn't remember everything about the evening, but he could remember everything about *her.* He could remember reaching for her with frantic, desperate hands, and then she'd touched him in her soft, gentle way. He remembered the taste of her, the feel of her and how they'd come apart in each other's arms. He'd never known anything like it.

Waking this morning to find Ashlynne still in his bed, gloriously naked and pressed sweetly, trustingly, against him, his memories had come flooding back. And with them came one undeniable truth: he had spilled every bit of his seed into Ashlynne's womb and, even now, she could be carrying his child.

Lucas withheld a bone-deep shudder. The thought of it scared the very devil out of him. It could never happen again.

He could never allow Ashlynne to grow heavy with his child. Never.

She's not Emily. The voice was insidious, tempting him with its tone of reasonable calmness. *She's stronger, not so dependent. She wouldn't be in Alaska otherwise. You've known that from the very beginning. And she's no tiny, frail miss to be easily hurt. Not like Emily.*

"It doesn't matter," he muttered to himself as he shot a moody glare toward the bartender. The man didn't notice.

It does matter, insisted the part of him that wished for…so much that he couldn't have. *You're a doctor. You know each woman has her own physical differences. Even here, in the backwoods of Alaska, Ashlynne is healthier than Emily ever was. She could give you a child.*

No! Lucas swallowed the word, clenching his jaw until it ached. Ashlynne would not give him a child, because making love to her as he had last night would never happen again. It couldn't.

And that meant that Ashlynne couldn't stay in Skagway. He could never trust himself around her again—and that reaffirmed his decision one last time.

He must kill Soapy. He had no choice.

Time had run out.

What if it's too late?

The possibility wouldn't be silenced, and how could he argue with the question? He'd made love to Ashe more fully and completely than he'd ever made love to another woman.

Lucas closed his eyes for a moment, two. It pained him to admit it, but he couldn't lie to himself about this. Emily had been his wife and he'd loved her with all his heart, but he'd never wanted her with the same depth of emotion that had overtaken him when he'd made love to Ashlynne.

He blinked and forced himself to face the truth of his

checkered past. There had been other women who'd come after Emily and before Ashlynne. Women like Candy, who had only provided him with a warm and convenient body, a chance to ease his physical needs and nothing more. He hadn't wanted anything more. He hadn't wanted Ashlynne to be anything more, either, but that had seemingly been out of his hands. From the moment he'd touched her, he'd lost control of things. Completely.

She was so very different from any other woman he'd known—and most especially Emily.

Ashlynne argued with him, irritated him, challenged him and pushed him. She disapproved of him and his life, that much was certain, and yet she helped him, worked with him, expected things of him that he would never expect of himself. She had a passion for life that allowed no room for reserve or detachment of any kind, and it extended to every part of her life.

Even to making love with him, and it had found an answering passion within him that had robbed him of the most basic control. It had left him without the common sense to use Mr. Goodyear's rubber product.

Lucas withheld another deep shudder. He'd given no thought to the future. He'd let need—desire—overpower every other sensibility. He hadn't used a condom, he hadn't pulled out before it was too late…and now he was left to pay the price.

And now, when it was too late, he realized that his instincts had been right from the very beginning. Going to Ashlynne's aid that night all those weeks ago might have been kind—the right thing to do from a humanitarian viewpoint. For him, personally, it had proved to be slow suicide. He had reopened his mind—and heart—to things that had damn near killed him once. He could hardly even think about it now after he'd barely managed to put it all behind him all those years ago. He very much doubted he had the ability—or the strength— to save himself again.

No, he could no longer pretend or delay. Ashlynne must leave Alaska, and as soon as possible.

Lucas flexed his shoulders, relaxing the tense muscles in his neck and back. Killing Soapy would give Ashlynne the justice she craved and the freedom to return to her life in San Francisco. With Soapy dead, she *would* go. Lucas was certain of it.

He counted on it.

And he…he would face the consequences of his actions just as he always had. Full-on and alone.

He deserved whatever might come his way—and more, if the truth be told. He would never argue that point any differently. If not for this sin, then he had myriad others as of yet unaccounted for.

"You want another whiskey, Templeton?"

Soapy's man behind the bar stared across the room and made no effort to disguise his sneer. Lucas dismissed him with little concern and instead peered at the shot glass left waiting on the table. It was full. At a loss when he found Soapy absent, Lucas had ordered the whiskey and settled in to wait.

Somehow he hadn't been able to take one drink.

How was it, he asked himself, after all the years he'd spent with a drink in his hand, he hadn't the least desire for one now? No craving for a taste, no…nothing. The idea of it almost made him sick.

No doubt his mission here explained it. He needed his wits about him today and alcohol would only dull the edges.

"No." He shook his head. "No more whiskey."

The bartender frowned but said nothing more.

Are you sure? asked a sudden, sly voice from the far corner of his mind. *It might build up your courage. And your hands, aren't they a little shaky? A drink might steady you.*

Yes…a taste of whiskey might do those things—and more, he thought with a flicker of momentary interest. But the appeal died a sudden death before he could so much as reach for the glass. He could wait. Once he'd finished what he'd come here to do, he could drink Skagway dry if he wanted to. The good stuff, the rotgut—all of it. But not now.

"When did you say Smith would be back?" he demanded shortly.

The bartender shrugged. "When he gets here."

Lucas slumped back in his chair and stared once more at the shimmering, amber-filled glass. Whiskey gold. The color of Ashlynne's eyes.

He dropped his arms to his sides and the unfamiliar weight of Willie's gun poked from under his suit jacket. Jesus. What did he think he was doing?

A sudden rattle accompanied the creak of a hinge and a draft of cold air snaked over his back. "Your wait's over, Templeton," announced the bartender. "Soapy's here."

"Read it, Willie." Ashlynne stared at the note as though it held the answers to the secrets of the world. And perhaps it did.

He unfolded the page slowly, as though his fingers didn't want to cooperate. His hesitation tweaked her already heightened nerves and her heart began to pound. She swallowed as Willie began to speak.

"'By the time you read this,'" he began in an awful, hushed voice, "'the deed will be done. It's time to take matters into my own hands. I didn't want things to turn out like this, but I don't see any other way. I have gone to take care of Soapy

Smith once and for all—whatever it takes. I expect one of us will end up dead.'"

"Dead?" It was no more than a whisper as all the air had fled from Ashlynne's lungs in one great rush. She choked back a sudden breathless sob and grasped the edge of the bar to keep her on her feet. Her eyes filled with tears. "He went after…Soapy?"

Willie nodded and continued to read. "'If I kill Soapy, Taylor won't let me live long. The Star is yours. You can make a good living but you might have to fight for it. Do whatever it takes to keep it away from Taylor or any of the other crooks in Soapy's gang. I've saved some money—you know where it is. No matter what happens, Willie, give it to Ashlynne and get her the hell out of Skagway. She'll have her justice and there will be nothing left for her here.'"

Willie's voice faded and Ashlynne gasped for breath. She couldn't think, couldn't breathe. Nothing made sense.

Lucas had gone after Soapy? But he'd wanted her to forget her quest for justice. Was it because of Ian?

No. The truth charged through her immediately and she fought back a wave of nausea. He'd gone after Soapy because of her.

"Oh, God." Her voice remained thin, her breath all but gone. But…she had to do something! "I've got to go," she muttered hoarsely. "I've got to find him."

"Ashe—"

"I don't expect you to come with me." She spun on her heel and started for her sleeping quarters. "But I have to go after him, Willie. I can't let him do this."

She ran back to her room, snatched her cloak from its peg on the wall and raced back into the saloon. "Where do you think he went?" she demanded as she pulled the cape around her shoulders.

He shrugged into his own coat and circled around from behind the bar. "Only one place I can think of. Jeff Smith's Parlor. Soapy owns it and he spends most days there."

"Take me there." She started toward the door without waiting for him, only slanting a gaze behind her to see that he followed. "And Willie. Hurry."

"You were waiting for me, Templeton?"

Lucas stood slowly and turned to face Jefferson "Soapy" Smith. They'd met but only rarely, mostly by Lucas's design. And as held true each time Lucas saw him, Smith's appearance was surprisingly average. He stood a few inches shorter than Lucas and was dressed in a broadcloth suit much like the one Lucas wore. His hat, light in color, had a wide brim, and his beard concealed the strength of his jaw. Lucas didn't make the mistake of thinking that made Soapy either weak or indecisive. Over the months he'd been in Skagway, Lucas had seen plenty of evidence to the contrary.

Smith carried a half-smoked cigar in one hand. The other he kept free. Lucas had few doubts about why. He couldn't see it; he knew damn well there was every chance that Soapy had a gun tucked under his suit coat, convenient to that free hand.

Just as Lucas did.

Lucas allowed a brief nod and said in a mild tone, "I wanted to…talk."

Word had it that Soapy would remain friendly and personable as long as the townspeople in Skagway stayed out of his business. Lucas was willing to believe such a rumor—to a point; Smith had never bothered him or the Star. For the moment he was willing to proceed as though they had something to discuss.

"All right." Soapy strode past Lucas to the bar. He pointed

at the drunks in the back. "Get them out of here," he said to the bartender.

He poured himself a whiskey and ignored the ruckus between the other men. Lucas concentrated solely on Soapy.

"What do you want, Templeton?"

Lucas hadn't thought much about what he would say and now the words came of their own accord. "It's about Ian Mackenzie."

"Who?"

"Ian Mackenzie," he repeated grimly. Ashlynne would hate it that Soapy didn't know Ian's name. "He died here in Skagway a few weeks back. He was gunned down in the street."

"And you think I'm responsible."

Lucas raised one eyebrow while a new and sudden uneasiness churned in his gut. Did Soapy suspect something?

"I've heard it said," Lucas admitted carefully.

"And I've heard a few things myself."

"Such as?"

"Such as that you've got it out for me. You and your new ladylove. It's her brother you're talking about, isn't it?"

Soapy's words sliced through Lucas with an edge of utter and icy coldness. There could be no mistaking Smith's sly tone or his matching expression. He was talking about Ashlynne. But what did it mean? And how much did he know about her?

Lucas neither moved nor answered. He delayed the moment by slanting a careful glance around the empty room. "You seem to think you know something that I don't," said Lucas finally, in a deliberate tone of amused disbelief. "Do you want to explain it?"

Soapy laughed with smug self-confidence. "You're right. Maybe I do know something. You have your Sugar Candy to thank for that."

"Sugar…Candy?" Lucas blinked and stared as the revelation whirled through his mind. "She—"

"She said you tossed her over for your new fancy piece. Mackenzie's sister. When Candy came looking for work, she was all too willing to tell me about the Mackenzies and their—" he paused and shook his head, pretending a regret that Lucas didn't believe for an instant "—run of bad luck."

"Bad luck? Is that what you call it?"

"I hear you took the Mackenzie woman in and without a cent to her name. She's a looker, though, I'll give you that."

"You've seen Ashlynne?"

Soapy offered his glass up to the bartender, demanding a refill. He swallowed the liquor before he answered. "I haven't seen her. Not yet. One of my men…visited for me instead. I had some questions Candy couldn't answer."

"You sent the man who attacked Ashe." It was no more a question now than it had been when Lucas had fought the intruder.

Soapy blinked and his expression seemed almost pained. "He was supposed to gather information—and he did a piss poor job. Your fancy piece, she distracted him, and when it all fell to pieces, he cut and ran rather than stay to take care of things." Smith shook his head sorrowfully. "I'm afraid Robby won't be working for me again."

Lucas swallowed back the sour taste that formed at the back of his throat. Soapy talked about the whole thing so easily, as though he felt no emotion over any of it. Not for ordering a man to break into the Star or the attack on Ashlynne. Certainly not about Ian Mackenzie's death. And not even over the fact that his man Robby was very likely dead himself.

"So tell me, Templeton…" Soapy paused and his gaze became strange, almost feral. "Now that I've spilled my secrets for you, why have you come here?"

There was, indeed, no more reason to delay. The game had played itself out long enough and they'd wasted enough time on useless banter.

"I came for this." Lucas snatched the gun from his waistband and leveled it at Soapy. "Don't move," he said, nodding at the bartender, "or I'll kill him before you can blink."

Smith stared at Lucas as though not particularly surprised to find a gun pointed directly at him—and not especially worried, either. "So you're going to kill me, are you?"

Lucas tightened his finger around the trigger. "Yes."

Soapy gave a scornful laugh. "You? Kill me?" He shook his head with clear amusement. "You'll never do it, Templeton. You've never done anything like it."

"You don't know anything about me."

Soapy shrugged. "I know enough. They say you're one of the *good ones*. You run a clean place and you rescue damsels in distress. Oh, you might have a taste for the booze, but you've got a damned annoying streak of honor that runs clear through you. I can see it from here."

Lucas couldn't say how he managed it, but he dredged up his own laugh. "I wouldn't be too sure about any of that, Smith. I might not have made my mark on Skagway in the same way you have, but that doesn't mean a damn thing. I haven't cared enough to try. I've got blood on my hands, the same as—"

"Lucas! Stop!" The words accompanied a sudden crash and a wave of cold air that signaled the door stood open. It was Ashlynne's voice, and the sound froze the very blood in his veins.

Ashlynne, here? Holy Christ, no!

"Well, well, Templeton. Looks like you've got company." Soapy smiled and pointed, but Lucas didn't turn to look. He kept the pistol aimed dead center on Smith's chest instead.

"Get the hell out of here, Ashe," he said. "Now."

"I will not. You can't do this, Lucas."

"You don't know anything about it." He ground out the words. "This is between Soapy and me."

"No. It isn't." He heard the waver in her voice but he hardened himself against it. "This is my fault," she insisted, "and it's…wrong."

"Wrong?" Lucas didn't turn to look at her but offered Smith a feral smile instead. "It's about justice. You said so yourself. You want it, I'll get it for you."

And solve a host of other problems, as well, but Lucas kept that truth to himself.

"Not this way, Lucas. Not for me. It's not worth it."

"Listen to her, Templeton." Even with a gun pointed straight at him, Soapy lost none of his confidence.

Lucas ignored them all. "Get out of here, Ashe," he repeated. "It's too late. You're too late. What's done is done."

"It's not too late! Nothing is done. I'm not going anywhere."

An edge of hysteria seemed to sharpen Ashlynne's voice and produced a new but very real fear to creep up along Lucas's spine. He'd felt little enough when facing Smith alone, but now, with Ashlynne here, subduing his emotions didn't come so easily. Worse, he knew her stubbornness, and that changed everything.

If he couldn't convince her to leave…well, there was no telling what could go wrong next.

"Ashe," he tried again, unable not to. "Just get out of here! I'll…see you later."

"Listen to your lady friend, Templeton." Soapy nodded as though agreeing with something that had been said. "If you don't put that gun away and get out of here now, you won't be going anywhere later. Except inside a wooden box. We both know it."

"And if I go now, I'll only find myself in that wooden box later, anyway. We both know *that*."

"Lucas, please." Ashlynne's voice broke, though he tried not to hear it. She surprised him when she touched him from behind, her hand tentative on his shoulder, and he caught a breath to steel himself against…everything. He could allow himself to feel nothing. Not now.

"This isn't worth it," she said, her fingers clutching tight. "I know that now. And I know what this will cost you. I can't let you do it."

"Ashe—" He dropped his gaze for an instant, just long enough to gauge exactly where she stood—and then everything unraveled around him.

"Drop the gun, Templeton."

Instantly he whipped his gaze back to Smith. Soapy had drawn his own pistol and trained it unerringly on Lucas.

"I can't do that, Smith. You know that. We need to finish this."

"Yes, maybe we do." Soapy raised one eyebrow. "But I don't think we need to bother with this outmoded sense of honor you seem so intent on following." He pointed the gun high over Lucas's shoulder—at Ashlynne? Lucas could only guess. "I've always believed in the motto 'all's fair.'"

Lucas had never seen things that way, but what choice did he have now? Seeing none, he held the pistol steady and started toward Soapy—and away from the others.

"Lucas, no!"

"Stop right there, Templeton."

"You stop me, Smith."

Forgive me.

The prayer came unexpected, but Lucas offered it up to a God in whom he no longer believed. Or perhaps he said it under his breath, hoping that Ashlynne would hear and understand. It made no difference. He could only take another step and another, and adjust the aim of his gun.

"Stop it! Both of you."

Ashlynne darted around Lucas and flung her arms wide. He tried to shout—something, but the words never came. Instead the sound of a gunshot erupted in Jeff Smith's Parlor and Ashlynne crumpled to the floor.

Chapter Nineteen

Darkness. Burning. Throbbing.

A tearing pain like nothing before.

The sensations crowded over Ashlynne, one after the other without pause, until all else retreated to nothing more than distant and vague impressions. She tried to think, to concentrate, but nothing made sense around the pain that consumed her.

She moved, or thought she did, but then she couldn't be sure as the pain burned hotter, deeper, like kindling added to a fire that now suddenly blazed. She gasped.

"Lucas."

She wanted to say his name, but she didn't think she actually managed it. He must be nearby—wasn't he? Or had he gone off? She couldn't remember, couldn't be sure. Ashlynne swallowed, trying to hold back a sudden fear, but she couldn't seem to do that very well, either.

It will be all right. Lucas will help you.

The certainty came from nowhere and everywhere at once. It started deep inside her and, while it didn't ease the pain, it comforted her somehow. Yes, Lucas would help her; he always had.

He would make the pain go away. He would hold her and kiss her and take care of her. He would make everything all right again. He had been doing that since she'd met him.

She must try again. Then he would hear her and he would come to her. He would make the pain go away. He was the one.

"Lucas?"

"I'm here, baby. Ashe?"

Relief flooded through her. Saying his name had taken all her strength, but a desperation to find him gnawed at her. Slowly, gradually, she managed to force open her eyes.

"Lucas?" She said his name again, a whispering sigh that barely made it past her lips.

"It'll be all right, baby. You'll be all right. I'll take care of you. I'll take care of everything."

She caught a glimpse of him, of tousled blond hair and vague features, but then it faded as her eyelids drifted down. She had known Lucas would help her, but he sounded so…worried. What would make him so frantic? So desperate?

Ashlynne wanted to reach for him, to reassure him with a gentle touch, but the instant she tried to raise her arm, arrows of hot agony shot through her. The renewed pain bore down on her relentlessly and she closed her eyes against it. An agonized groan rumbled low in her throat.

"Shh, baby. Just lie still."

His hands brushed over her cheek, her forehead. She knew it was Lucas; she would never mistake his touch.

Her Lucas.

Her Lucas…and she had to tell him.

A new urgency charged through her suddenly and she found herself stiffening against it. It hurt—she hurt—but he must know the truth. Nothing was more important.

"Lucas. I have…to tell…you."

"Shh, baby. Later."

"No!" She tried to swallow another grunt of pain.

"Yes. You can tell me later."

"No. Now. I have…to tell…you. It's…important."

His hand brushed over her forehead. "All right. I'm here, darlin'. What is it?"

Ashlynne wanted to smile. *Darlin'*. He'd called her darlin'. She liked that, and the other soft endearments he used. But she couldn't both smile and say what she must—and the words were what mattered.

"Lucas…you have…to know. I…love you."

There. It was done. She allowed herself a soft sigh of satisfaction and then she gave up the struggle.

Oblivion stole her from the pain.

Lucas had dropped his gun when he'd sunk to his knees, but he didn't care. He disregarded that and everything else in the room. Noise vibrated all around him, a constant irritation that grated on his nerves. His breath came sketchy and uneven.

Ashlynne had fallen unconscious and she lay motionless before him. A dark hole tore through the fabric of her cloak and now he pressed his fingers there. Carefully. He knew before he looked at them what he would see.

Blood. Some might be fooled that it wasn't much, but it didn't surprise Lucas.

"She stepped in the way, Templeton! You saw it. I didn't mean to shoot her."

Smith's voice penetrated Lucas's consciousness, sounding more anxious than he would have expected. He ignored it, as he did everything else, and tore at Ashlynne's clothing. Under her cloak, her dress was soiled with the same astonishingly small, bloody stain. Beneath that, her camisole revealed more red, and there, in her upper chest, below her collarbone, was the hole punctured by Soapy's bullet.

Even having anticipated what he would see, Lucas's heart clenched and the air rushed from his lungs. Somehow he managed to raise his gaze. "You son of a bitch," he said to Smith.

"She stepped in the way! You saw it. I didn't mean—"

"I know what you meant. You meant to kill me," Lucas snapped, and he looked back at Ashlynne's pale face. "Just as I meant to kill you. And now look what we've done."

Lucas leaned down, pressing his ear close to her mouth, her nose. She was alive—thank God!—but her breathing trickled both irregular and shallow. He pressed his fingers against her neck and found her pulse. Fast. Too fast.

He looked up and around, searching for…something. What? His mind seemed to go suddenly sluggish and a fine trembling had started deep within him, gradually extending itself up and throughout his body.

"Willie." Lucas didn't think to wonder about it when he caught sight of his bartender. He motioned the other man close. "We have to—"

The door to the Parlor crashed open and a crowd of men interrupted as they pushed their way inside, all talking at once.

"What happened?"

"We heard a shot."

Willie answered, "Soapy Smith shot Ashlynne Mackenzie."

"I didn't mean to!"

No one seemed to pay much attention to Soapy's denial, least of all Lucas. He returned his attention to Ashlynne, watching for any movement, any change, as he tried to regain control of his nerves and to think.

But how could he do that with all the chatter around him?

"Did you hear that? Soapy Smith shot a woman!"

"How did it happen?"

"Nobody shoots a woman. Not even in Skagway."

"Soapy did."

God, he needed to get away from here. He needed to get Ashlynne away and safe.

Safe.

The word seemed to free something within him and Lucas settled on a decision with abrupt certainty. He scooped her up in his arms and stood, turning for the door. As though he'd been waiting for a signal, or perhaps simply understanding, Willie joined him.

Those in the crowd seemed to hold a variety of opinions about what they should do next.

"You gonna take her over to the hospital?" asked one.

"We got one now, you know. That preacher, Reverend Dickey, he started it," said another.

"I heard they was full at the hospital. Ain't you heard about the epidemic?"

"Meningitis, I heard, and people are dyin'."

Willie glanced at Lucas, as though looking for direction. "The Star," Lucas said, and started for the door. "We'll take her to the Star. She'll be safe there."

Ashlynne lay unmoving on her cot, relocated to the main room of the Star. She wore only her ruined camisole and petticoat. Lucas had undressed her himself with all the care of a lover, while he'd had Willie stoke up the fire in the stove and light the lamps and chandelier to blazing.

Now Lucas sat in a chair next to the bed and Willie sat behind him. They'd been that way for hours, and the Star of the North was closed.

"Is there any change?"

Lucas continued to smooth a cool, damp cloth over Ashlynne's face and neck. "No."

"She's so pale, and she hasn't woken up. I don't think—that's not good."

Lucas swallowed an errant hiss as he tried to wrestle back the fear that sat in his chest, but it refused to budge. It remained there like a living being and gave him no peace. It made breathing difficult, inhibited movement and thought. It allowed room for nothing more than raw emotion and pure instinct.

"Is she still bleeding?" Willie asked after a moment. The bartender remained outside the periphery of Lucas's vision, much to his relief. Somehow he couldn't tolerate anyone too close. Not to him and not to Ashlynne.

He splayed his hand wide over the bandage he'd fashioned over the wound, checking to make sure it stayed secure. "No. This type of wound doesn't bleed all that much, and I got it stopped. But…"

"But?"

"She's running a fever."

"Maybe I should go for the preacher. Maybe Dickey—"

"We don't need Dickey. *I don't want him here.*" Lucas bit off the words with an absolute fury that boiled beyond his ability to control. "The preacher hasn't been around to see Ashe since her brother died, and he doesn't need to come around now."

"It's the meningitis epidemic, Lucas." Willie sounded both oddly patient and urgent at the same time. "He's been busy at the hospital. You understand that, don't you?"

Reverend Dickey—the preacher—had been tending to the sick while Lucas—a doctor—had refused to acknowledge his training. A sick feeling churned in his gut. He'd turned his back on medicine and been glad to do so, but now, for the first time, he wondered what he'd done. People were dying and he had done nothing to stop it.

And what about Ashlynne? Would she pay the ultimate price because of his selfishness?

"Ashe doesn't need a goddamn preacher. *She's not going to die.*"

"Lucas." He flinched when Willie put a hand on his shoulder, but the hand stayed, even tightened for a moment. "I…know. I believe you, but she needs a doctor. And the sooner the better."

"She'll be all right." The words sounded sharp and desperate, precisely as Lucas felt. Ashlynne would be all right. She had to be.

"Maybe so. I hope so," Willie added. "But if she does need a doctor, I don't know where to find one. There's probably one in Skagway—hell, more than one—but they're not here doctoring. They're going for the gold. And if Dickey's at that hospital, then maybe he's the best we've got."

"No." Lucas said it flatly and plowed a hand through his hair, shoving it back from his face.

"He might be her only hope."

"Not yet."

Willie didn't answer and the room went silent except for the crackling fire. Finally he dropped his hand and said, "All right, Lucas. What can I do?"

"Take that." Lucas nodded toward the basin that sat among the clutter on the table only an arm's reach away. "Fill it with snow. We'll melt it, and I'll see if I can bring her fever down."

Willie hesitated; Lucas knew because the basin didn't disappear. Finally the other man asked, "What about the bullet?"

"What about it?"

"It's still in there. It didn't go through."

"Get the snow."

Lucas didn't move. He waited until he heard Willie leave by the back door, listening to each distinct sound as though he'd never before heard the creak of a door, the click of a latch. Any distraction had to be safer, easier, than acknowledging the litany of doubts.

God, how had it happened? But he knew. He'd taken matters into his own hands and he'd brought them to this. He'd made a holy mess of things. And then Ashlynne had completely devastated him.

Dear God, she loved him? How could that be? He'd done nothing but make her life miserable. He represented everything she hated in life. He drank too much and made his livelihood—his *life*—in a saloon, while she was there only because she had no other choice.

And now…would she pay the ultimate price for loving him? Just as Emily had?

His heart clenched in his chest and his breathing staggered. Thank God he wasn't standing; his legs wouldn't have supported him.

Could he be responsible for another woman's death?

The differences in circumstances seemed so obvious and yet the results were the same: two women fighting for their lives because of his actions. Emily had lost the struggle, but Ashlynne still lived…still loved.

You've lived off stubbornness and self-pity for years now. Isn't it time you let Emily rest in peace? You loved her, but she's gone. Does that mean you can never love again?

The question shook him as nothing else could have at the moment. He *had* loved Emily and she'd loved him. But she was gone…and how had he honored their love? By turning his back on everything that had ever meant anything to him. By drinking and gambling and whoring. By refusing to open his emotions up to anything but bitterness and anger.

By being a coward.

Lucas hauled in a weak breath and blinked. He looked at Ashlynne, so still and pale on the bed. Her own breathing remained hoarse and labored. What next? he asked himself. Could she survive on her own? And if not, could he help her? Dare he try?

Wasn't it time to put cowardice and fear behind him? Could he take the chance of losing Ashlynne, just as he'd risked everything else in his life?

Lucas waited another hour, but by then he knew he could delay no longer. Ashlynne's fever wasn't coming down on its own and he'd given up hoping that it would. Not as long as the bullet remained in her chest.

"Willie," he called before he could reconsider.

"What?" Willie came immediately.

The bartender had been more than a friend, Lucas realized with a twinge of surprise. He hadn't left the Star except on Lucas's orders, and he'd done everything Lucas had asked of him. Now he would have to do even more.

"Go into the back room—Ashe's room," Lucas amended. His heart pounded and a lump settled at the back of his throat. He tried to swallow past it.

"All right. Then what?"

"There's a trunk. It's in the corner opposite the window and shoved behind the chair. My name's printed on it. It has some...personal items in it. One is a black leather bag. Bring it to me."

"Lucas, what—"

"Just bring me the bag."

Lucas allowed neither resignation nor uncertainty to color

his tone and Willie didn't argue further. But why would he? He couldn't know what Lucas meant to do.

How can you even consider it? demanded a sharp voice of disbelief, and he closed his eyes wearily. But how could he not? It was the only choice Ashlynne had.

"Ashlynne. Baby." Lucas bent low to whisper near her ear. She couldn't hear, couldn't see, but still he held out one hand that betrayed him with weak, damning tremors.

"Do you see that, darlin'? I don't know if I can do this. I shouldn't even consider it, sure as hell shouldn't try. But…I have to. Don't I? I can't lose you, baby. It's… I…" He swallowed a low, agonized groan. "Goddammit, Ashe. *I love you.*"

"Is this it?"

Lucas straightened abruptly and looked over his shoulder. Willie had indeed found what he was looking for and had returned carrying what could well be Pandora's box. The black leather bag that Lucas had once considered much like another limb. A hand, an arm. It had been invaluable to him.

It had been a curse to him.

He nodded. "That's it."

He wanted to reach for it—and he didn't want to touch it ever again. Ashlynne made a soft little sound, a labored search for breath, and Lucas blew out a long breath of his own, as though that would help her. Swallowing, he dug deep within himself for the resolution to stand and take the bag.

He turned to the table where he'd arranged all the other sickroom paraphernalia and placed the bag smack in the middle. "Get that board," he said over his shoulder. "The one Ashe uses for a counter. We'll put it over a couple of tables, right here under the light."

Lucas didn't look to see if Willie cooperated but instead began rearranging tables to put them just where he wanted them. He and Willie adjusted the board to its proper place and then Lucas pulled close the table that held the supplies he'd accumulated.

He closed his eyes, gathering his strength, and then he opened the bag. Carefully, reluctantly, he peered inside. What a mess! Everything was tossed around willy-nilly, as though he'd thrown it there in a fit of anger…and likely he had. He hadn't opened it in four years. Not since Emily and baby Rose had died. But now he spied most of his instruments and half-empty bottles of chloroform and laudanum. Thank God, at least he had something to work with.

He plucked a basin from the clutter and filled it with water kept hot on the stove. Next, he rinsed his hands. "Get me a bottle of whiskey. No, get several."

"Whiskey?"

Lucas glanced up, recognizing the sharp tone in Willie's voice. "Get it, Willie." He caught and held the bartender's gaze. "If ever I needed whiskey in my life, now's the time."

"But, Lucas—"

"Get it, dammit!" His patience ran thin and he turned his back on Willie. He went to Ashlynne instead. "I need it."

Slowly, as gently as he could, Lucas scooped Ashlynne up into his arms. She uttered a soft, wheezing moan. How could she feel so light, so delicate, almost ethereal? Almost as though she no longer remained of this world. Fear pounded through Lucas and his heart beat harder and faster. For a moment he couldn't breathe.

"Here's the whiskey," said Willie, his tone heavy with disapproval.

"Put it there." Lucas nodded toward his worktable. "Then cover the plank with that sheet."

Thank God, Willie cooperated, and finally the surgery, as Lucas tried to think of it, was ready. He laid Ashlynne on the table with great care, then turned to his assortment of supplies.

He stared at them all, at the black bag and the meager provisions he'd managed to accumulate. He had little more than nothing to work with…only a will for Ashlynne to live.

Lucas sucked in a deep breath, then fished inside the bag until he came up with a scalpel and forceps. He pulled the cork from the closest bottle of whiskey and poured it over everything, including his hands. He allowed the excess to run into the basin, where he left the instruments to soak. Then he turned once more toward Ashlynne.

"Willie, I'm going to need your help," he said as he dampened a rag with chloroform. "I'll need you to hold this over her nose for a bit," he said as he handed over the rag. Wide-eyed, Willie took it from him without a word. "I'll tell you when to take it away."

Lucas pushed Ashlynne's camisole aside and began to unbandage the wound. Revealing the red, angry-looking bullet hole, he swallowed and then carefully poured whiskey all around it.

"Lucas?" Willie spoke softly, his voice almost nonexistent. "What the hell are you doing?"

"We're going to take the bullet out. It might be the only chance she has."

Lucas picked the scalpel out of the basin and dried it with a clean towel. Remarkably, it fit much more easily in his hand when he didn't clutch it so tightly. It felt…odd. Unnatural and yet right. Almost as though the years since he'd touched his instruments were beginning to fall away as though they'd never been.

"Jesus Christ, Lucas, you're a doctor!" said Willie as understanding finally dawned.

Lucas spared a glance for nothing but Ashlynne as he bent over her. "We'll see if I am," he muttered hoarsely, and positioned the scalpel against Ashlynne's skin.

Chapter Twenty

Awareness came to her awkwardly, distantly, in sketchy bits and pieces that made little sense with their jumbled order. Ashlynne didn't mind. She preferred it, in fact, to coming too close to *real* consciousness. The moment she moved too far from the protection of her dreams, pain roared forward and warned her away.

It was better here, in this special place, anyway. It was safer, without the raw, throbbing ache that waited out there, in that other place. But it was odd, as well. Nothing made sense and yet it seemed exactly right. For now, she decided, she liked it well enough to stay.

"Look, Ashe, that's it."

Ian pointed from behind her at the sheer rise of the mountains looming high into the sky. Snow covered them while a few wispy clouds decorated the peaks as though they'd become caught on the jagged edges. And there, squatted at the edge of the water, sat a ragged little town.

"That's Skagway?" she asked.

"That's it," Ian agreed, glee dancing in his voice. "And be-

yond those mountains is the Klondike. And the gold." He laughed with clear delight. "We're almost there, Ashe. And then..."

"Then what?" she asked when he didn't finish.

"Who knows?" Ian flung his arm wide. "Anything can happen in Alaska."

Ashlynne pulled back the satin coverlet and silky sheets that covered her bed, then sat on the edge of the mattress to remove her slippers. She smiled as she glanced around the bedroom, much like she did most nights. She had slept in this room since she'd been a child. It had always been her favorite place in the house, at times the only place she could feel safe.

The room was large, dominated by a bed big enough to sleep two. She slept in it alone. A matching dresser and heavy armoire filled one wall, while a dressing table and comfortable stuffed chair occupied the opposite side of the room. The draperies, carpet and fabrics had been expensive at one time and were well-made, but the years of use showed if one looked closely. Ashlynne didn't care. She loved this room.

"Ashe, are you in here?" Ian's voice sliced through her gentle contemplation and she narrowed her eyes as she glared at the door.

"Yes," she snapped. "So what if I am."

"Open the door." He rattled the doorknob.

"Go away. I'm ready for bed."

"Ashe! Open the damn door! It's important."

Ashlynne blinked. Ian rarely sounded so...passionate about anything. Well, nothing other than drinking and gambling and women. Certainly nothing that went on at home.

"What do you want?" she asked warily.

"Goddammit, Ashlynne!" He pounded on the door. "We have to talk. It's...Mother and Father."

*Mother and Father? Ashlynne swallowed and found her-
self standing without quite realizing the impulse to move.
Both Ian and her parents had gone out for an evening's entertainment—whatever that might have been tonight. Ashlynne never asked and the others rarely confided in her. If Ian
was here now...*

She jerked the door open. "What happened? What's wrong?"

*Ian stood in the hallway, dressed in an elegant, tailored
suit. Whether or not he could pay his bills, he always seemed
to find money for the latest fashions. His mahogany-brown
hair was disheveled, as though he'd raked his hands through
it, and his eyes flared wide. He stared at her, as though suddenly unable to do anything more.*

"Ian, what is it?" she demanded, harshly this time.

*"It's Mother and Father," he repeated. "There—it was an
accident."*

*The breath dropped from Ashlynne's lungs as though she'd
been hit in the chest and her head suddenly throbbed. She
wrapped her arms around herself and muttered hoarsely,
"How bad?"*

*"Bad enough," Ian said in a voice much like hers.
"They're dead."*

Consciousness forced itself on her, whether or not Ashlynne was ready. She didn't want to wake up. Not yet. Some
of her dreams had been wonderful. Heavenly. She might have
smiled, if she'd been able. Lucas had held her and kissed her
and made love to her, and she never wanted it to stop.

But...the warm feelings fell away. There had been other
dreams. Horrid dreams, painful dreams. She'd hated them. If
she could only escape them by waking, then she would tolerate the dull, throbbing pain that accompanied true consciousness.

Ashlynne touched her tongue to her lips. She'd never felt so weak, and her mouth tasted terrible, all dry and cottony—and something else she couldn't identify.

Oh, dear Lord. She hadn't gone and gotten drunk again, had she?

She tried to open her eyes but found the effort almost too much. Still, she didn't want to risk the oblivion of sleep again so soon. She tried again and finally managed to pry open one eyelid, then the other.

She was in the Star, but not her room or even Lucas's sleeping area upstairs. Someone had moved her cot into the main room. Why would they do something like that?

Ashlynne blinked, a slow and laborious process, but finally she was able to look around her again. Yes, it was the Star, just as she had thought. Lucas slumped in a chair next to her bed, curled in on himself as he slept, while Willie snoozed in another chair, his arms and legs spread akimbo and his head tipped back and to the side.

How could they sleep that way, all twisted and uncomfortable-looking? She should wake them or they'd be very sore.

Ashlynne swallowed, only to remember the dryness in her throat. The longer she remained awake, the more she identified other aches and pains she hadn't realized before. A tender soreness weighed down her muscles and a different burning pain throbbed high in her chest.

"Lucas?"

His name came out as little more than a dry, croaking sound. She took a breath to try again, but the ache in her chest shot fire clear through her. Her head throbbed.

With little other choice, she resigned herself to that awful voice. "Lucas?"

"Ashe…"

It sounded as much like a low groan as her name and she watched as Lucas slowly came awake. He blinked those marvelous, brilliant blue eyes, then blinked again and peered about him sleepily. The instant he caught sight of her, he sat up straight, his eyes suddenly wide.

"Ashlynne!"

He snatched up a lamp from the table at his elbow and brought it close. She squinted against the bright light. "Willie, she's awake!" he called in an oddly spirited voice that had her opening her eyes again. She looked at him curiously.

"How do you feel?" Lucas asked.

She tried to swallow, but it still did little good. "Thirsty," she whispered.

He smiled, an oddly triumphant expression that made no sense to her. "I hoped you would say that."

He slipped an arm beneath her neck and raised her head with gentle care. Once she was steady, he brought a blue-enameled cup to her lips and held it there.

"Water?"

He nodded, this time all seriousness. "Water. *Just* water." She lifted one corner of her mouth, all she could manage for a smile, and sipped from the cup. The water soothed her dry lips, her mouth, her throat. Nothing had ever tasted better.

"There. That's enough." He pulled the cup away. "You can have more in a little while, but I don't want you to get sick. You've been through an ordeal and you don't want to upset your stomach."

"An...ordeal?" She glanced at him, puzzled.

"Ashlynne! You're awake, girl!" Willie loomed up behind Lucas suddenly, his smile wide and welcoming. "We were so worried about you."

"What—" Without thinking, she tried to sit up and the words died abruptly. Tendrils of pain shot up into her head and down to her stomach. Her chest throbbed with it and she gasped for air.

"Shh, baby. Just lay back." Lucas was there immediately, fussing over her and stroking a gentle, soothing hand over her forehead, her cheek, settling her back against the mattress. "Don't move, darlin'. Just rest."

"What…happened?"

Lucas and Willie exchanged glances; she recognized the silent communication but it made no more sense than her being confined to this bed in the middle of the saloon. Or the obvious worry the men shared.

"Lucas?"

He returned his attention to her and the haunted darkness in his usually lively blue eyes almost convinced her to recall the question. Then he said in a rough voice, "You were shot."

"Shot!" Ashlynne stiffened, frowning as she tried to make sense of Lucas's words.

Memories came flooding back suddenly, some clear and some with no more substance than a melting snowflake. On the whole, it made a sketchy picture at best—but it was enough to give her a glimpse.

"You…I woke up and you were gone," she said softly as she watched Lucas and saw the truth on his face. "We didn't know where you were, but then Willie found the note." She glanced aside to see the bartender nod. "You—" she located Lucas again. "You took his gun. We went after you. And you—"

Tears filled her eyes and her voice grew thick. "Oh, Lucas. You were going to kill Soapy Smith!"

"Shh." He moved closer and brushed his hand across her temples, her forehead. "It's all right, Ashe. I didn't kill him. Everyone's still alive."

But the grief in Lucas's eyes…oh, God, his eyes carried

such torment. Ashlynne's heart broke. She should say—do—something for him…but what? The little strength she'd awoken with seemed to be fading and her mind remained sluggish at best.

"It was Soapy who shot me." She knew that much.

"You got right in the thick of things, honey." Willie added that detail and she turned her head to look at him. He stepped forward. "I don't think Soapy meant to hit you, but it happened, all the same. He's not a very popular man in these parts right now. You don't shoot a woman. Not even in Skagway."

"That's enough," said Lucas, drawing Ashlynne's attention once more. "We'll talk about all this later, when you're better. Right now you need to rest. And to not think about any of this."

Her eyelids drifted down and sleep beckoned, encouraged by Lucas's approval, but for the moment Ashlynne refused to give in to it. She couldn't trust the release of sleep—yet. She'd seen the agony in Lucas's eyes, understood the pain in his heart and knew full well that danger remained.

"Lucas!" She struggled to full awareness and would have tried to sit up had he not been right there.

"Ashe. Please, baby, just lay back. You need to rest."

"I can't. Not unless you promise me you'll stop." She didn't even try to keep the plea from her voice. "You can't go after Soapy again. Please."

"Ashe—"

"Please, Lucas! You can't go after him for me. Especially not for me."

He brushed his fingers along her temples again and she found herself relaxing under the soothing gesture. She turned her head against the touch of his hand.

"I'm right here, baby," he murmured softly, "and I'm not going anywhere."

"And you'll stay here with me?" She forced herself to keep his gaze trapped by hers. "You won't leave me?"

"I won't leave you."

Her eyes fell closed as she searched for a last semblance of strength. Gradually, willfully, she found enough to raise her arm, to find Lucas's hand with hers. His fingers twined with hers immediately and she pressed the back of his hand against her cheek.

"You must never consider something like that again." She spoke softly, implacably, using her strength for that and not opening her eyes. "The cost is too great. More for you than most men."

He moved their joined hands in a small circle that caressed her cheek. "You just go to sleep and don't worry about such things."

Ashlynne smiled, or she thought she did. Lucas's touch always gave her that melting, tender feeling. He had wonderful hands.

A doctor's hands.

A doctor...

Had he told her that or had she dreamed it? There were other things that made no more sense, and she tried to think back. Events, moments, slipped in and out of her consciousness faster than she could follow them. Still, it seemed as if it should be important—if only she could grasp the truth.

"There's more I should remember," she whispered, unable to drag open her eyelids. "I just...can't."

"Don't worry about that now." A soft brush against her ear—his lips?—followed the words. "You can think about it all later."

"Yes. All right."

Her fingers loosed from his as she relaxed, but she didn't quite let go. Her thoughts began to drift and she wanted to let them go where they would. She just couldn't. Not yet. Something still troubled her.

"Lucas?"

"What, darlin'?"

"Did you promise me?"

"Promise you?"

She swallowed and pulled in a shallow breath. "That you wouldn't go after Soapy again. That you would let it go."

"Ashlynne—"

"You have to let it go, Lucas. I'm sure of it. I don't think I've ever been more certain of anything in this life. You have to promise me." Finally, slowly, she dragged her eyes open. *"Promise me."*

"Yes, all right."

He sounded none to happy about it, but Ashlynne wanted to smile. She would have, if she'd had the energy.

"I promise," he added, his tone thoroughly disgruntled.

"Good." Satisfaction—relief—relaxed her and she felt herself fading. "You've sacrificed too much already. No justice in the world is worth the price of your soul."

And then she lost herself to the summoning darkness.

Chapter Twenty-One

∞

"What do you think you're doing?"

Ashlynne stopped immediately, feeling much like a child caught in the midst of a prank. But she wasn't doing anything more than trying to sit up, she reminded herself firmly.

And Lucas wasn't her father.

She frowned at him. "I want to get up."

"No." He crossed the room and shook his head with utter disapproval. As she had come to expect, his blond hair fell into his eyes and he pushed it away with unthinking irritation. "You aren't ready to get up yet. It's only been three days."

"Three days is long enough," she insisted.

"Three days is nowhere near long enough to recover. Ashlynne, you were shot!"

She frowned at Lucas and his absolute decree, but he didn't seem to notice. Instead he turned to tidying up all the sickroom paraphernalia that had accumulated over the past few days. He was very careful, she noted, about the way he handled the instruments and other supplies that he returned to the black leather bag he'd produced from…somewhere.

His doctor's bag. His bag of miracles.

The bag—and the man—had saved her life.

Lucas, however, didn't seem to want to talk about it.

She had awoken several times—and stayed awake for a bit longer each time—before she could put the pieces all together. Now she understood his pain; she had her own heartaches, her own secrets that she'd rather forget. But peace, it seemed, never came easily. How long had Lucas spent keeping his pain hidden inside of himself?

Wasn't it time to begin anew? With her as she found herself facing her own fresh start, her second in as many months.

"If I have to lie here any longer, I'll have bedsores." She frowned with the words. It gave her an outlet for some of her frustration, not only at being confined to bed but because she never seemed to have any answers, only more questions.

Lucas glanced up from his chores, but his gaze carried little enough sympathy. "You won't have bedsores. But you squirm around enough that I'm beginning to wonder if you've got bedbugs."

"I don't have bedbugs."

"Well, whatever it is, if you keep moving around, it'll keep you from getting bedsores well enough. And it just might reopen your incision."

Ashlynne pressed her lips together and glared at him. How could she have fallen in love with such a stubborn, infuriating man? Not only did he refuse to discuss her injuries except in the most clinical of ways, but he had been acting strangely, as well.

Almost as if they hadn't made love.

As if she hadn't told him that she loved him.

Or had she?

It was one of the things Ashlynne couldn't say for sure. She had remembered most everything else with stark clarity up to the moment she'd stepped between Lucas and Soapy. Then it all went hazy. Since then she'd welcomed the growing moments of lucidity. The comfort of her earlier dreams and a temporary lingering in the hazy world between being awake and asleep had left her not quite able to distinguish for certain among any of it.

But if she had said it, would he have believed her? And even if she had said it, it was also entirely possible that he didn't love her back. And yet…if he didn't care for her at least a little bit, why would Lucas have put himself through the ordeal of practicing medicine again?

And even if those things were true, was it enough?

Ashlynne frowned. It had to be. For now. She—and Lucas—could do nothing more than take things one day at a time.

Besides, she was recovering nicely. Her frown faded. Lucas had been forced to admit it last night when she'd pressed him. So if she deserved to be sick of anything, it was being in this bed, she decided anew.

"Where's Willie?" she asked suddenly.

Lucas closed his medical bag and slanted an irritatingly distant gaze in her direction. "He went out. I think he felt like he was cooped up here long enough." He surprised her when he hiked the corner of his mouth up in a crooked smile. "He said he needed to get out and blow the stink off himself."

Ashlynne gave in to a soft laugh. The remark sounded exactly like something Willie might have said. "He deserves to get away," she agreed. "He's been a godsend."

And he had been. He'd stayed with her from the very beginning, when she'd discovered that Lucas was missing and as she'd tracked him down. He'd extended the same friendship to Lucas, even helping with the surgery, or so he'd boasted since then.

Ashlynne allowed herself a small, tender smile. Even with

his bragging, Willie had turned white every time she tried to ask him about it.

"He might have gone to find Candy." Lucas's tone was brittle with disapproval. "I think she broke his heart."

He didn't look at Ashlynne but kept working instead. He picked up one of the displaced tables and carried it back to its original position.

"Lucas…" She hesitated. She'd learned of the other woman's part in bringing Ashlynne to Soapy's attention—and, in turn, the intruder he'd sent to attack her—but only because she'd pestered the men with questions until they'd finally given in. Since then, Lucas had fought her every time she tried to bring it up again.

"Lucas," she said, more insistent this time. "I don't think you should blame Candy. I don't think she knew what would happen."

"Of course she knew," he snapped, dropping the table into place with a crash that made Ashlynne jump.

She swallowed a grunt of pain that the unexpected movement produced. He couldn't know about any small aches and pains that continued or he'd never let her out of bed.

"If she didn't, she should have guessed."

"How could she?" Ashlynne's voice sounded a bit more breathless than she would have liked, but she forged ahead. "I'm sure she never imagined—"

"Don't be naive, Ashlynne." Finally, Lucas looked at her, but it was with a determined glare. "Candy's an experienced who—woman. She knew damn well what it could mean if she went to Soapy. If she hadn't done it, then that man might not have broken in here and attacked you."

And, Ashlynne supposed, he was right. "If that hadn't happened, then we might never have made love."

The words were out before Ashlynne could think better of

them. Heat crawled up her neck, flushing her cheeks with a warmth that gave away her embarrassment. The woman—no, the *cheechako* girl—who had come to Skagway would have never had the courage to say such a thing, but a new woman seemed to have awakened to life in Ashlynne's body. After Ian's death and now since she'd been shot herself, she had come to recognize just how fragile life could be. She had come to accept a willing determination to take this life that had been returned to her and make it her own, no matter what the risk.

This Ashlynne couldn't sit here in bed, waiting for permission to live again. And if the new Ashlynne truly loved Lucas, then she might have to fight for him.

"Ashe—" he began, but she interrupted without giving him a chance to finish.

"I want a bath," she said.

He blinked once, twice, then shook his head. "You can't. You aren't strong enough."

"I'm plenty strong…" she began, ready to argue, but on second thought, she smiled. "All right. I'll make you a compromise. A sponge bath. That won't exhaust my strength. Especially if you help me."

Lucas's mouth went dry at just the thought of it and he found himself swallowing, wetting his lips with his tongue.

He leaned forward, resting his palms on the nearest table as though that would eliminate the problem of his erection. It didn't—but he hoped it might keep Ashlynne from seeing the evidence. *Don't be depraved,* he told himself with a hint of firm desperation. He had no business allowing himself to entertain such licentious thoughts about her. Not now. She had only just begun her recovery from the double trauma of the shooting followed by surgery.

But that didn't stop him from wanting her. Just like he always wanted her.

The idea of it scared him like nothing else.

He'd almost lost her because of his own selfish stupidity. How could he allow himself to get close to her again, when it meant that he might someday face that risk again?

And if he didn't, if he held himself aloof and turned away from her, didn't he lose her anyway?

"Please, Lucas?" If she realized his torment, Ashe gave no indication of it. She offered wide eyes, whiskey-gold and pleading instead. "Willie's gone and we're here alone. I just feel so…dirty."

She gave an abbreviated shudder but cut it off with a quick frown. Lucas recognized the response; her first movement had likely produced a twinge of pain at her wound. How many other spasms would she have to suffer before she settled down to rest again?

"All right." It was against his better judgment on several levels, but he couldn't seem to deny her. Maybe if she got her sponge bath, she'd take his advice and give in to a nice long nap. Or maybe he should sneak her a small dose of laudanum. Surely that would put her to sleep. "But you'll listen to me," he warned. "And you won't overdo it."

She smiled again. "I promise." But did there seem to be something almost seductive in her expression?

It must be his imagination, he told himself as he put a kettle of water on the stove to heat. And his randy, uncontrolled attraction to her. But—dammit! Where had she gotten this idea for a bath?

At her urging, he searched through her things for a clean nightgown and a piece of French soap she'd insisted was there. He also located a soft piece of cotton toweling and washcloth and collected everything all together.

With things prepared and Ashe carefully propped up with extra pillows under her back and neck, Lucas could only sit on the cot next to her and stare. His thigh pressed against hers with soft, human warmth that reminded him of the likelihood that she still had a bit of a fever.

"It's all right, Lucas." She smiled, equal parts demure lady and bold temptress. He swallowed hard and stared. "You've seen me in a much more compromising position," she added when he didn't move. "And more than once."

It was true. He'd made love to her and his body was primed to do so again. But something seemed so very different about this. Incredibly, he realized, his nerves had set his fingers to trembling. He swallowed, imploring himself to relax as he carefully reached for her. How could this seem more intimate than making love to her?

But it did.

She wore one of his shirts and, concentrating as though his life depended on it, Lucas unfastened the first button at her neck, then the next and the next. Each revealed a bit more of her skin—flushed a healthier pink now and not the mottled red of a fever or even the pale, bloodless color she'd been for so many hours. He stopped the moment he could see the bulky white bandage that covered her injury and marred the smooth flawlessness of her skin. His gut churned, as it did each time he saw the evidence of her wound. Doctor or not, he simply couldn't seem to respond in any other way. He recognized the sickly fear, remembered the sight of her as she had stepped in front of him, arms outstretched…and then crumpled to the floor.

He swallowed and closed his eyes against the image.

"Lucas?"

Slowly he raised his eyelids and looked at her.

"Don't worry, darlin'." She smiled, genuinely and wholly.

Oddly enough she'd seemed more open and understanding—and had smiled more—since she'd been shot than in the whole time he'd known her.

And she'd called him—darlin'?

"I'm all right," she added. "Because of you."

He dropped his gaze and returned to his task, careful to keep his eyes focused on the work of his fingers and nothing more. He dipped the washcloth in the basin of warm water, squeezed out the excess and lathered it with soap.

"I owe you more than anything I've done for you so far." He found an answer from somewhere, though he couldn't be sure that what he said made sense. He could only keep moving, behaving as though everything was...normal. It wasn't and he wasn't sure it ever would be again.

"It was my fault you were shot," he added, the admission out before he could stop it.

"It was not!" She started up off the bed but seemed to rethink the movement and settled back down again.

"Yes. It was."

He stared at her throat, at the tiny, fluttering pulse that beat there, and touched the washcloth to the very same spot. He stroked it across her skin, dipped down near the place where her shirt—his shirt—parted open and then back up the side of her neck.

"You were not responsible for anything." She wrapped her fingers around his wrist and held him steady, the heel of his palm resting just below her collarbone, where he could feel the first rise of her breast through the fabric of his shirt. "Certainly not that I was shot—and nothing else I did, either. You were honest with me, about Soapy and about Ian. After that, I did what *I* wanted to, even though I didn't want to admit it. I was angry and frightened, and I wanted things to be safe and familiar. I should have known better."

He didn't want to talk about this. "That doesn't sound like such an unreasonable thing." Was that gruff, hoarse voice his?

"Of course it is! This is Alaska. The frontier. The edge of the earth, it seems sometimes." She offered him a small smile. "It shouldn't have come as any great surprise that nothing about life is safe or familiar here."

She uttered a soft sigh, more forlorn than he might have expected, and despite his better judgment, Lucas raised his gaze to meet hers. Seductive since he'd first seen it, that shimmering whiskey-gold peered back.

"Ashe, you did your best." And, Lucas realized, it was true.

"No, I only made things worse when I insisted I needed justice for Ian's death." She sounded as resigned as she was saddened by the admission. "You warned me it would be difficult or—worse—even dangerous, but I wouldn't listen. Instead I blamed a man who wasn't even there to pull the trigger."

Lucas pulled his wrist from her grip and tossed the washcloth back into the basin with some irritation. "You know Soapy was probably involved as well as I do."

"Yes, I do." She held his gaze with hers. "But that doesn't change things, Lucas. Or it doesn't change them enough."

"How can you say that? Of course it does."

"No. I was on a quest for vengeance and it simply wasn't right. Oh, I called it justice, but if you look clearly, there's little enough difference. I refused to see the truth and that… stubbornness—" she offered up a self-deprecating smile and gestured carefully around her "—put me here.

"And you know that wasn't the worst of it. It almost cost you your soul, Lucas—and that is unforgivable."

She reached for him then, moving carefully to cup his cheek with her palm. "The price is too high and I'm letting it go."

"You're…what?"

"Letting it go. All of it. It's time. I'm going to let Ian rest in peace."

"But…" Lucas shook his head. Did that mean she would be leaving Skagway?

"You stayed for justice," he said, hating the vulnerable thread that weakened his voice. "For Ian."

"Yes, I did. At least partly. But there were other reasons, as well. I had nowhere else to go, no one to care." She dropped her hand to her lap, twined her fingers together and trained her gaze there. "Except you."

"Ashe—"

"My parents are dead, Lucas." She spoke over him, continuing almost as though she must, though she raised her gaze to his. Even so, he saw little enough emotion there. Just…determination. "They were killed in an accident last year. My father made some sort of bet—I don't know what it was. He often did things like that. My mother was with him, and they were racing another carriage. The fog came in and he missed a curve. They died instantly."

"I'm sorry."

She smiled, soft remnants of grief coloring the expression. "If they'd had a choice, I think they would have preferred to go that way. Doing something wild and exciting. And together. Ian was very much like them. And I…well, I wasn't."

She shook her head and the light in her eyes faded, as though she had retreated to the memory of days gone by. "My parents were gone frequently, and I didn't like it as a child. They frightened me when they came home from parties, all giddy and excited. My grandparents helped to make up for any…shortcomings in my home life, but they died years ago. After that, I was left much like a fish out of water."

Lucas sat stiffly, not certain he wanted to hear more. She described something absolutely different than his upbringing—a very ordinary childhood with two devoted parents who always thought of others' needs above their own wishes. And yet, by the time he'd returned from medical school and settled down with Emily, he had begun to feel oddly disenfranchised himself.

As though he didn't belong.

"I tried to fit in with them," Ashlynne continued. "I tried very hard, in fact, but in the end, it was a disaster. There was a man, of course."

Lucas's stomach clenched. A man. The man who'd taken her virginity.

"Elliott—Elliott Sanders—was a friend of Ian's. They gambled together—among other things, I'm sure. My grandfather had just died and I was feeling…vulnerable. My father always said that he and Grandfather were alike in one way— they lived life to the fullest—and so I decided that I would adopt their philosophy. It was the least I could do—a tribute to Granddad, I suppose.

"I didn't see, until it was too late, the many ways that *living life to the fullest* could be interpreted. I took it at the face value my parents had given it and tried to be more like them. I went to parties, stayed out late and generally tried to behave as though nothing mattered but the moment."

"And that's when you met—Elliott?" Lucas bit off the name.

Ashlynne nodded, seeming caught up in the memories. "Ian introduced us. I'm ashamed to admit that Elliott swept me off my feet. I was…smitten."

A charming flush turned her cheeks a dusky rose and

Lucas could almost imagine a younger, innocent Ashlynne enraptured by an older, more worldly man. Something like the very way in which Lucas himself might have overtaken her life?

"I found out later that Elliott had lost a considerable sum to Ian. Drinking, card playing, I don't know what else. Elliott thought that Ian had cheated him and he wanted—" She paused as she swallowed visibly. "He wanted revenge, and he found it when he...seduced me."

"And then?" Lucas didn't doubt the answer.

"And then he lost interest. He'd gotten what he wanted. And he had the final say when he made the round of parties and other social gatherings. He told everyone that Ashlynne Mackenzie was an unprincipled slut just like the rest of her family."

"And people believed him." It wasn't a question.

"Why not?" Ashlynne blinked and settled back against her cushion of pillows, as though she'd only just realized how tense the retelling of the story had made her. Unthinking, Lucas would bet, she reached across her chest with her good arm to massage her wound gently.

"My parents worked very hard to earn their reputations," she added after a moment. "Ian had done his best to follow in their footsteps. Who would ever believe I might be any different? I stopped going out after that and never saw Elliott again. I kept to myself and managed the household. We were..." She paused, then shook her head with a shrug. "We were short on funds by then, in any case. And then, when my parents were killed, everything changed again."

"And so you came to Alaska to recoup your fortune."

"That may have been what Ian was thinking. But me?" She shook her head. Emphatically. "I came to find my own way. I didn't care about any fortune. I only wanted to find a way to earn—and keep—my own money. I might have worked with Ian once we got to Dawson, but I had no plans to pool our finances."

"You were going to be an independent woman."

"I was. I wanted to never depend on another person—man or woman—again."

"And now here you are, stuck with me."

She smiled softly, her attention returned fully to him and the present. "You did something amazing. Something no one had ever done for me. You took me in. You cared for me and gave me a job. You did more than my own family did for me, and I didn't know how to accept that. How to trust another's consideration.

"And, Lucas." She blinked and peered at him through the fan of her lashes. "I fell in love with you."

"Ashe—"

"I don't expect you to love me back," she hurried on, interrupting as she'd done so often during her confession. Somehow, Lucas couldn't fault her for it.

"Not now. Not yet," she said softly. "I know life hasn't always been kind to you, and none of this can have been any easier for you. But please understand. I've spent my whole life trying to make people—my parents, Ian, Elliott—love me. I tried to make myself into what I thought they wanted me to be, and in the end, all it did was break my heart. I don't want that to happen again, Lucas."

She straightened and raised her head as though she had found a new source of inner strength. Her hair spread about her shoulders like a mink pelt and he found himself reaching for her, weaving his fingers through the tendrils that curled down over her shoulder. She followed his every movement with her eyes, her expression completely trusting.

"I love you, Lucas," she said with gentle sincerity. "It's important to me that you know that, no matter how you feel. You deserve to be loved, my darling."

"How can you say that you love me?" he asked hoarsely. "After all I've done to you?"

Her eyes, her mouth, softened. "What you have done *for* me." Her cheeks flushed, but still she continued. "Best of all you made love to me in the way that every woman wants to be made love to. It wasn't something rushed and illicit and painful."

Lucas moved his hand, traced the pads of his fingers over the arch of her cheek. "He hurt you."

She shook her head. "It doesn't matter. What's important is the gift you gave me. The ability to look past the outside of a person and see the soul inside. You taught me to love without conditions or expectations. I can never repay you for that."

"What you feel is gratitude."

"What I feel is love. And even if you don't love me back, it's worth everything. But, Lucas…" She paused as though reconsidering whatever else she'd started to say. "I can't deny it—your drinking…it scares me. It worries me."

Lucas dropped his hand and got up. He wasn't the man she thought he was, no matter what had happened between them. He crossed the room and stopped at the bar, staring at the array of liquor and champagne bottles lined up along the shelves.

"I haven't had a drink since the day you were shot," he said hoarsely. "I've wanted to so badly my hands shake and I sweat like I have a fever. I've even poured a glass more times than I can count. Then I smell it and remember everything, and it makes me sick to my stomach."

"Are you giving it up?"

"I don't know. I want to, but…"

"But what?"

"You know I'm a doctor," he said without turning to face her. If he'd wanted to, he could have seen her face in the mirror; it reflected everything that happened in the Star. He didn't look. He couldn't.

"Yes."

"Hell, the whole town knows by now." Lucas tried to laugh, but it was a rough, disbelieving scrape of sound. "There are no secrets in this place. Didn't I say that once?"

"And I know why you gave it up, Lucas."

He slanted her reflection a careful glance but looked away before she could notice. "You're the only person in Skagway—in all of Alaska—who knows about Emily."

"You must miss her very much."

He shrugged. "I did. I suppose I always will. But…after a while, I think missing her became a habit. An excuse. It was easier to feel sorry for myself than go on with life."

Lucas half turned from the bar and finally let his gaze settle on Ashlynne—his beautiful, spirited, loving Irish. "She would have been furious with me."

"She would have wanted you to be happy." Ashe said it without a doubt in her voice.

He nodded. "She would have. She was…sweet. Small, fine-boned, beautiful."

"Nothing like me."

He couldn't help but smile. "No, nothing like you. She would have liked you—very much, I think. But she'd have been jealous of you, too."

Ashlynne's eyes grew wide. "Jealous of me?"

"She was…small," he repeated for lack of a better word. "I always had to remember the differences in our sizes. I teased her that I would break my back bending down for her, but I don't think she appreciated the reminder. She was…

meek, I suppose. Submissive. She would have been terrified of coming to Alaska. I'm not sure she would have done it, even with me." And not virtually alone, as his brave, self-sufficient Ashlynne had done.

"She had antiquated ideas," she said with a crooked smile.

"Yes. She had antiquated ideas." He nodded with his own sad, sweet smile as he remembered their conversation that very first night. No wonder Ashe had been such a surprise to him.

"But I loved her." He softened his tone as he remembered. "I'd loved her from the time I was ten years old and I suppose I never got over it. I went away to medical school and when I came home again, I married her. But...I'd changed. I can see that now. I said things, did things that she never understood. I thought then it was just the difference between men and women, but I'm no longer so sure."

Lucas blinked and shook his head. He didn't understand it all yet. "I think we were very different, beneath it all. And though I really did love her, it was also...easy. Comfortable."

"That's not such a bad basis for a marriage."

"I didn't think so then. But now I'm not so sure."

He looked around him, at the room that had given him so much over the months he'd been in Skagway. The Star of the North had provided him with a place to live, to work, an escape from the rigors of the outside world. It had brought him Ashlynne and it had sheltered them through the storms, both physical and emotional. It was almost like another entity that had offered them both its protection.

But now, there was more to be said. One last explanation, something Ashe must understand. The Star couldn't protect them from the truth.

Lucas approached the cot, skirting the disarranged tables and chairs until he stood at the foot of her bed. He caught and held her gaze, telling himself that the whiskey-gold color had warmed and softened. Telling himself that she would understand.

"Emily wanted a child. Desperately. I've come to realize that she, too, was disappointed in our marriage and she thought a child would…fix things. Bring us closer together. She didn't like the physical side of marriage. We both realized that from the very beginning. But she was willing to endure it for the sake of a child. Unfortunately she had a difficult time conceiving, but when it finally happened, Emily was ecstatic."

She'd been like a child at Christmas, delighted and euphoric. Lucas didn't remember ever seeing her so excited. As pleased as he'd been by the news, he'd been worried, as well. "I'd delivered a few babies by then and I knew she wasn't built for childbirth. When her time came, it seemed like everything went wrong. The labor was long and hard, the baby wouldn't come. Finally, when Emily had no strength or anything else left to her, my daughter was stillborn…and there was nothing I could do to save either of them."

"But you tried."

His hands clenched into fists of impotent rage. What else could he do? He couldn't change the past, any more than he'd been able to stem the approach of death as first his daughter and then Emily had faded from this life.

"What good did trying do?" he demanded. "I was a doctor, I'd had the finest medical training available and still I couldn't save them."

"You *tried*."

Ashlynne grimaced as she struggled to sit forward, as though she needed to reach out to Lucas. Not quite willing to move, he couldn't just let her thrash about that way and take the chance of hurting herself, either. Awkwardly he took the place he'd occupied earlier, next to her on the cot.

"Lay back." He urged her to recline against the pillows, his grip firm but gentle on both of her shoulders. "You'll reopen the wound and then I'll have to play doctor again."

She raised her eyes to meet his, her expression as regretful as it was sorrowful. "You did everything you could, Lucas. For Emily and for me. You should never have any regrets about that. You're a doctor—a wonderful, talented doctor—but you aren't God."

"Maybe not." He dropped his gaze, staring at the potbellied stove that kept the room so toasty warm. Why couldn't he feel that same heat inside of him? "I'm still responsible," he added in a distant voice. "I did things that put you right in Soapy's way. And I gave Emily that child. If I'd done things differently, if I'd controlled myself—"

"I told you," Ashlynne interrupted, grabbing Lucas's wrist, tightening her grip until he could no longer avoid looking at her. "I made my own mistakes, my own choices. And Emily made hers. She was desperate for a child—you said it yourself. She was willing to take any chance to have that baby, Lucas. She wanted to have your child."

"How can you be so certain?"

"Because I'm a woman. And…I feel the same way."

"No." Abject fear tore the word from him.

"No?" Ashlynne looked at him with confusion—and so much love it made his heart ache. "What do you mean, no?"

"I don't want you to have a child. Not my child, not any child. I…we can't risk it. I won't risk you."

She reached for him then, stroked soft fingers over his cheek and brushed his hair back from his forehead. "The risk isn't the same, my darling. You said it yourself. Emily was small, not built for having children. I'm not small or frail or any of those things. I'm—"

"We can't take the risk," he repeated, stiffening against her touch. He could do nothing to keep the desperation from making his tone harsh.

"All right." She smiled softly and brushed her fingers across his lips. "But I don't know how we can prevent it. If we're together, I'm not sure it's up to us. Unless…" Her smile died along with the words.

"There are ways. Don't worry so, darlin'." He tried to reassure her with a crooked smile. "We'll talk about it later."

"But, Lucas—"

"Not now, Ashe honey." He took her hand in his. "First you have to get well. And then…I don't know. We'll figure something out."

She looked at him, a long, steady gaze that seemed to see clear through him, to the places and things he might have liked to have kept hidden. Somehow, with Ashlynne, there seemed to be no secrets.

And maybe it was time.

"Lucas," she said softly. "There's something you must remember, must accept. Doing your best—*trying*—is all we have. We can offer our hearts, our understanding, our talents, our encouragement, but in the end, we can't do anything more. It took me a long time to come to terms with the truth of how life— and love—works, but that's the answer. Now…" He'd never seen a smile so full of love. "Let me make it all right for you."

She looked so earnest—and so beautiful—with her hair spread about her shoulders, his shirt unbuttoned to reveal the shadowed rise of her breasts and her eyes shining clearly with a love he couldn't mistake. "You make me want to believe," he said hoarsely.

"Come here, Lucas."

He blinked. "I *am* here."

"No, I mean *here*." She released his wrist and patted the bed next to her. "Lay down with me."

"I will not. You're still recovering!"

She pursed her lips and narrowed her eyes. "When did you get to be such a prude?"

"I am not a prude."

"Then lay down here with me."

He blinked and looked between her and the width of the narrow cot. "There isn't enough room."

"We'll make room."

He could see the care in her movements as she scooted aside to make room for him. Still he hesitated until she took his hand and pulled him forward.

"Lucas, I don't know what's going to happen. Not tomorrow or the next day. None of us do. But for this time, right now, I want to lie next to you. I want to hold you and I want you to hold me. I want to pretend everything will be all right."

Carefully, gingerly, he did as she asked. He lay on her un-injured side and gathered her close. She wrapped her arms around him.

"I've lived my whole life for this," she said softly, "and I can't regret anything that happened. If things had been different, we might never have met and this moment might never have happened. And that would be unforgivable."

"Ashlynne?"

"What, my love?"

"You didn't get your bath."

"Later." She stroked a fleeting touch up and down, over his back. "Maybe by then you'll let me have a real bath."

"With me in it?"

She pulled back just a bit and stared at him. "Do people do that?"

Lucas smiled in spite of himself. "People do that," he agreed. "Among other things. After everything we've been through, we can do anything we want."

She snuggled close again. "All right. Then we will. One day at a time."

He liked the sound of that, as though it would go on and on. He could do almost anything…one day at a time.

"Ashe?"

"Hmm?"

He swallowed. "I love you."

And he knew that he did and always would.

Epilogue

Ashlynne knelt by the recently turned-up ground and rested a gentle hand on the plain wooden cross that identified the grave. Her brother's grave.

"Ian," she said softly but she smiled when she said his name. "It's over now, and you have your own place for all eternity."

The breeze, not so cold now that it was summer, brushed across her forehead, her cheek, and she could almost imagine Ian was there, telling her that he understood. After everything that had happened, she believed that it would be true.

"Lucas ordered a real monument for you." She traced two fingers over the outline of the cross. "It's large and ornate and should be quite beautiful. I think you'll like it."

She paused. "Ian, you'd like Lucas, too. He…loves me as much as I love him. He takes care of me, and he's shown me so much about myself and about life. I'm sorry I didn't understand when you were alive. I'm sorry if I judged you too harshly. But it's all right now. I see things differently, and I try to remember only the good things. I know you did the best you could. It's what we all do."

Ashlynne stood but took a moment to reposition a small

bouquet near the cross. It contained a colorful arrangement of Alaskan wildflowers that she'd picked: dainty blue forget-me-nots, Sitka roses with their soft pink petals, the dark pink, almost purple, of fireweed and tall purple spires of lupine. A square of newspaper held them together in a tidy bunch.

"I'm sorry, Ian, but I have to go. Lucas is waiting for me. But I'll come back soon and I'll bring him with me. We're staying here, you know. We're going to make a life in Skagway, in Alaska, just like you wanted to do."

She took a step away from the gravesite, then turned back once more. "You were right, you know. Anything can happen in Alaska." It still surprised her to realize just how prophetic Ian's words had been.

"I love you," Ashlynne whispered and walked away to meet her future.

The Skagway Sentinel
July 10, 1898

Gunfire erupted at the Juneau Company Wharf in Skagway Harbor late in the evening when ruffian Jefferson Randolph "Soapy" Smith met his match in Frank Reid, one of Skagway's founding fathers. Tempers had been running high since prospector J. D. Stewart, newly arrived in our fair city, was promptly swindled of his $2,800 in gold. Smith died in the exchange of gunfire, while hero Frank Reid clings to life. Doctors fear his wound is mortal.

Meanwhile, Judge Sehlbrede, arrived from Dyea, has sworn in Si Tanner as the new acting deputy marshal. Twenty-six accused gang members and former Deputy Marshal Taylor have been arrested.

In other, happier news, Dr. Lucas Templeton and Miss Ashlynne Mackenzie were united in holy matrimony on July 1, 1898. The private ceremony was held in the Union Church. With the departure of Reverend Dickey for the Klondike in April, the Right Reverend Peter T. Rowe, Episcopal Bishop for Alaska from Sitka, performed the ceremony. The newlyweds will be at home in Skagway, where Dr. Templeton has opened his medical practice. Mrs. Templeton will assist him in his calling. Dr. Templeton's former business, the Star of the North, has been purchased by Mr. Willie Seltenrich, an employee of that saloon since first arriving in Skagway.

* * * * *

Harlequin Historicals®
Historical Romantic Adventure!

FROM KNIGHTS IN SHINING ARMOR TO DRAWING-ROOM DRAMA HARLEQUIN HISTORICALS OFFERS THE BEST IN HISTORICAL ROMANCE

ON SALE MARCH 2005

FALCON'S HONOR
by Denise Lynn

Desperate to restore his lost honor, Sir Gareth accepts a mission from the king to escort an heiress to her betrothed. Never did he figure on the lady being so beautiful—and so eager to escape her nuptials! Can the fiery Lady Rhian of Gervaise entrance an honor-bound knight to her cause—and her heart?

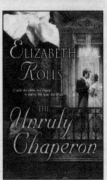

THE UNRULY CHAPERON
by Elizabeth Rolls

Wealthy widow Lady Tilda Winter accompanies her cousin to a house party as chaperon and finds herself face-to-face with old love Crispin, the Duke of St. Ormond. Meant to court her young cousin, how can St. Ormond forget the grand passion he once felt for Lady Tilda? Will the chaperon soon need a chaperon of her own?

www.eHarlequin.com

HHMED41

Harlequin Historicals®
Historical Romantic Adventure!

**ESCAPE TO A LAND LONG AGO
AND FAR AWAY IN THE PAGES OF
HARLEQUIN HISTORICALS**

ON SALE APRIL 2005

THE VISCOUNT
by Lyn Stone

Lily Bradshaw finds herself in a dire situation
after her husband's death and seeks out the only
person she knows in London: Viscount Duquesne.
Guy agrees to marry Lily to protect her and
her young son from harm's way. Will their
marriage of convenience turn to one of true
happiness and love?

THE BETROTHAL
by Terri Brisbin,
Joanne Rock
and Miranda Jarrett

Love is in the air this spring, when Harlequin
Historicals brings you three tales of romance in the
British Isles. *The Claiming of Lady Joanna* features
a beautiful runaway bride and the man who is
determined to claim her for his wife. In *Highland
Handfast*, a Scottish lord agrees to a temporary
marriage with an old childhood love, but plans
on convincing her to make it permanent! And in
A Marriage in Three Acts, a noble lord finds himself
enchanted by a beautiful actress when her troupe
of traveling players arrive at the lord's estate.

www.eHarlequin.com

HHMED42

If you enjoyed what you just read,
then we've got an offer you can't resist!

Take 2 bestselling
love stories FREE!
Plus get a FREE surprise gift!

Clip this page and mail it to Harlequin Reader Service®

IN U.S.A.	IN CANADA
3010 Walden Ave.	P.O. Box 609
P.O. Box 1867	Fort Erie, Ontario
Buffalo, N.Y. 14240-1867	L2A 5X3

YES! Please send me 2 free Harlequin Historicals® novels and my free surprise gift. After receiving them, if I don't wish to receive anymore, I can return the shipping statement marked cancel. If I don't cancel, I will receive 6 brand-new novels every month, before they're available in stores! In the U.S.A., bill me at the bargain price of $4.69 plus 25¢ shipping and handling per book and applicable sales tax, if any*. In Canada, bill me at the bargain price of $5.24 plus 25¢ shipping and handling per book and applicable taxes**. That's the complete price and a savings of over 10% off the cover prices—what a great deal! I understand that accepting the 2 free books and gift places me under no obligation ever to buy any books. I can always return a shipment and cancel at any time. Even if I never buy another book from Harlequin, the 2 free books and gift are mine to keep forever.

246 HDN DZ7Q
349 HDN DZ7R

Name	(PLEASE PRINT)	
Address	Apt.#	
City	State/Prov.	Zip/Postal Code

Not valid to current Harlequin Historicals® subscribers.

Want to try two free books from another series?
Call 1-800-873-8635 or visit www.morefreebooks.com.

* Terms and prices subject to change without notice. Sales tax applicable in N.Y.
** Canadian residents will be charged applicable provincial taxes and GST.
   All orders subject to approval. Offer limited to one per household.
   ® are registered trademarks owned and used by the trademark owner and or its licensee.

HIST04R   ©2004 Harlequin Enterprises Limited

eHARLEQUIN.com

The Ultimate Destination for Women's Fiction

The ultimate destination for women's fiction.
Visit eHarlequin.com today!

GREAT BOOKS:
- We've got something for everyone—and at great low prices!
- Choose from new releases, backlist favorites, Themed Collections and preview upcoming books, too.
- Favorite authors: Debbie Macomber, Diana Palmer, Susan Wiggs and more!

EASY SHOPPING:
- Choose our convenient "bill me" option. No credit card required!
- Easy, secure, 24-hour shopping from the comfort of your own home.
- Sign-up for free membership and get $4 off your first purchase.
- Exclusive online offers: FREE books, bargain outlet savings, hot deals.

EXCLUSIVE FEATURES:
- Try Book Matcher—finding your favorite read has never been easier!
- Save & redeem Bonus Bucks.
- Another reason to love Fridays— Free Book Fridays!

Shop online
at www.eHarlequin.com today!

INTBB204

Harlequin Historicals®
Historical Romantic Adventure!

CRAVING STORIES OF LOVE AND ADVENTURE SET IN THE WILD WEST? CHECK OUT THESE THRILLING TALES FROM HARLEQUIN HISTORICALS!

ON SALE APRIL 2005

THE RANGER'S WOMAN
by Carol Finch

On the run from an unwanted wedding, Piper Sullivan runs smack into the arms of Texas Ranger Quinn Callahan. On a mission to track outlaws who killed his best friend, Quinn hasn't got time to spare with the feisty lady. But he can't help but be charmed by Piper's adventurous spirit and uncommon beauty....

ABBIE'S OUTLAW
by Victoria Bylin

All hell is about to break loose when former gunslinger turned preacher John Leaf finds himself face-to-face with old love Abbie Moore. Years ago, John took her innocence and left her pregnant and alone. Now Abbie's back and needs his help. Will a marriage of convenience redeem John's tainted soul and bring love into their lives once more?

www.eHarlequin.com

HHWEST37

Harlequin Historicals®
Historical Romantic Adventure!

FOR RIVETING TALES OF RUGGED MEN AND THE WOMEN WHO LOVE THEM CHECK OUT HARLEQUIN HISTORICALS!

ON SALE MARCH 2005

THE BACHELOR
by Kate Bridges

At the town harvest festival, dashing bachelor Mitchell Reid is raffled off for charity—and lands in the unlikely arms of no-nonsense, hardworking Diana Campbell. Ever since the Canadian Mountie mistakenly tried to arrest her brothers, she's attempted to deny her attraction to the roguish Mitch. Twenty-four hours spent in his company just might change her mind....

TURNER'S WOMAN
by Jenna Kernan

Rugged mountain man Jake Turner rescues Emma Lancing, the sole survivor of an Indian massacre. Burned by love in the past, he's vowed to steer clear of women. But the young woman in his care is strong and capable— and oh, so beautiful. Can this lonely trapper survive a journey west with his heart intact?

www.eHarlequin.com

HHWEST36